A Fatal Night

FAITH MARTIN

ONE PLACE. MANY STORIES

HQ
An imprint of HarperCollins*Publishers* Ltd
1 London Bridge Street
London SE1 9GF

www.harpercollins.co.uk

HarperCollins*Publishers*
1st Floor, Watermarque Building, Ringsend Road
Dublin 4, Ireland

This paperback edition 2021

1
First published in Great Britain by
HQ, an imprint of HarperCollins*Publishers* Ltd 2021

ISBN: 9780008410520

Readers love the Ryder & Loveday series

'... insanely brilliant ... return or

'I absolutely loved this book'

'Faith Martin, you've triumphed again. Brilliant!'

'If you haven't yet read Miss Martin you have a treat in store'

'I can safely say that I adore the series featuring Dr Clement Ryder and Probationary WPC Trudy Loveday'

'This book is such a delight to read. The two main characters are a joy'

'Yet another wonderful book by Faith Martin!'

'As always a wonderful story, great characters, great plot. This keeps you gripped from the first page to the last. Faith Martin is such a fantastic author'

FAITH MARTIN has been writing for nearly thirty years, under four different pen names, and has published over fifty novels. She began writing romantic thrillers as Maxine Barry, but quickly turned to crime! As Joyce Cato she wrote classic-style whodunits, since she's always admired the golden-age crime novelists. But it was when she created her fictional DI Hillary Greene, and began writing under the name of Faith Martin, that she finally became more widely known. Her latest literary characters, WPC Trudy Loveday and city coroner Dr Clement Ryder, take readers back to the 1960s and the city of Oxford. Having lived within a few miles of the city's dreaming spires for all her life (she worked for six years as a secretary at Somerville College), both the city and the countryside/wildlife often feature in her novels. Although she has never lived on a narrowboat (unlike DI Hillary Greene!) the Oxford canal, the river Cherwell, and the flora and fauna of a farming landscape have always played a big part in her life – and often sneak their way onto the pages of her books.

Also by Faith Martin

For all my readers. After nearly thirty years of being published, I feel more grateful than ever for their continued support.

Prologue

Oxford 1962

It was Christmas Day and the citizens of the beautiful university city of Oxford were feeling replete with turkey and plum pudding. Most of them were looking forward to Boxing Day, thinking only of a lazy day spent by the fire, with nothing more onerous to focus on than the inevitable return to work and the normal, humdrum routine of living.

But the twenty-sixth day of December that year brought with it a blizzard of epic proportions, presaging a period of bad weather that would rage and rage and never seem to end. It was the start of what would later become known as 'The Big Freeze', when the whole of the United Kingdom would be locked in the grip of snow and ice for nearly four months.

The people first saw the snow as a welcome representative of a white Christmas; the children and the adults alike played in it, starting snowball fights and gleefully building snowmen. But they had no idea of the nightmare that lay ahead of them. No concept of what it would be like when roads would be blocked for weeks on end, when trains couldn't run, when winter fuel became scarce, and food in the shops dwindled alarmingly.

Nor could they have anticipated the wearying, will-sapping tedium of constant freezing temperatures, day in, night out, until only and finally on the sixth day of March of the brand-new year of 1963, did the country finally record its first frost-free day.

Of course, by then, there had been death, and plenty of it – the elderly, the unwary, the unlucky, the ill.

But not all of the deaths were natural or accidental, or could be blamed solely on the pitiless winter …

Chapter 1

WPC Trudy Loveday felt her right foot sliding out from under her in a way that was becoming only too familiar, and instinctively reached out to grab at a railing beside her. It belonged to a small front garden currently blanketed in white, like everything else as far as the eye could see, and obligingly kept her upright. Luckily she was wearing warm woollen gloves, otherwise her bare skin might have stuck to the metal, it was that cold.

All around her, the city of Oxford lay shivering and miserable. Much like one young, lone WPC, who was resolutely walking her beat.

Trudy looked around and sighed, her breath, as ever, appearing in front of her in a small puff of vapour. They were in those 'dead' days between Christmas and the New Year of 1963, when all thoughts of Father Christmas seemed like weeks ago instead of mere days, and the time to sing 'Auld Lang Syne' seemed as if it would never arrive.

Most of the shops around her were closed, some because the proprietors weren't convinced that any customers would be foolish enough to venture outside when the roads and pavements were so slick with ice and the dark days so uninviting. Others belonged to owners who lived out of town rather than over the shop, and were themselves snowed solidly into surrounding villages, unable to come in and oversee their business premises. No buses ran, and most trains were either hours late, cancelled, stuck on frozen points, or halted by last night's snowfall, which a nasty wind had driven into drifts that covered open spots on the railway tracks.

She set off down the pavement again, her calves aching from the constant slipping and sliding she was doing, although so far she hadn't taken a total tumble. By dint of shuffling and hardly lifting her feet, she was managing to get along, but her lower back was starting to feel the strain of walking so unnaturally. She would be glad when she could return to the station and thaw out with a hot cup of tea.

Although it was nice to have a white Christmas, or so everyone kept saying, she'd be glad to see the back of snow. Pretty though it might be – and it had certainly given the already lovely city an almost magical appearance, covering spires and clinging to rooftops like a layer of icing on a cake – there was no denying it was beginning to cause serious issues.

Traffic that did manage to take to the streets seemed to end up in ditches, or ploughing into other stationary vehicles when traction was lost on the ice. Old folk were accumulating in hospitals with their fragile bones broken after a slip on the garden path, or with hypothermia after they huddled too long in inadequately heated homes.

And to make matters worse, a nasty cold or flu bug was going around, incapacitating not only members of the general public, but also decimating the ranks of the police and other emergency services, just when more and more calls were being made on their resources.

Not surprisingly, her inspector was not in the best of moods.

Trudy sighed, but DI Harry Jennings's foul temper notwithstanding, she headed determinedly for the police station with its noisily clanging but blessedly warm radiators.

*

In his Victorian terraced home, with a pretty view over the nearby park, Dr Clement Ryder, city coroner, watched his son move around the kitchen, preparing breakfast. It wasn't often that either of his two children, now long grown up, visited him for any amount of time, so he was making the most of it. Not that he didn't heartily approve of them living their own lives, for he'd always thought that was how it was meant to be.

When his wife had died a number of years ago, the twins had been twenty years old, and already both away at university, getting ready to begin their own journeys through life. His daughter, Julia, had taken her mother's death particularly hard though, and he was glad that she was now happy and well and settled. He'd seen her on Christmas Eve, and had hoped to see her again for New Year's Day, but he doubted, unless there was a sudden thaw, that she'd be able to make it. The roads were still impossible to navigate.

As if reading his mind, Vincent, waiting by the toaster, sighed heavily as he looked out of the window. 'I've checked, but there's no chance of making it back to Cheltenham any time soon, Dad. No trains or buses and the roads are blocked everywhere. What's more, the weather forecast last night said that there would be more snow flurries in the next two days. So it looks as if you're stuck with me for a while yet.'

Clement grinned. 'I'll cope! There's no problem with your office, I hope? You being snowed in here, I mean?' His son was a junior member of a small but well-respected architect's firm. Fortunately, he'd brought with him some plans for a private boys' school that he was currently working on, so it wasn't as if he didn't have something to be getting on with.

'No, I managed to get through to Chris on the telephone at last. Apparently nearly everyone is stuck at home. And it's not as if I can't continue to work on the plans here. The new pavilion for the indoor sports facility isn't urgent or particularly taxing.'

Clement grunted. 'Don't worry. You'll be designing power stations by the time you're my age,' he prophesied proudly.

Vincent grabbed the toast as it popped up, laughing and juggling the hot bread onto two nearby plates. 'Hope I won't have to wait that long!'

'Cheeky pup!' his father mock-growled.

Vincent glanced at him then quickly away again. Like his father, he was six feet tall. Unlike his father though, whose hair was steel-grey with touches of white, his own light brown hair had near-golden touches here and there, and he'd inherited his mother's rather striking green-flecked hazel eyes. A former girl-friend had told him that he had an expressive face, and he hoped that none of his growing concerns about his remaining parent were on his face when he brought the buttered and marmalade-bedecked toast to the kitchen table.

'You going into the office today?' he asked, careful to keep his voice casual. When his father confirmed that he would, he was even more careful to keep his face blank.

'You're not going to try and take the car though, are you?' he added casually. He thought he'd managed to sound nonchalant and offhand, but the quick, sharp look his father sent his way made him wonder if he'd succeeded.

'No, there's no point. The roads are like an ice rink right now. And I'm not sure that last night's snowfall will have been cleared everywhere in the city. Besides, Floyds Row isn't that far.' His workplace was handily located next to the city's mortuary. 'The fresh air and exercise will do me good,' he concluded, his own tone having a definite ring of finality to it.

And his son knew better than to say anything more. Besides, what *could* he say? *Be careful to wrap up warm. Remember to take the stick. Don't fall over again. Do you want me to come with you?* He'd sound ridiculous. And his father would almost certainly snap his head off, and say something cutting about not being in his dotage just yet!

Nevertheless, after consuming their breakfast over some more father-and-son banter, Vincent Ryder went to the window of the sitting room to watch his father's figure as it set off into the snow. Clement, he was relieved to see, was wearing his heaviest overcoat and a fur-trimmed hat, and had on a pair of warm sheepskin gloves. And he had, indeed, taken a walking cane. This was something new, for he'd never known his father use a walking stick before, and he'd like to think his father was carrying it solely because of the weather conditions.

But something about the familiar and confident way he used it made him wonder.

And although the former surgeon and now city coroner seemed to step out with all the verve and vigour that Vincent had always associated with his parent, he felt a trickle of unease nonetheless.

For there was no getting away from the fact that he'd become rather unnerved when seeing his father this Christmas. Clement had seemed more than a year older somehow. A little frailer, and perhaps a little thinner too? What's more, Vincent was sure that he'd seen his father's hands tremble – once when he'd been carving the goose that they'd enjoyed for their Christmas dinner, and once when they'd been playing backgammon and he was moving his counter.

And, though it might be comforting, he didn't think he could put the shakes down to the old man imbibing a bit too much of the Christmas spirit either. Although he liked the odd drink, his father had never been one to overindulge in alcohol, his former career as a surgeon no doubt having a lot to do with it.

Perhaps Vincent was just imagining that slightly slurred word last night too? It had, after all, been late, and both of them had been tired. And perhaps all the times that he'd imagined he could see fatigue in his father's eyes were actually no more than a reflection of the harsh white light bouncing off the snow that lay everywhere outside the windows.

Still, Vincent shifted uneasily at the window as he watched his father's figure until it was out of sight. Perhaps he was just kidding himself, not wanting to face up to the fact that Clement was getting older, just as everyone did.

As Vincent Ryder watched his father disappear, he felt himself shiver. Which was silly – the fire in the grate was roaring away.

And his father was invincible, indomitable, even. Everyone knew that. Right?

Chapter 2

A few days later, the dawn was cold but bright.

Finally, New Year's Eve at last, thought Millie Vander as she rolled over in bed, a happy smile on her face. She had been planning her party for weeks now, and everything had to be perfect for her guests, the rotten weather notwithstanding.

She could just feel in her bones that this was going to be a night she'd never forget. For tonight, surely, he would finally propose.

She climbed out of bed and went moodily to the window, scowling out at the relentlessly white vista that lay outside. She'd been hoping all week that there'd be a thaw and the snow would have gone by now, so the sight of it made her lips curl in something that was part pout, part sneer. She could almost believe that nature had conspired against her on purpose to put this annoying obstacle in her way.

Already five of her guests who had to come from outside Oxford had called to cancel, saying they dared not risk the roads. Still, at least she'd had the good fortune to hire a famous local caterer, and she'd already had the evergreen arrangements delivered for Christmas Eve, so they were in place. They'd just need a little sprucing up.

She sighed and went out onto the landing, crossing over to the

9

largest of the bathrooms, glad that her daughter, Juliet, was still in bed. She liked to have the best bathroom to herself for a good hour or so in the morning. At the age of forty-three (thirty-eight to her friends and acquaintances) she needed just that little bit more time nowadays until she felt ready to face the world.

Not that she hadn't done well, she mentally congratulated herself. She stood in front of the long mirror that hung on the back of the bathroom door, turning her figure this way and that, checking for any signs of sagging or unsightly bulges, and finding none.

At only five feet and three inches, she could almost see her entire length, and she liked what she saw. She'd always been curvaceous in all the right places, and slender where it mattered. A proper pocket Venus, George, her late husband, had always called her. Bless him.

She sighed and turned away from the mirror, her mind going instantly to the day ahead. So much to do, but she was confident it would all go well. She only hoped her nineteen-year-old twins, whom she'd reluctantly agreed could bring one friend each to the party, would have been careful in their choices.

Although she loved them dearly, they could be a bit of a handful sometimes. Her best friend Frances told her she'd spoilt them rotten, but what did Frances know? Her own kids didn't like her one little bit! At least Juliet was fond of her, and Jasper adored her. So what if they had a reputation for being a little wild? When she was young, she'd been a bit reckless too. That was what youth was for – to enjoy.

She met her satisfied reflection in the normal-sized mirror over the sink and regarded her face hopefully. Even without her make-up she didn't look her true age, she was sure. Everybody said so! Having the fair skin that came with red hair helped, but she leaned forward closer to the mirror to check for crow's feet either side of her eyes and found none. Well, not obvious ones, anyway.

She'd been barely out of nappies before she'd learned that

her jade-green eyes were her best feature, along with the dark red (definitely not ginger) hair, which she kept stubbornly long, even now. Who said it was girlish? With long hair you could do wonderful things – French pleats, chignons, all sorts. Only middle-aged women who couldn't be bothered to make the effort anymore cut their hair short, and she was definitely not that over the hill yet.

Pleased to see that the cold cream she smoothed on her face every night seemed to be working, she tied up her long hair into a topknot to keep it dry and ran the taps for a hot bath, happily contemplating the glorious evening to come.

And most of all, thinking of Terry – tall, dark, good-looking Terry. Terry – who was more than ten years her junior.

But really, what did that matter in this day and age? she mused. Angry with herself for thinking negative thoughts about their age difference *yet again*, she poured her favourite, prohibitively expensive, jasmine-scented bath salts into the water, and after slipping off her peach satin negligee, sank with a sigh of bliss into the scented water.

The hairdresser was coming at four, and would be putting up her hair in a delightfully 'messy' chignon that left attractive curls 'straggling' around her ears and neck. The very latest thing – she'd seen the style in a magazine from France that autumn. Her newest dress, acquired from Harrods earlier in the month just for the occasion, hung waiting for her in the wardrobe. The cleaners would arrive soon and make sure that her house, a fine, gracious five-bedroom, white-stuccoed mansion in a desirable leafy street just off the bottom end of Banbury Road, was spic and span and sparkling.

Her late husband had been a whizz with investments and stocks and shares and all that sort of thing, and had left her very well off indeed, not only with sizeable bank accounts, but also with a steady and regular income that barely touched the sides of her capital. Bless him.

She frowned uneasily and pushed the thought of George away. She'd loved him and been a good wife to him, given him the twins and entertained his business friends over the years, even though she'd found them mind-numbingly boring. So she really had nothing to feel guilty about. And he *had* been gone for nearly five years now. A woman who was still young and had much of her life ahead of her couldn't mourn and live alone forever, could she?

And Terry was so nice. She was sure that George would have approved of him. Of course, George had been born to well-off parents, as had she, so he might have raised his eyebrows a bit that Terry was, to some extent, a self-made man; but George was no snob, and he'd always admired get-up-and-go. And Terry was part-owner in a thriving and glamorous business!

No, she was sure she had nothing to reproach herself for, no matter what others might think! She shook her head, again angry with herself for letting negative thoughts invade her happy mood. She must let nothing spoil this special time. Today was going to be a great day – she just knew it! It was the last day of the old year, and 1963, which started tomorrow, was going to be just wonderful. Especially if, as she thought he might, Terry finally plucked up the courage to ask her to marry him.

She didn't think she was fooling herself to hope for a proper engagement ring soon. It wasn't as if they didn't have an 'understanding', after all. They'd been seeing each other for nearly a year now. And she wore the lovely gold heart-shaped pendant that he'd given her for her birthday all the time. Surely that was a big enough hint about how she felt? But if not, then tonight she'd be sure to encourage him even more – leave him in no doubt whatsoever that she was ready for him to get down on one knee. It would be so romantic – with snowflakes falling outside and the bells ringing out for a brand-new year and everything …

She sighed and reached for a sponge, absently rubbing it down her pale, slightly freckled arms. Of course, she knew why he might have felt reluctant to ask her before now. Her children, the scamps, were at times barely civil to him. But they were teenagers still, as she'd pointed out to him time and time again, and everyone knew that teenagers could be a bit emotional and trying. They would change once they'd had their twentieth birthday and began to act like grown-ups. And if they didn't … well, indulgent mother though she usually was, she knew how to put her foot down if she really needed to, Millie thought, with a tightening of her lips and giving a cross little shrug.

No matter what, she wouldn't let them spoil things for her tonight. They would just have to be made to understand that, whilst they *had* been her whole life, especially since George had passed away, they couldn't be the centre of her universe forever. Soon they would marry themselves, and move away, and she would need someone in her life. Did they expect her to be lonely forever? she would demand of them. Well, did they?

For once, she would put herself first. No matter what anyone thought. And her snide friends could go hang as well! She gave a gurgle of delight at the thought of Frances's face when she flashed her new engagement ring at their next lunch at the Randolph!

With a smile, Millie Vander leaned her head back against the rim of the tub, and sighed.

Tonight *was* going to be magical. She was going to make sure of it.

Chapter 3

The first guests for Mrs Millicent Vander's New Year's Eve party arrived at her door promptly at eight o'clock.

Millie didn't mind. It would never have occurred to either of the Wainwrights to be fashionably late, and she'd been prepared for that. They'd been her next-door neighbours for all her married life, and she knew their little ways. Not the most sophisticated of people, either of them, but you couldn't have a party and not invite your immediate neighbours, could you? It wasn't polite.

She showed them straight into the large living room, where tables groaned with food. There, she poured Mary her favourite 'snowball' – inwardly wondering how anyone could actually like advocaat – whilst merely drifting a hand towards the help-yourself bar rife with spirits, indicating that Mary's husband was to pour his own. William, like George, preferred brandy or cognac to mixed drinks – and like George, he liked to pour his own measures. George had always thought she'd never realised how much he consumed that way! Bless him.

After a quarter of an hour of rather dull chat, others began to arrive, and Millie relaxed slightly. In spite of the weather, the vast majority of her guests were within walking distance of her home, and those who weren't had found various means of getting to her, regaling her with jokes about skis, snowshoes and a farmer's tractor.

She laughed gaily, circulating, flirting, showing off her new dress and keeping glasses topped up, her eyes always on the lookout for one guest in particular.

*

He came just after nine-thirty.

Jasper Vander was the first to spot him, and swore softly under his breath. At only five-feet-six, Jasper often cursed his mother's small frame, wishing that he'd inherited his father's more manly five-feet-ten-inch stature instead. All through school he'd suffered jibes of 'shorty' and 'pipsqueak' and the chip on his shoulder was fast growing to boulder size.

Some of the more prescient adults who had been a part of his life might have wondered if his lack of inches was responsible for his rather nasty personality, but most people preferred not to contemplate him at all, and simply avoided him whenever possible.

Only his mother and his twin loved him. A fact that worried Jasper not one whit. He was clever, handsome and funny, and (best of all) came from money. Any one of those advantages would have been more than enough to enable him to carve a comfortable place for himself in the world that he was happy with.

He'd been head boy at school, (indulging in a few nasty tricks and using his old noggin had secured him that position of power), and captain of the cricket team, having a slender, graceful form that was almost balletic. And what he might have lacked in actual sporting talent, he'd more than made up for in aggression.

He was also quite a success with the opposite sex, having inherited his father's black hair (not his mother's awful red mop) along with the late George Vander's large grey eyes and handsome, square-jawed face. He wore clothes very well, and spent almost as much on them as his mother did.

A sharp and funny wit earned him both approbation and condemnation in almost equal measure (depending on his audience) and he regarded either reaction as a victory.

Now, though, he was feeling not at all sanguine as he noted Terrence Parker's arrival with a narrowing of his eyes and a snort that he hid by taking a sip from his cocktail glass. It contained something blue and was the latest fad, which he thought appropriate, since it tasted just like paraffin.

He watched as his twin also followed the latest arrival with her eyes. Juliet's red-painted lips twisted into a predatory smile that made her brother almost laugh out loud. He could always count on good ol' Jules to help him take down his prey.

*

Terry Parker headed into the noisy, crowded room of partygoers with an easy smile on his face. He had eyes only for the hostess, watching the moment she spotted him and came towards him at once, her eyes lighting up with gratifying pleasure.

'Terry! I was beginning to worry you couldn't make it! Is the weather still frightful? It was snowing again last time I looked. I hope you didn't come in one of those death traps of yours,' she teased.

Terry smiled. 'I left the E-type Jag in the garage, I promise,' he said. Which was true enough. 'I brought a beast of a Riley instead. Old, ugly as sin, but heavy and reliable as a tank. Satisfied?'

'Very,' Millie said, taking his arm and leading him to the bar. On the record player Elvis Presley's number-one hit 'Return to Sender' was playing at its loudest setting. 'Have a drink. Do you want that latest cocktail, or a glass of my best port?'

*

Millie Vander's resentful children were not the only ones watching the discreet lovers that night.

Patsy Arles also watched them avidly. At eighteen, Patsy looked perhaps slightly younger, a fact that often caused her serious resentment. She blamed it on her long, curly, ginger-blonde hair, but her heart-shaped face and big blue-grey eyes didn't help. She often thought that she looked more like a puppy dog begging for treats than a mature, slinky femme fatale, intent on breaking hearts.

Her icons were the glamorous and often scandalous actresses of the golden Hollywood era – Myrna Loy, Rita Hayworth, and, of course, now Marilyn.

She'd left school three years before, where she'd always had a serious crush on Juliet Vander, who, at just one year older, seemed to the adoring Patsy to be the epitome of everything that she herself was not. Stunning black hair, flashing cat-green eyes, tiny shapely figure and a knowing way that seemed to radiate out, making everyone turn their heads to look at her as she walked past. Not only that, she had family money, a vinegar tongue that could reduce teenage boys to jelly at will, and a reputation for playing with fire. Not that she ever got caught out by the school authorities, of course.

Juliet was the girl everyone wanted to know and, of course, she didn't look at you twice. Aloof, curiously friendless, Juliet was queen!

So Patsy couldn't believe her luck when, out of the blue, Juliet had sought her out and invited her to her mother's swanky party this evening. Everyone knew that Mrs Vander threw the best parties in north Oxford, Patsy mused now, almost swelling with pride at being here, in the Vanders' mansion. Her own mother did her best to keep up appearances, but she simply didn't have Mrs Vander's elan. Or social contacts. In fact, she had only managed to get Patsy into the same prestigious school as Juliet by the skin of her teeth – and a lucky win on the Premium Bonds!

Not that Patsy had been able to take advantage of that piece of good luck and do well at the school – unlike Juliet, who passed all her exams with a sneer and no revision at all. Patsy knew she wasn't the brightest button in the box. Still, Patsy thought happily, hugging her secret joy to herself like a precious diamond, none of that mattered now. She was *here*, at this fabulous party, and Juliet Vander, *Juliet Vander* of all people, had confided in her and drawn her into a real adventure. Just like her heroines on the silver screen, here was danger, excitement, romance, and thrills. At last, she could say goodbye to her boring, mundane life. Because, once she'd done the favour asked of her, and become Juliet's best friend, who knew what the future could hold?

She only hoped she didn't fluff it! It sounded simple enough. A bit … well, risqué as their French teacher would have said, but not really difficult. Just as long as she held her nerve …

She watched Terry Parker nervously but avidly. She knew how much Juliet despised him, of course – she and Jasper had made it clear just what the jumped-up little Lothario (Jasper's description) was up to, and she had to agree it was a bit thick! Cosying up to Mrs Vander like that, who was heaps older than him, just to worm his way into her life so that he could marry her for her fortune!

Well, not if they could help it! Patsy was determined not to let Juliet down. They would beat him at his own game! She felt almost like Grace Kelly in a Hitchcock film.

Patsy saw her quarry smile at Mrs Vander, and almost squirmed in embarrassment for Juliet as Juliet's mother smiled back. Mind you, she thought wistfully, she couldn't really blame Mrs Vander. He *was* very good-looking, not that she'd ever dare say so to Juliet or Jasper! Over six feet, she thought, if only by an inch or so. (She did *so* like tall men, perhaps because she was five-feet-ten herself. It was so embarrassing having to look down to meet a boy's eyes …) And with all that lush dark hair and melting dark-brown eyes … Oh my!

She pulled herself up with a start, and turned away. She mustn't be caught staring at him. Juliet would be angry with her if she gave anything away.

But later, once all the bells had chimed for midnight and the party broke up, she would do what she had come here for. Her heart thumped in trepidation, and she quickly swallowed back her anxiety. Nothing would go wrong, she reassured herself. They'd planned it all out – Juliet, Jasper and herself. And Jasper, like his twin, was so clever. They'd gone over and over it, until they were sure that Patsy knew it all off by heart. And she did – she really did! She knew just what she had to do … And it was so exciting and wonderful and very daring. Even maybe a little dangerous …

For a moment, eighteen-year-old Patsy Arles felt a frisson of fear snake through her, and a small voice at the back somewhere far away hissed at her that she was in way over her head.

But then she caught Juliet's eye, and saw her nod at her with a small secret smile, and her heart swelled with pride. She pushed the small voice away. It would probably turn out to be easy as anything after all, and she was worrying for nothing.

Besides, Grace Kelly wouldn't be such a rabbit, would she?

*

Just before eleven o'clock a gate-crasher made an unobtrusive entrance and ate some canapés happily, enjoyed a very nice glass of expensive French wine, and circulated amiably, earning friends here, there and everywhere.

Millie Vander was perhaps the only one, at first, to be puzzled by the newcomer, for she had no idea exactly who the stranger was. But she was, naturally, far too polite to enquire. No doubt one of her guests had invited someone to come along and had simply forgotten – or been too embarrassed or tipsy – to admit it to their hostess.

Besides, it would be utterly déclassé to make a scene about a mere gate-crasher, Millie knew. In this modern new age, weren't parties deemed to be something of a failure if they didn't attract some scandalous behaviour?

*

If Patsy Arles was suffering from nerves and a surfeit of hot blood, the other woman who watched Terry Parker so thoughtfully that night was as cold as the snow that was falling outside, and felt perfectly calm.

She felt only slight distaste as their clearly enamoured hostess laid a hand possessively on his arm, and carefully sipped from her champagne cocktail before whispering something into his attentive ear.

She thought that Terry Parker seemed to be enjoying himself. So alive, and contemplating a happy future, spending the silly woman's fortune …

Her mind drifted to other, darker, things … and brooded.

*

As midnight inevitably drew nearer, the noisy party grew ever more boisterous. And when the countdown finally began, everyone stood around, most holding hands and lifting their arms up and down in time with the chanting. 'Eight,' they called merrily, 'seven, six, five …'

The twins, Juliet and Jasper, whispered together in a corner. The 'star guest' – a local celebrity artist – had clearly drunk just a little too much, but ever the lady, she held her liquor well. She had once, famously, drunk Dalí (or was it somebody almost as famous?) under the table somewhere in Budapest. (Or was it Luxembourg?)

Most people were feeling pleasantly hazy. Everyone present considered the party to be a great triumph. The food had been wonderful, the drinks copious and varied, and the records had been just the right mix of big band, jazz, and the modern stuff that was so popular with teenagers nowadays.

As the last chimes of midnight came and went, the streamers flew, champagne corks popped, people kissed, and 'Auld Lang Syne' was sung with the proper amount of maudlin relish. Indeed, as it was later agreed by all those who had cause to think back on that night, a good time had been had by all.

It was such a pity that, later, all of those present would be suspected of having just taken the necessary steps to execute a very simple, neat and near-perfect murder.

Chapter 4

Trudy was asleep when the banging began on her front door. She opened her eyes with a snap, still feeling groggy from having had too much sherry last night. What on earth …? She lifted her head from the pillow and looked out of the window, feeling confused. It was still dark. What time was it?

She groped for the bedside lamp and switched it on, blinking in the sudden light, and reached for her watch. She had a slight headache, but nothing worse.

Her tin alarm clock assured her that it was not quite seven o'clock – hardly the middle of the night. Soon even the mid-winter dawn would break, although her room had that now familiar pale glow from all the reflected snow outside. For a second, she wondered if she'd overslept for work, and it was her mother banging on the door … and then she remembered.

It was New Year's Day! And she wasn't due in to work until two o'clock that afternoon. No holidays for her – but at least she hadn't been landed with the early shift! With the weather like it was, and so many officers trapped in their homes or off sick with the wretched bug that was going around, she had been wondering if her luck would continue to hold.

Perhaps it hadn't?

She groaned, stuck one leg out into the cold air of her bedroom, shivered and quickly slipped her feet into slippers before her toes could become icicles. She shrugged thankfully into her warm quilted housecoat (a Christmas present from her father) and padded rapidly downstairs as another spate of knocking echoed through the household.

She went to the door and cautiously opened it. She recognised the blond, good-looking man on the doorstep at once and scowled at him, shivering as the wind blew some flakes of the softly falling snow onto her slipper-clad feet.

'Mornin', sunshine,' PC Rodney Broadstairs said with a wide, unrepentant grin. 'Get dressed, darlin'. The big cheese wants you at the station right away.'

Trudy sighed but nodded. 'Give me five minutes,' she muttered.

Reluctantly, she let him in to wait in the kitchen. It wasn't much warmer in there than it was outside, since neither of her parents had risen yet to light the fires, but at least the penetrating wind didn't reach that far into the Lovedays' small council house.

When she came back down again, she discovered that he'd at least had the decency to make a pot of tea – even though she suspected that it was probably incidental that she got to benefit from it too. He was already on his second cup. Still, she was able to gratefully gulp down several hot mouthfuls of it before she had to dash out to the police-issue Land Rover that was waiting outside.

Even though she'd now passed her driving test (thanks to her friend Clement Ryder, giving her driving lessons) she knew that Rodney wouldn't let her drive it, and went straight to the passenger seat and climbed aboard. She sat beside him, shivering in her winter uniform and winter coat, and blowing on her hands to try and keep some feeling in her fingers.

The ancient vehicle had been requisitioned from who-knew-where (since a lot of the police cars were all but useless in streets where the council had been unable to clear the snow) and its heater definitely wasn't working. And from the way that Rodney had to struggle to keep it on the icy roads, she wondered nervously what other, more vital bits didn't work either!

Every now and then they saw cars abandoned in snowdrifts, where their unlucky owners or the AA had failed to dig them out. In St Aldates, a milk lorry was stuck, and the driver and one or two others (irate customers?) were trying to dig it out.

'Any idea what the inspector wants?' Trudy asked tiredly, tucking a stray strand of her long dark hair back under her police cap.

'He didn't say,' Rodney said shortly.

Trudy wondered if he'd been one of those stuck with the night shift, and wisely kept silent. She wasn't up to coping with Rodney's continuous complaints today.

*

The station seemed deserted. She was so used to seeing old Walter Swinburne at his desk, drinking tea or hogging the fire, that it felt quite odd how quiet it was. She guessed that the few officers who had managed to make it in were now out and about attending to their many duties – even poor old Walter!

She supposed that, given all the parties that must have been going on last night, the drunk tanks all over the city were now probably full to bursting, and the paperwork for that alone would be mind-boggling. She hoped that wasn't what she'd been called in early to help with.

'Go on in, the inspector's been in since six. He's in a foul mood though, so watch out,' Rodney advised her gruffly.

Duly warned, Trudy checked her cap was on straight, knocked on Inspector Jennings's door, and heard the familiar bellow for her to come in.

She flinched, but put a bright smile on her face.

Harry Jennings raised his head as she entered and gave her a jaundiced look. He was a fair-haired man of medium height and build, with a rather large nose and hazel eyes. Right now, his eyes appeared rather bloodshot and Trudy wondered if he'd been partying himself last night and now was suffering from the subsequent hangover.

'Oh, so you're here at last,' he said flatly.

'Sir,' she said smartly. She wondered, briefly, if she should point out that she wasn't due in for a good six hours yet, but knew better.

'Well, you'd better get yourself off to Five Mile Drive then,' he said grimly. 'We've got a dead body.'

Trudy blinked and stiffened in surprise. Had he really just said what she'd *thought* he said? 'Sir?' she asked timidly. Usually the inspector wouldn't let her handle cases more important than shoplifting or old ladies mugged for their pension money. Well, apart from the odd occasion when Dr Clement Ryder needed her official police services, and the inspector was given no other choice but to comply.

Was it possible that the inspector was taking her seriously at last?

'Oh, don't get excited, Constable,' Jennings said wearily, catching the excitement in her eye. 'We've got reports of someone being found dead in their car in a snowdrift. Almost certainly he was out drinking and partying last night, crashed, and either died of his injuries or exposure. If I had the men, I'd send—' He broke off and sighed as he contemplated his depleted forces. 'Bloody snow!' he muttered.

He slumped back in his chair and eyed her belligerently. 'I just need you to go to the scene, organise the paperwork, oversee the removal of the body and make general inquiries. *General inquiries, mind!*' he emphasised. 'Although when a medical officer will be able to get out to confirm death with everything they've got on their plate … it'll probably take them hours.' His eyes glinted in malevolent, sudden good humour. 'So try not to freeze to death, Constable.'

'Sir,' Trudy sighed.

'Once someone more senior becomes available you can hand it all over to him,' Jennings informed her. 'If I can get Sergeant O'Grady on the phone, and if he's feeling better, he might be able to take it on,' he muttered, but didn't sound very hopeful. 'If not, you might have to carry on doing the basics until I can find someone.'

'Yes, sir!' she said eagerly. Even if it did turn out to be something so run-of-the-mill, this was the first time her superior officer was willing to trust her with something substantial, at last!

'All right then, off you go. You know the drill,' he added vaguely. 'Preliminary inquiries only, mind,' he repeated.

'Yes, sir. Er …' Trudy hesitated.

'Well?' Jennings snapped.

'I was just wondering, sir, if the police surgeon's office is so busy … Might it not be a good idea to call on Dr Ryder? In a pinch, he'd have the authority to confirm death, and allow the mortuary people to move the body? Otherwise …'

The inspector's first thought was to roar out, 'No, you bloody well can't call on the old vulture!' This was the nickname for the coroner that most members of the police force (and several not in the police force) often used behind Clement Ryder's back. The inspector didn't like it when his WPC and the coroner got together – they very often discovered more trouble than he would like.

But then he caught back the knee-jerk reaction, and instead a crafty smile spread across his face. It was blowing freezing snow out there, and he doubted Dr Clement Ryder would be pleased at being winkled out of his cosy home on New Year's morning to go to the scene of a road traffic accident, and perform so humble a task as to pronounce a death. The former surgeon would think it well beneath his status and dignity.

Serve him right!

'Of course, Constable,' he said sweetly. 'A good idea. It might not be very orthodox, but given how much the police surgeon has been complaining how backlogged they are, I'm sure I can square it with their office.'

'Thank you, sir,' Trudy said, beaming, and shot out the door before he could change his mind.

Jennings chuckled, then winced as his head began to throb. Glumly, he saw the day stretching grimly ahead. Just how many of his officers could he expect to straggle in?

He sighed heavily. Well, at least this time not even Dr Ryder and his troublesome WPC would be able to make anything out of something so straightforward as a dead motorist.

Chapter 5

Trudy very rarely had cause to visit Dr Clement Ryder at his private residence, and she felt a moment of apprehension as she walked up South Parks Road towards the attractive Victorian terrace where he had his home. She was pushing her bicycle somewhat awkwardly, as the roads here hadn't been totally cleared yet, but she was confident that the main Woodstock and Banbury roads to the north of the city would have been. And that Dr Ryder's heavy Rover would probably be able to cope with the conditions.

But what if he wasn't interested in her new 'case' – if it could even be called that? She doubted that there'd turn out to be anything actually criminal going on, and he might not appreciate being dragged out into the cold just to do the police surgeon a favour. On the other hand, they hadn't investigated anything together since last May. She couldn't be the only one who was looking forward to getting together again – could she?

She sighed as she opened his gate, relieved to see that the short front path had recently seen the attentions of a snow shovel. She was dressed in wellington boots (not regulation, but the weather had made even the most hardened stickler for uniform turn a blind eye) and as she rang the doorbell, she conscientiously stamped her footwear clear of clinging snow. If she had misjudged things, the last thing she wanted to do was track unmelted snow into the house.

She was still looking down at her feet when the door opened, and she looked up with a bright smile, already saying 'Happy New Year, Dr Ry …' when she realised that the man standing in front of her was not, in fact, the coroner.

Somewhere in his late twenties, he was around six feet tall, with light brown, almost blond hair and large, hazel eyes. He was good-looking in a foxy-faced kind of way, and at the moment he was looking over her uniform and frowning. 'Yes, officer? Is there something I can help you with?'

Trudy quickly wiped the smile off her face, feeling like a fool, and stiffened slightly. 'I'm sorry, sir. I was wondering if it would be possible to speak to Dr Clement Ryder?'

The stranger on the doorstep looked at her with wary puzzlement. Her complexion had become reddened by the coldness of the day, but she couldn't know that he thought she still managed to look quite lovely. 'It's New Year's Day,' he said flatly, apparently unimpressed by the caller's charm. 'I believe he's not officially on duty until the beginning of next week?'

Trudy flushed. She was right to be worried – she shouldn't have come. 'I'm sorry, I'll …'

'Who is it?' she heard Clement call from somewhere in the hall beyond.

'Not sure, Dad. It seems to be the police. Hope you haven't been misbehaving,' the young man said teasingly, but still regarded Trudy without any particular benevolence.

'Who?'

Trudy, who was already turning away, swung back as she heard her friend's voice calling her. Clement's face had appeared over one of his son's shoulders and he was now smiling widely in welcome. 'Trudy? My dear girl, come in out of the cold. I was just about to make some cocoa,' he lied. He never drank the stuff, and Vincent, who clearly knew it too, shot him a quick look of puzzlement. 'This ill-mannered oaf is my son Vincent,' he added mildly.

Trudy saw the younger man shoot her a slightly shame-faced look.

'Oh, no, it's all right. I have to …' she began, still eyeing Vincent nervously. By now, she'd worked out why he was being so antagonistic of course. The family members of public servants must get used to protecting them from intrusion and unwarranted calls on their time. The children of GPs, she suspected, learned at an early age how to sort the wheat from the chaff when it came to out-of-hours callers.

'I won't take no for an answer. Come on in,' Clement said firmly, more order than suggestion, and Vincent hesitated only a moment longer before reluctantly stepping aside, opening the door wider to admit her.

'Well, just for a moment then,' Trudy said uncomfortably. Why hadn't she realised that the coroner would probably have family in residence? It was the holiday season after all. She was just so used to thinking of him being alone in the world, she supposed.

'Happy New Year,' she said, flicking her gaze between Clement and his son.

Trudy knew little about the coroner's private life; only really the basic facts that he'd been a widower for some time, and had a son and daughter – twins – who had long since grown up and moved away from the city.

'Happy New Year to you too,' Clement responded, ushering her ahead and leading the way to the kitchen. There he went straight to the refrigerator where he extracted a milk bottle and began to pour some milk into a pan. 'Vincent, you want some?' Clement asked his son, who stood leaning against one side of the doorway, arms crossed over his chest, watching them.

'No thanks,' he said quietly.

'Sit down, Trudy,' Clement said as he noticed that his young friend was hovering uncertainly by the kitchen table.

30

Trudy had already noted that he was dressed in a heavy tweed suit, but no tie, and looked to have a lost a little weight since she'd last seen him. She obediently drew out one of the kitchen chairs and sat down. 'I really can't stay long, Dr Ryder. I have to make my way to Five Mile Drive. We've had a fatality,' she added.

As she'd known it would, Clement's handsome head turned swiftly to look at her, eyes already alight with interest, and she felt a small but distinct sense of satisfaction at his reaction. 'Oh?'

'A driver found dead in his car.' Whilst she had been pleased to discover that her mentor was as eager as she was to work another case together, she felt as if the rather prosaic nature of it let them down somewhat.

Not that he seemed to feel the same way. 'You need me?' Clement asked eagerly. He put the saucepan of milk onto the stove and turned on the heat and glanced at her.

Trudy shot the young man hovering in the doorway a quick look and wondered what to say. If Vincent Ryder hadn't been there, she'd already be eagerly giving him all the details, including Inspector Jennings's strict and limiting instructions (and how they could get around them!) but now she felt as if she really *was* intruding. What if Dr Ryder wanted to stay at home in the warm with his son? Before she could think of a way to frame a polite refusal, however, Clement was already talking.

'Sorry, that was stupid of me. Of course you need me. I heard from Dr Robbins only yesterday that he was up to his eyes in cases, with half his staff off with this bloody bug and others snowed in out in the suburbs. He'll have no manpower to spare for something so routine. I'll give him a call now and offer to have a look and pronounce death. That way, they can at least move the body, tow the car and get the obstruction cleared before the day gets really started.'

Vincent moved out of the doorway to allow his father to pass by, and a moment later Trudy heard a door open and close somewhere in the front of the house. Presumably a study or library?

'Do the police really need to call on my father for something so basic?' Vincent asked resentfully. His dad was no spring chicken anymore, and they'd had a late night, seeing in the new year. He should be taking it easy today. 'He is on holiday you know.'

'I'm sorry,' Trudy said uncomfortably.

Vincent sighed, and began absently ladling two heaped spoonfuls of cocoa into a mug and mixing it with a little milk. From somewhere further back in the house they could just hear the coroner's deep, rumbling voice.

A short while later, it fell silent and then Clement reappeared in the kitchen, rubbing his hands with satisfaction. 'Well, that's all sorted. Robbins was delighted to have one less thing to worry about, as I thought.'

Vincent smiled grimly, wondering if that was the case or if, as happened so often, his father had simply told the poor man what was going to happen and expected to be obeyed. He noticed that a similar smile was hovering around Trudy's own lips and Vincent's gaze sharpened on her.

He felt an unexpected but definite sense of anger creep over him. Just who was this attractive girl, to know his father so well? And think she could smile about it?

'The milk's about to boil over, Dad,' Vincent said sharply and watched as Clement made a brief noise of annoyance and reached for the saucepan on the stove.

Vincent handed over the mug, and he and Trudy watched as Clement poured out the milk. His hand shook slightly as he did so, spilling some milk on the draining board. Clement looked up quickly, no doubt checking to see if either of his guests had noticed, and Vincent saw the pretty young police officer glance carefully away. There was something in the way she pretended not to see it that made his hackles rise in growing alarm. Just what the hell was going on here? Who *was* this young woman, and how well did she know his father?

'So, do you often get called out by the police to do their

32

work for them?' Vincent asked, careful to keep his voice light and teasing.

Clement grunted, stirring the cocoa mix and handing the mug to Trudy, who took it and sipped from it nervously. In truth, she didn't really want the hot drink, welcome though it was. There was something increasingly odd in the atmosphere between father and son now that made her feel distinctly uneasy.

She couldn't for the life of her have said why, but she was sure that the coroner's handsome son had taken against her for some reason, and she wanted only to make herself scarce.

'As a matter of fact, Constable Loveday and myself are old hands at it,' Clement said cheerfully. Things had been pretty dull for him of late, and even if a dead, probably drunken driver, wouldn't amount to much of an investigation, it beat staying indoors, listening to the wireless and rereading Tolstoy.

Vincent's head came up sharply. 'Sorry? What do you mean, exactly? Old hands at what?'

Clement smiled at his son, and began to explain their previous cases. Trudy, whilst proud of their successes, couldn't help but feel that Vincent Ryder was less than happy to hear that his father fancied himself as a detective and had actively been working with her to investigate actual crimes.

'So you and … er …' Vincent looked at the pretty young girl incredulously. 'Er … Constable …'

'Loveday, sir,' Trudy supplied helpfully.

'Yes, thank you, Constable Loveday. You've been actually working on *murder cases*?' Vincent said, his voice rising higher in sheer disbelief.

He stared at Trudy, trying to guess her age. She looked to him to be barely out of her teens!

'Well, not quite,' Clement said. 'That is, nobody knew they were murder cases at the time. Let's just say,' he added on seeing his son's puzzled features, 'that sometimes things happen that need looking into, but they don't really seem to require an official investigation, as such. If I get a case in my court where I feel that a verdict of accidental death, for instance, isn't really justified, that's when I make a fuss and we're allowed to dig about a little. Question suspects, follow leads, that sort of thing. And recently, we were asked by the police to do some undercover digging in what was an active murder investigation.'

'Dad! That's a job for the police, surely?' Vincent objected.

'Trudy is the police,' Clement pointed out placidly and with impeccable logic.

'But *you're* not!' he objected. 'You're supposed to work in an office or the courtroom.' Where the old man would be safe and not getting himself into trouble, he mentally added.

Clement shot his son a knowing look. 'I'm not a complete old duffer yet, Vincent. And you could argue that making sure people don't get away with murder does fall under my purview as a city coroner.'

'Don't give me that,' Vincent snorted. 'You're just having a ball running around playing Sherlock Holmes!' he accused.

Clement threw his head back and laughed. 'And what if I am, son, hmm?'

Vincent opened his mouth, but catching the steely glint that lit his father's eye, thought better of the pithy reply that hovered on his lips. Instead, he looked across at the young girl sitting silently at the table, patently unable to meet his eye, and felt another jolt of alarm hit him.

He remembered, a few months ago now, talking to his sister on the phone, and her remark that their father seemed to have got some of his old vim and sparkle back during the last couple of years. He had to agree, but hadn't really thought much about why that should be so at the time. Now he suspected that he knew exactly why.

His father, who liked to be in the thick of things, had found a new way to amuse himself. Tracking down murderers, and ordering people about. It would be just the sort of thing he would relish.

But what if there was more to it than just that?

His father had been a widower for some time now. And he was at that age when men could make a fool of themselves over a pretty girl. Worse still, a man like Clement, who had both independent wealth and status, would represent a very attractive proposition to anyone on the lookout for a wealthy husband.

Just how long had this dark-haired, doe-eyed demure little WPC and his father been working together?

And exactly how 'friendly' were they?

Chapter 6

'I thought the old girl was never going to start,' Clement Ryder mused ten minutes later, and patted the dashboard of his Rover P4 as they finally and carefully pulled away from his house. There was barely room in the middle of the road for the big car to push past the snowdrifts on either side and even in low gear, the car's rear end had the unnerving tendency to head off in odd directions.

Trudy, who was merely grateful that it had started (otherwise she'd have had to cycle up the freezing Woodstock Road) smiled distractedly.

Once they'd made their way to the more recently cleared and wider carriageway of Banbury Road, Clement glanced across at her thoughtfully and frowned. His young friend wasn't her usual ebullient and sparkling self today, and he suspected he might know why. He hadn't exactly been oblivious to the chilly atmosphere in the kitchen earlier – a chill that had nothing, for once, to do with the atrocious weather.

'You mustn't let Vincent worry you,' he said casually. 'He's always something of a grump in the mornings. It takes him time to warm to people.'

'Oh, I didn't mind,' Trudy said hastily. 'And he might have been right to be unhappy with me. I didn't even stop to consider whether you might not want to be dragged out of your warm home on a national holiday!'

'Nonsense! I'm glad you did,' he said, evidently meaning it.

Reassured, Trudy began to relax.

Clement frowned once more as he turned the windscreen wipers on. The snow was coming down again, faster than ever, but it wasn't the thought of yet more snow that concerned him.

His son was no fool, and Vincent had seen him take that tumble last week – a result of his Parkinson's disease getting worse. It had happened in the house too, without even the excuse of a slippery pavement to disguise it. He had simply failed to lift his feet properly – his own fault entirely. Although he tried to make a conscious effort to think about walking normally, sometimes he just forgot.

Bloody disease!

It had ruined his career as a surgeon. When he'd first noticed a fine trembling in his hand, and went overseas to confirm his diagnosis, he'd resigned immediately from the medical profession – to the astonishment of everyone who knew him – and retrained as a coroner. At least, in that profession, his medical knowledge didn't go to total waste.

So far he'd been able to keep his condition a secret from everyone around him, having travelled abroad to get properly diagnosed and treated. Nowadays, he tracked the progress of the disease himself, and self-medicated when necessary. He'd been confident that no one in his intimate circle even suspected that he might have a problem.

But now he was worried that Vincent might have begun to wonder if there was something his father was keeping from him. He was a sharp-eyed lad, and not unintelligent. And much as he loved him, Clement wished this bloody snow would stop so that his son could return to his own life, which was lived many miles away from Oxford, before …

'I think this must be it, just ahead. I can see the constable on guard,' Trudy's voice interrupted the direction of his morose thoughts.

They had just approached and made the turn into Five Mile Drive, and up ahead, only a few yards on the opposite side of the road, they could just see, sticking up through a mound of snow, one angle of the rear end of a car. 'It looks as if he turned the corner and overshot it and hit the tree,' Trudy mused. 'He might have hit a really bad patch of ice, perhaps?'

In front of the snowdrift was the bare trunk of a denuded cherry tree. The whole length of road was lined with them, and they looked lovely in April or May, when all the blossoms were out. Now this particular tree seemed to stand as a sad sentinel over the place where a man had lost his life, its bare twigs hanging heavily with icicles.

'Either that, or he was going too fast for the conditions and lost control of his car,' Clement agreed, automatically looking for a place to park, and then realising how pointless that was. The snowploughs, whilst furrowing a path through the road, had simply heaped snow at the kerbside. Instead, he just turned off the engine where they were – in the middle of the road – and opened the door. It was not as if it was likely that traffic would be queuing up any time soon. It was still relatively early on New Year's Day. Most sensible people would still be in bed – and likely to stay there for some time to come!

'Would he be driving fast? In this weather and the dark?' Trudy mused.

'Depends how much he'd had to drink.' Clement shrugged. In his line of work, he was hardly unfamiliar with people who thought they could drink and drive.

As Trudy stepped out of the passenger side, a young constable, looking miserable and perishing, stepped forward.

'You my relief then?' he asked hopefully, looking Trudy up and down without much favour. He was probably the same age as Rodney, and from the dismissive look in his eyes, shared Rodney's opinion of women in the police force.

Trudy smiled wearily. 'Inspector Jennings has asked me to do the preliminaries,' she said brusquely and got out her notebook. As she began to take down the particulars from the local beat bobby, Clement approached the crashed car cautiously.

It was a Riley, he thought, and a path through the foot or so of snow surrounding it had already been cleared somewhat to the driver's side door – probably by the constable who'd originally been called out to the scene.

He bent down and peered through the frosted glass of the door's window. It was hard to see much, as the icy film on the glass distorted the picture of what lay within, but Clement could make out the bare details.

A man in a fashionable coat lay slumped forward, forehead resting on the steering wheel and looking, incongruously, as if he'd decided to just take a nap. His arm on the nearest side to where Clement was looking in, hung down by his side, his bare hand and fingers pale against the darker interior of the car. Clement's own hands, clad in thick warm gloves, tingled in sympathy for their cold, blue nakedness.

The coroner knew that it had been well below freezing last night, but he'd have to get the exact temperature from the local meteorological people. If they could find out when the victim was last seen alive, it might be possible to make a fairly accurate guess at time of death.

He opened the door and crouched down, feeling a twinge in his lower back as he did so. Ignoring it, he peered closely at the dead man. Then he lifted his gloved right hand to his mouth and, using his teeth, pulled his glove off by the fingertips. He made a quick check for any pulse or other sign of life, unsurprised when he didn't find any.

Young, around thirty or so, Clement guessed. Good-looking too – for in spite of the fact that his face was a ghostly white, his features hadn't been affected much. Lots of dark hair, in need of a good cut, in Clement's opinion. But the trend among the

39

young nowadays was to wear their hair longer, he knew. There was no obvious blood or sign of severe injury. Gingerly, Clement leaned in closer to peer at the forehead where it was lying against the wheel. He could see no sign of significant bruising yet – but that, as he well knew, needn't necessarily mean anything. Some bruising only became obvious on cadavers after twenty-four or more hours.

But on first glance, it didn't look to him as if the driver had sustained fatal injuries from the crash. Although the front of the car rested against the tree trunk, it didn't look all that dented in, and he suspected the bank of snow at the side of the road had softened the actual impact. But perhaps it had been enough to jolt him forward, banging his head against the wheel? Enough to knock him out? Especially if he was already three sheets to the wind anyway? Clement gave a mental shrug. Most likely it would turn out to be the cold that had finished him off, poor soul.

With a grunt, Clement leaned even further forward, putting his nose close to – but not touching – the dead man's lips. He sniffed and thought he detected just a faint whiff of alcohol. In the intense cold, he couldn't be sure. Delicately, he reached out and lifted one of the man's closed eyelids.

And for a long, long, moment, he regarded the large, darkly dilated pupils thoughtfully. Then he gave an almost imperceptible nod, closed the man's eyes again respectfully and stood up. He again ignored the twinge in his back.

He put his glove back on, and carefully closed the door.

By the time he'd finished all this, Trudy and the other constable were watching and waiting for his verdict in silence.

'I can confirm death,' Clement said flatly, glancing out of habit at his watch.

Trudy too made a note of the time in her notebook, and nodded at him. 'Constable Wilkins here was called out just after six-thirty this morning, by a man who'd been walking his dog and found the car.'

'Beats me why anybody would be up at that hour on New Year's Day, let alone walking a dog. And in this weather too!' the constable muttered resentfully.

'People are often creatures of habit,' Clement commented mildly, looking at the scene. All around, white, hard-packed frozen snow, overlaid with a softer blanket of the snow that had fallen recently, made everything look uniform and ill-defined. Trudy, also looking at the scene, pointed to the obvious set of footprints leading to the car.

'These the dog walker's?' she asked.

'Uh-huh,' Wilkins agreed. 'He was waiting by the passenger door when I got here. When I cleared a path to the car myself, I made sure not to disturb them,' he added smugly, clearly expecting praise. Receiving none, he sighed.

'What are these, do you know?' Trudy asked, hunkering down and looking at some slight indentations in the snow that also seemed to circumnavigate the stranded vehicle.

'Dunno,' Wilkins said, looking at where she was pointing.

Trudy frowned. Two sets of tracks – the dog walker's in deep snow, and the constable's where he'd trampled down a path – were clear enough. Both men, sensibly, had come and gone using the same set of tracks each had made. If you had to plough through nearly two feet of snow, it was hard work. Instinctively, you'd put your feet in the same holes coming as going, and in the bottom of each set of tracks, she could just make out the individual boot patterns of each man. Those of the dog walker, though, were fast disappearing in the falling snow.

But the other indentations in the snow had no marks in them at all – nor were they so deep. 'It looks as if someone might have been here already – perhaps last night when it happened – and then fresh snow partially filled in the holes?' she hazarded, looking up at Clement.

'Or they might have been caused more recently by someone or something that was not heavy, and didn't sink so deeply into the snow?' Clement pointed out. He glanced at the constable. 'What was the breed of dog?'

'Sorry?' Wilkins blinked at the older man in consternation.

'The dog walker's? Was it a small dog, or a big one? Could it have been prancing around, making these marks?'

'I don't see any pawprints,' Trudy said, peering into one of the smaller indentations. Might a fox have made them in the night, she wondered, sniffing around and disturbing the scene?

'It was a collie,' Wilkins said to the coroner, sounding bored. 'One of those daft, friendly, black-and-white ones.'

Trudy shrugged and stood up. 'Well, Dr Ryder has confirmed death. Why don't you see if you can find someone up in one of these?' She glanced around at the houses. 'And ask to use their telephone and get the mortuary van out here? I'm sure someone will give you a cup of tea – maybe even offer you breakfast if you're lucky,' Trudy added quickly, when it was obvious that Wilkins was about to object to having to hang around.

She saw the allure of bacon and eggs work its magic and the constable nodded and walked off, looking almost jaunty, to the nearest house.

Trudy braced herself then walked to the car, stepping in Dr Ryder's footsteps, and inspected the body inside. She was glad it wasn't gruesome, but she still felt slightly queasy as she reached into the dead man's coat pockets in search of identification.

She found it in his wallet.

'Terrence James Parker,' she said, glancing down at the dead man sadly. 'I wonder what he was looking forward to doing in this brand-new year?'

Clement shook his head. Although he heard her comment, he wasn't feeling in a philosophical mood.

'Trudy, I don't like the look of his eyes,' he said flatly.

Chapter 7

When Trudy shot him a quick, surprised look, he explained about the dilated pupils.

'Could too much drink be the cause of that?' she asked, after a startled moment of thought.

'I don't think it's particularly likely,' the doctor in Clement proclaimed cautiously. 'Of course, he could have hit his head far harder than it appears he has. Head injuries are notoriously hard to quantify until a proper post-mortem has been performed. Concussion *might* be the cause of it.'

'But?' Trudy asked, one dark eyebrow raised quizzically.

'But,' Clement echoed with a small smile, 'I have to admit, my very first thought was that he might have ingested some kind of drug.'

Trudy thought about that for a moment, then sighed. 'We really need to find out what he'd been doing last night then, don't we? And if he was at a party, as his clothes suggest, just what *kind* of a party was it?' So far in her career, she had seldom come across problems caused by drugs – as a lowly beat cop, she was kept well away from the investigation of narcotics cases. But she knew that drugs weren't exactly unheard of in the city – especially among the student body and the bored and wealthy set, to which their corpse seemed to belong.

His clothes were all good quality, she'd noticed, as were his shoes. He'd also been wearing an expensive watch. 'At least he wasn't robbed,' she added as an afterthought, checking his wallet again and finding a lot of folded paper notes, confirming her hypothesis.

Clement grunted. 'Got an address for him?'

Trudy waggled the wallet happily. 'Inspector Jennings did tell me to start on preliminary inquiries,' she agreed, eyes sparkling with anticipation.

＊

Terrence James Parker lived in a small terraced house near the turn-off to the very desirable village of Wolvercote, and opposite the entrance to another road full of north Oxford mansions. Not quite close enough to be able to boast that he lived in either area, but his street was not exactly downmarket either.

Unfortunately, this smaller side street had not seen the attentions of the snowploughs yet, so they had to abandon the Rover on the nearest clear road and make their way as best they could through the snow on foot.

Luckily, the coroner kept his wellingtons in the car boot, but even so, both of them were aware of numb toes and clammy, cold legs as they made their way up the short path to the front of his house. In addition, Trudy's cheeks felt as if they were burning – a product of profoundly icy air that she'd always found rather baffling.

Made of red brick with attractive cream details over windows and door, the residence still had its curtains firmly drawn. Trudy pressed the doorbell, hoping her instincts were right, and that their victim lived alone. Surely, if he'd had a spouse, she would have reported him missing last night – or in the early hours? Or, more likely, she'd have been at the same party with him – in which case, what had she been doing after the car accident?

There were no sounds coming from inside the house, but she rang the bell again just to make sure. She hated having to deliver bad news to the relatives of people who had died, and she couldn't help but smile slightly as she turned to the man beside her. 'Looks as if nobody's home.'

'No,' Clement agreed. 'Let's try next door.'

It was starting to get fully light now, but Trudy wasn't sure if anybody would be up yet. Especially if the neighbours either side of Terrence Parker had stayed up to see the new year in.

Still, that couldn't really be helped.

They walked back up the path, choosing the house on the right first. She banged on the doorknocker and waited. Its sharp, peremptory noise sounded ominous, even to her ears, and she could only wonder what the householders felt at being awakened like this on such a cold, dark morning.

She knocked again, and was finally rewarded by the sound of someone obviously coming down the stairs. From that she surmised that the front door led straight into the hallway, with the stairs facing them. Whoever it was descending sounded heavy.

The door opened with a yank, and a large, fleshy woman dressed in a pink flannel housecoat wrapped tightly around her figure, glared out at them. She was probably in her early fifties, Trudy gauged, with short curly brown hair that was almost certainly the result of a permanent wave, and large brown eyes that looked slightly red-rimmed.

'Yes?' the woman said, her eyes growing wider with alarm as she took in Trudy's uniform, and then looking even more worried as she regarded the unmistakable figure of authority that was Dr Ryder, standing slightly behind and to the left of her.

'Oh no, it's not my Frank, is it?' she said, swallowing hard, all the colour leaching out of her rounded face.

45

'No, it's about your next-door neighbour,' Trudy reassured her hastily, assuming that Frank was a family member.

'Oh, him!' The woman sagged against the doorframe, breathing out in obvious relief, then instantly looked guilty. 'Sorry, I didn't mean … What's up with Terry then? He's all right, is he?' Her eyes went from Trudy to the coroner, then back again.

'No, I'm afraid not, madam,' Trudy said, thinking that there was very little point in beating about the bush. Although it was hardly ever a good idea to give out information, she knew that the news of the fatal accident would be out and doing the rounds before lunchtime. Snow or no snow! And she needed this woman's help. 'We're trying to locate his next of kin. Have you been neighbours long, Mrs …?' she probed gently.

'Kirk. Kitty Kirk. Er, nearly four years now. What happened?' the woman asked again, looking eager and curious now that her initial fright had passed.

'We're still investigating, Mrs Kirk,' Trudy said firmly. Just because the local grapevine would soon be in overdrive, she saw no reason to add her own tuppence's worth. 'Is Mr Parker married?'

'Oh no, love, not him!' Kitty Kirk said with a sudden and knowing smile. Trudy nodded, taking on board the tacit message. Their victim was something of a ladies' man. Probably not relevant, but still interesting to know.

'I don't suppose you happen to have an address for his parents?' Trudy asked next, but without much hope.

'Oh no, love,' the older woman said, right on cue. 'He's not one to be over-friendly like. Well, not with his neighbours anyway,' she added, with another knowing smile.

Trudy sighed. 'Is there anything you can tell us about where he might have been last night?' she asked, again without much hope.

But this time, her luck seemed to be improving. 'Oh, he was sure to be at that fancy party,' Kitty said, her lips twisting into yet another smile that was just a little crooked. 'I heard from

Doris three doors down that he'd been invited. Well, I'm not that surprised. He was the sort who would be, if you know what I mean.'

Trudy didn't, but she definitely wanted to find out. 'Fancy party? Do you know where this was?'

'Oh, Doris said it was in one of those mansions down along Banbury Road. A widow-woman,' she added with heavy emphasis. 'Mrs … Oh, what was the name? Doris said everyone who was anyone was going … well, that rules me out then, don't it, love?' Kitty added with a laugh. 'Mrs Vander!' she suddenly squealed loudly, making both Trudy and Clement jump. 'Yerse, that was her name. Mrs Vander … like I said, a widow-woman. Well-heeled. Just Terry's type if you ask me,' she added, nodding with satisfaction at her ability to recall the name. 'Terry's a nice enough lad, but he's got ideas above his station, you ask me.'

'I don't suppose you know the exact address of this party?' Trudy asked.

'No, but Doris will,' Kitty predicted smugly. 'Do you want me to go round and ask her?'

'No, thank you,' Trudy said hastily, then added, more gently, 'It's perishing out here, and I don't want to inconvenience you more than necessary. If you can just tell us which house belongs to Doris?'

Reluctantly, Kitty Kirk pointed out the house, then watched them as they retreated up her garden path. She continued to watch them all the way to Doris's house, Trudy noted, and almost certainly she was still waiting and watching as they knocked on the door and got her friend out of bed.

No doubt, the moment they left the area, she'd be dressed and around Doris's house to compare notes, Trudy mused with a wry smile.

*

The helpful Doris didn't know the address as such, but *was* able to give them such an accurate description of the house, and its position on Banbury Road, that they were able to find it without much trouble. It was slightly nearer St Giles than Summertown, which put it somewhere around two miles from the scene of the crash.

It was now fully light. The house was large, whitewashed and maybe Georgian, with big wide windows and the simple, elegant dimensions that a lot of the houses in this part of the city seemed to prefer. The wide, semicircular gravel drive had obviously been cleared last night for the event, but that morning's fresh snow was starting to lay another blanket on top of the cleared spaces.

It was clear that a few cars had been parked on the spacious driveway recently, and as they approached the impressive front door (oak, painted dark blue) Trudy was sure she could see movement in an upstairs window.

'Somebody's up and about,' Clement said, indicating that he too had noticed. 'We're being watched, I think.'

Trudy turned around to regard the large garden, full of laurels and several other evergreens, now bowed down under the weight of snow. Clement, doing the same, murmured thoughtfully, 'This is a long way, socially, from his own place, isn't it? Any idea, from his identification, what he did for a living?'

'No,' Trudy said, then tensed as the door opened behind her.

The woman who stood on the threshold looking at them was small – not much more than five feet, Trudy gauged. She had long red hair left loose around her shoulders, and wore some sort of fancy silk black lounge pyjamas with a matching black-and-gold floating negligee thing that she now pulled tightly around her. Unlike Kitty Kirk's warm housecoat, she doubted it gave the woman much protection from the freezing air.

But something told Trudy that this woman would rather look good and freeze, than be warm but look dowdy.

'Yes, what on earth is it?' the woman asked, looking at Trudy in her uniform with some trepidation.

'I'm sorry to bother you … is it Mrs Vander?' Trudy asked.

'Yes, I'm Millie Vander.'

'Can we come in please? You must be freezing,' Trudy said, following up the suggestion with a small forward step. She couldn't have said why, but she had the feeling that the petite redhead didn't want them in her house, which only made Trudy all the more determined to conduct the interview inside.

Millie Vander visibly hesitated a second, then stepped aside to let them in. The house was warm everywhere, and Trudy realised they had central heating. She'd heard about it, but no one she knew had it in their own homes. But chilly draughts and inadequate real fires were not for someone who lived in a house like this! The hall was otherwise small but nicely proportioned.

'I've only just risen, as you can see,' Millie began. 'I hope this won't take long – whatever it is?'

She eyed Clement curiously, and Trudy saw her preen a little in the presence of a handsome man. It seemed to come from a habit born of a lifetime's practice.

'I hope we won't have to take up much of your time, Mrs Vander. I'm WPC Loveday, and this is Dr Clement Ryder.'

'Hello, Doctor,' Millie said at once, holding out a slender, pale hand to the coroner, who took it and shook it with a smile. Trudy noticed Mrs Vander was wearing pink nail varnish. She was also, Trudy noted, wearing a certain amount of make-up. So much for having just risen, she thought. The lady of the house must have been up for at least a quarter of an hour and had been in the process of making herself presentable for the day.

'We understand you threw a New Year's Eve party last night,' Trudy began gently.

'Oh, for heaven's sake,' Millie said, tossing her long red hair in annoyance. 'This can't be about a noise complaint? I simply can't believe it of my neighbours – besides, most of them were here themselves!' She laughed lightly, throwing another smile somewhat perfunctorily at Dr Ryder.

Beneath the veneer of gaiety, however, Trudy was sure she could detect nervousness in their witness. Of course, that didn't necessarily mean much – most people, even thoroughly law-abiding people, felt nervous when they had an unexpected visit from the law.

'No, I'm afraid I have more serious news than that. Could we talk somewhere more …?' Trudy glanced around the hall, which had a small grandfather clock ticking pretentiously in one corner, a marble console table with a black Bakelite telephone on it, and a staircase, sweeping up and around to the top floor.

'Oh, come on through to the morning room,' Millie said with a slightly petulant sigh, turning and heading to the second door on the right. Here, the curtains were still drawn, and she went straight to the window to let in some light. The room was square, the walls painted a duck-egg blue. A large gilt oval mirror reflected the room back at them over a marble fireplace. The air smelt faintly of cigarette smoke. A large sheepskin rug lay in front of a small walnut coffee table and a two-seater settee. If any of last night's party had overspilled into this room, it had either been cleaned in the interim, or else the guests had been very well behaved.

'Please, take a seat,' Millie said, indicating the Queen-Anne-style settee and chairs. Clement chose the sturdiest-looking chair, and Trudy another. After a moment's hesitation, their hostess chose the two-seater settee and settled herself in it. She tossed one silk-clad leg over the other. On her feet were backless mules, fluffy with dyed black feathers. With her unbound long red hair and exotic (to Trudy) outfit, she looked a bit like one of the stars of the silver screen from a decade or two ago. She should, Trudy thought cynically, ideally be holding a cigarette holder, and saying something witty.

Instead, she looked wary and unhappy. Her green eyes danced around the room, seemingly unable to settle.

'So, what time did your party break up last night?' Trudy asked, getting out her notebook. The sight of such officialdom made Millie go slightly pale under her face powder, and her brows puckered.

'Everyone had left by around one o'clock, because of the awful snow, of course. People were worried they might not get back … Look, do you mind telling me just what this is all in aid of?' she said, definitely petulant now. She jogged her loose foot in the air in agitation, the ridiculous slipper threatening to fall off.

'I'm sorry to say that we have reason to believe that one of your guests was the victim of a fatal accident last night,' Trudy began gently. 'You don't happen to have a guest list, do you?'

Millie abruptly uncrossed her legs and leaned forward on the settee. 'Who?' she cried, her face growing ever more pale now. 'Who died?'

'Did you invite a man named Terrence Parker to your party, Mrs Vander?' Trudy asked gently.

And then she watched, stunned, as the pretty green eyes rolled back in the woman's head, and the petite figure of her witness pitched forward and landed with a graceful fold onto the sheep-skin rug.

Clement was the first to move. He took the few steps necessary to get by her side, then knelt on one knee. Trudy, by now, was also on her feet, her heart thumping in her chest. She had expected the woman to be upset – after all, nobody liked to think a guest in their house had left it only to meet their end. But she had not anticipated such a strong reaction.

She watched nervously as the coroner lifted one of Mrs Vander's hands, his expert fingers quickly searching for a pulse on her wrist, and held her breath as she waited for his verdict. If her witness had had a heart attack …

'She's only passed out,' Clement said calmly. 'She'll soon start to …'

It was then that a young man walked in, took in the scene at a glance, and snarled, 'Who the hell are you? Get away from my mother before I rip your damned head off!'

'That'll be enough of that, sir,' Trudy said sharply, moving forward hastily and putting herself between Dr Ryder and the newcomer.

The young man reared back in surprise, not having realised she was there, his mouth falling open. He was very good-looking, Trudy noticed clinically, with black hair and grey eyes, but he wasn't particularly tall. At five-feet-ten herself, she thought she had a good four or so inches on him, and he took a step back and watched her resentfully, his eyes narrowing.

'Police?' he said, noting her uniform with a brisk, unimpressed glance. 'What have you been saying to my mother? Why is she lying on the floor?'

Just then, Millie gave a sigh and opened her eyes. 'Hello, Mrs Vander, don't be alarmed,' Clement said, still kneeling beside her. He'd paid barely any attention to the young man, his focus on the woman he suddenly considered as a temporary patient. 'You've had a bit of a faint that's all. You've had a nasty shock. Just lie still for a moment and take some deep breaths. When you're ready, I'll help you back into your chair. All right?'

To the young man standing uncertainly in the doorway, he added crisply, 'Your mother's had a shock. Go and make some hot sweet tea. Now,' he ordered curtly as the newcomer continued to stare at him blankly.

The young man flushed, his anger at being spoken to so peremptorily making him look ugly for a moment, before he nodded without much grace and stalked back out into the hall.

Trudy hadn't realised she was so tense until she felt her shoulders slump in relief.

With the son of the house gone, she turned her attention back to Millie, who was beginning to turn on her side, putting a hand out and levering her elbows upwards so that she could sit up.

Trudy rushed forward and helped her lean back against the

settee, and with a nod from Clement, they both put a hand under each of her armpits and helped her up and back onto the settee. She was so slight it didn't require much effort.

Under her make-up, however, Trudy could see that she was still deathly pale.

'Did … Did I hear you say that Terry … Terry's d-dead?' she asked, the last word little more than a whisper.

'We don't yet have a formal identification, Mrs Vander, but yes it seems very likely,' Trudy said with genuine sympathy. 'A car was found crashed earlier this morning. A Riley.' She cited the number plate, which she had written down in her notebook, but it was clear from the dazed look in her eyes, that Millie was in no state to either confirm or deny that she recognised it. 'The man inside had a driver's licence made out to Terrence James Parker. Did he attend your party in a Riley, Mrs Vander?'

'Yes, oh yes, he did,' Millie confirmed miserably.

'I take it he's a good friend?' Trudy persisted softly. 'Have you known him long?'

Millie drew in a long, shuddering breath, and closed her eyes for a moment. Then her shoulders straightened and her lips pinched tighter together. Trudy recognised all the signs of a woman getting herself firmly under control. A long, tense moment passed in silence, then the older woman pushed back the hair from her face and hugged herself around the middle.

'No, not really,' she finally said. And now Trudy was sure she could sense caution in the woman's manner. 'I met him last year … No, sorry, of course we're into a new year now, aren't we, so it'll be the year before last. I'm sorry, I don't seem to be … Oh, Jasper, thank you.'

Her green eyes fastened on her returning son like a drowning woman spotting a ship in the distance. She reached out with unsteady hands for the cup he held, and Trudy wasn't surprised to hear the cup rattling against the saucer as she drew it towards her.

Somewhat to Trudy's surprise, her son sat down beside Millie, gently took the crockery from her and helped guide the cup to her lips. 'Come on, old girl, take a small sip and then tell me what's up then, hmmm?' he asked.

He shot Trudy a savage glance, then Clement a more thoughtful one.

'Oh Jasper, something t-terrible happened,' she said. 'T … one of our guests crashed his car on his way home last night. Oh, darling, he's dead.'

For a moment Trudy saw an extraordinary expression cross the young man's face. That whatever feeling had prompted it went deep, and was ferocious, she had no doubt, but she couldn't for the life of her have placed it. Anger? Fear? Hope? Guilt? It might have been any of these, or a combination of all of them, or none of them.

'What do you mean? Who are you talking about? Who's dead?' Jasper demanded, but he was not looking at his mother. Rather he was looking at Trudy. His face was now perfectly composed, but his grey eyes seemed to darken in shade a little.

'Mr Terrence Parker,' Trudy said simply.

Jasper blinked once, then again, and both Trudy and Clement who were watching him closely, saw his lips curl into a faint smile.

'Is he now?' Jasper said evenly.

Chapter 8

For a moment there was a long, odd sort of silence. Jasper was clearly thinking furiously, whilst his mother's glazed expression said she was probably not thinking at all. Clement was watching the young man with a carefully neutral face, and Trudy wondered what she should do and say next.

On the one hand, she was here simply to get details about their victim, and begin the preliminary investigation. Apart from Clement not being sure that Terrence Parker's dilated pupils could definitely be attributed to a brain injury of some sort, she had absolutely no reason to suspect that they were dealing with anything other than a tragic but (in the circumstances) under-standable road fatality.

But instinct and observation was telling her in no uncertain terms that something odd was going on here.

'Can you remember what time Mr Parker left the party last night, sir?' Trudy fished delicately, turning her attention to Jasper Vander.

'Can't say that I do,' Jasper said unhelpfully, holding the cup to his mother's lips again, giving her no option but to take another sip.

'Did you know him well?' Trudy persevered.

'Can't say that I did,' Jasper repeated, shooting her an amused glance. Since it was obvious that he knew that he was being deliberately annoying, Trudy smiled back at him sweetly.

'Did he come alone or did he arrive with a partner?' she asked mildly, taking care that she kept her tone distinctly light. No way was she going to let this little toad get under her skin!

'Oh, I'm sure he was alone,' Jasper said drolly.

Beside him, Trudy saw Millie stiffen slightly at this.

'I was asking your mother if she had a guest list,' Trudy said. 'Would you mind getting it?'

'Oh, I doubt Mother had anything so organised,' Jasper said, staying obstinately in his seat.

At this, Millie waved a self-deprecating gesture with her hand, as if sensing that her son's manner was not winning him any friends. 'I'm afraid he's right about that you know – I'm not very well organised. But I think I can probably remember most of those who came. The immediate neighbours, of course, and the women from my bridge club, you know, along with the usual crowd. Oh, and Katherine Morton, such a coup getting her to come,' Millie added, for a moment the pride of a society hostess shining through.

Trudy had a feeling she was supposed to know who Katherine Morton was, but she had no idea.

'If you give me a little time, I'm sure I'll be able to write out a list for you,' Mille promised. 'Jasper will help, won't you, darling?' She looked at her son appealingly. Yet something about the look that passed between them made Trudy feel uneasy. Although, on the face of it, Millie seemed to be asking for help, there was something else, something hovering just on the edge of her tone and in the look in her eyes that verged on something much harder and steel-like. Almost as if she was giving him orders.

And Trudy wondered, was this woman really as needy as she appeared to be?

'Sure,' Jasper said shortly, and the fact that he said nothing more, Trudy also found very interesting. He hadn't struck her as the type to take hints from his mummy and keep quiet.

'Was Mr Parker a local man?' Trudy tried next. 'Did he come from an Oxford family?'

'Oh no,' Millie said at once. 'He came to study as a student, I think … or no, I have that wrong. I'm sure he told me once that he actually went to Cambridge, but he liked living in a university city so much, that when he graduated he relocated to Oxford. He was originally from Birmingham, I believe.'

'Funny, he never had a Brummie accent,' Jasper commented mildly. 'But then, he probably worked very hard to get rid of it,' he added snidely.

Trudy, who was wondering why, if their victim had studied in Cambridge and liked university towns so much, he simply hadn't stayed in the city in the Fens, shot the man of the house a quick, questioning look. There had been no disguising the dislike in Jasper's tone, and his mother shot him a stricken look.

'Oh, Jasper, not now!' she said. 'I keep telling you! You might think it amusing and oh so modern to be mean about people, but I think it's the height of ill-breeding.'

Jasper spread his hands in surrender.

'What have you done to upset our lovely mother now, Jasp?' a voice drawled behind him, and all four of them turned to watch as the latest entrant to the drama made her appearance.

It wasn't hard to recognise the daughter of the house. As petite as her mother, she had the same attractive green eyes, but her hair was as black as that of her brother. She was quite astonishingly beautiful, and dressed in a long white nightgown and peignoir set. Trudy, in her wellingtons and heavy-weight uniform, immediately felt about as huge and unattractive as an elephant.

'Oh, Juliet, it's terrible. Terry is dead,' Millie wailed. She said it fast, as if needing to warn her daughter of the situation before she could say anything that Millie didn't want said in front of strangers.

Juliet didn't look at her mother though, but rather looked straight at her brother. Again her expression was impossible for Trudy to fathom. Accusing? Questioning? Amused?

Trudy was getting annoyed at her inability to read these people. They seemed to have their own language, and she felt resentful about it. She knew she would have to keep a tight hold on her manner.

She glanced at Clement, who was watching the show silently, his eyes alert but calm.

Jasper shrugged slightly at his sister's questioning, arched his brows and stretched out lazily on the sofa. He didn't look particularly relaxed though, Trudy thought with some satisfaction.

'Dead?' Juliet said flatly. 'Really?'

'He crashed his car, in the dark and the snow,' Millie said, her voice trembling now.

'Finish your tea,' Jasper said sharply, clearly brutally determined to cut off any approaching histrionics. Again, a strange lightning-quick unspoken conversation seemed to go on between mother and son, after which she lifted the teacup obediently and sipped from it.

'We're trying to find out more about Mr Parker.' Trudy kept plugging stubbornly away. 'His next of kin, for instance? Do you know of any family members that we need to contact?'

'I don't think his parents are living,' Millie said forlornly. 'He never spoke of brothers or sisters either, now that I think of it. I think he might have been raised by an aunt or something, but she's probably old and dead by now,' she added vaguely.

'Poor orphan Terry,' Jasper drawled.

'Shut up,' Juliet said to her brother, without any kind of heat. 'Sorry, but we can't help much, as you can see,' she said to Trudy. Her green eyes swept over her appraisingly, rather like someone who has only just noticed another female presence besides her own. They lingered on Trudy's pinned, lustrous dark hair for a moment, before dismissing her and moving on to Clement.

The green eyes looked far more impressed with him, and Trudy could feel the back of her neck begin to burn in a mixture of humiliation and anger.

'Is there anyone you can think of who might help us?' she asked through gritted teeth.

'Oh – of course, how silly of me. Geoffrey Thorpe! His business partner,' Millie suddenly said. 'Terry had his own business selling top-of-the-line sports cars.'

'Used cars,' Juliet corrected her. 'A rather tawdry trade, I've always thought. Selling silly little cars to middle-aged men who can't properly afford them, and certainly don't need them.'

'And can't drive them properly,' Jasper added with a laugh.

Millie flushed at this evidence of her children's contempt, but said nothing. Her lips, though, had tightened into a thin, stubborn line.

Trudy got out her notebook and jotted down the name of the garage and the address that Jasper dutifully recited for her. She also made a note to contact her counterparts in Birmingham and ask them to see if they could find a next of kin for their victim. But she wouldn't hold her breath. The whole country was covered in snow, and she doubted that her request would be a priority.

'Thank you, sir. Perhaps your sister could also help in making up that guest list?' she added.

'Sure, but we're not going to thrash that out right now,' Jasper told her bluntly. 'You'll have to call back in a couple of hours for it. Right now, I think Mother needs to rest and get over the shock a bit. I'll run you a hot bath, shall I?' he added to his mother, who nodded gratefully.

'Perhaps her daughter could stay in the bathroom with her?' Clement said quickly. He didn't want Millie to remain unchaperoned in a bath full of water.

'Yes, she can make herself useful for a change,' Jasper said sardonically, looking at his sister mockingly, who promptly poked her tongue out at him.

'Twins,' Millie said to Clement with an unhappy smile, embarrassed by their behaviour. 'They've always been like this. They don't mean anything by it,' she added feebly.

'I'll just see you out, shall I?' said Jasper, getting to his feet and looking thoroughly unabashed. It was not an offer so much as an order, and one Trudy was in no position to quibble with. Well, not yet anyway, she mused grimly.

Once on the doorstep, however, she had a few last questions. 'Did anything unusual happen at the party, sir? Was Mr Parker, shall we say, a little worse for drink?'

'That would hardly be unusual at a party, Constable dear, would it?' Jasper drawled.

'So he *was* drunk then?' Trudy snapped.

'Not that I saw. But then, I wasn't paying that much attention to him,' Jasper snapped right back.

And then he shut the door firmly in their faces.

Chapter 9

'Well that was interesting,' Clement said mildly, the reverberation of the slammed door still echoing in their ears. He was looking at her with a half-smile on his lips. The handsome, cocky young pup had really riled her, he could see.

'Hmph!' Trudy grunted. 'Did you get the impression that our hostess had, shall we say, a distinct fondness for our victim?'

'Oh yes, it was as clear as a pikestaff,' Clement agreed. 'As was the fact that both of her children most definitely did not!'

'Scared he might be about to upset their very comfortable apple cart no doubt,' Trudy said bitterly. 'If either of those two spoilt brats do a day's work in their life, I'll eat my hat!'

*

According to the information Jasper had provided, Terry Parker's place of business – Regal Cars – had set up their forecourt out near Osney Mead, but Trudy was sure that they wouldn't be open on New Year's Day. In fact, given the weather, she doubted they'd open tomorrow either – especially if it kept on snowing and the snowploughs didn't get out that way.

Luckily, it didn't take her long to get a home address for one

Mr Geoffrey Thorpe, who lived less than a quarter of a mile away from the centre of town.

Unlike the dead man, Geoffrey Thorpe lived in a larger, more obviously family-friendly terraced house, with a bigger front garden. Now that the morning was advancing somewhat, they'd seen just a few more people out and about as they drove, but when Clement was forced to leave the car, yet again, in the middle of a road piled high on either side with snow, nobody was around to object.

As they made their way with some difficulty up a path that, as yet, hadn't been dug clear of the latest snowfall, they could hear the sound of children's excited voices coming from inside the Thorpe residence. So Trudy wasn't surprised when a middle-aged, somewhat harassed-looking woman opened the door to them.

She looked instantly surprised, then alarmed, to see Trudy.

'Good morning, madam, is this the Thorpe residence?' Trudy asked, wishing her uniform didn't have to scare everybody so whenever she called on them. Although she understood why it did, it made her feel like a proper pariah.

'Yes. Is everything all right?' the woman, presumably Mrs Thorpe, demanded quickly. She was a fleshy but pretty woman, with fading fair looks but nice blue eyes.

'We need to speak to Mr Geoffrey Thorpe as a matter of some urgency,' Trudy prevaricated carefully.

'Oh, please, come along in – you must be freezing,' the woman said, casting an apologetic glance at Clement, who had begun stamping his feet as his toes threatened to go numb. They followed her gratefully into a small hallway.

'Head on right in here.' She led them to a door, which opened off to the right. It was clearly their 'best' room, because it had that seldom-used feel to it. There was no Christmas tree here, or children's toys scattered around. Only lace antimacassars on the backs and arms of the furniture and a nice Oriental rug on the linoleum in front of a Draylon sofa. It was also freezing.

'Oh, let me put on the fire,' the woman said, scuttling over to the fireplace where a three-bar electric fire stood in the grate. She put in the plug and turned it on, and then hurried to the door. 'I'll just fetch Geoff,' she said, casting them one last anxious glance and then closing the door behind her.

The electric fire began to make ticking sounds and finally glowed with a promising red heat, before infusing the room with that nose-wrinkling scent of burning metal. Clement nevertheless went over to it, took off his gloves, and held his hands gratefully over the bars.

The noise of children abruptly abated, and Trudy could imagine their mother – or possibly she was their grandmother – demanding that they pipe down.

A moment or two later the door opened and a man walked in. He was in his late forties or maybe very early fifties, Clement gauged, around five-feet-ten, with grey hair and eyes. He was starting to thicken around the middle, and was wearing warm tweed trousers and a matching blazer with a knitted V-neck jumper underneath.

'Hello, this is unexpected,' the man said, holding out his hand first of all to Clement, then to Trudy. 'Geoffrey Thorpe. My wife says you need to see me?'

'Yes, sir, I'm afraid I may have some bad news,' Trudy said. She saw the man stiffen and his eyes fixed on hers steadily.

'Oh?'

'About your business partner. You do own a used car business with a Mr Terrence Parker?' Trudy lifted her voice at the end, to make it a question. As she did so, an undeniably wary look, perhaps tinged with imminent panic, fleetingly crossed the other man's face, before it was almost instantly smoothed out again.

'Terry? Yes? Why, what's he done?' Geoffrey Thorpe asked mildly. He looked, in some puzzlement, at Clement.

It was, Trudy thought, an interesting way of putting it. What had he *expected* the dead man to have done?

'I'm sorry, I should have introduced myself sooner,' Trudy apologised. 'I'm WPC Loveday, and this is Dr Clement Ryder, city coroner.'

'*Coroner*?' Geoffrey echoed, startled. 'Is Terry dead then?'

'We believe so, sir,' Trudy said. 'A man was found dead in his crashed vehicle early this morning. His wallet had documentation in it, which leads us to believe it was Mr Parker. Naturally, we need a formal identification, and so far we've been unable to track down any next of kin. I was wondering if you would mind making your way to the morgue at Floyds Row to view the body?'

Mindful of her need to obey the inspector's orders to get as much of the preliminary work done as possible, she was relieved to see Geoffrey blink, then nod and mutter abstractly, and a little reluctantly, 'Yes, of course I can do that. Yes … er …'

He looked around, as if not sure what to say next, and Trudy said gently, 'There's no immediate rush, Mr Thorpe. But if you could do it today, sometime, that would be very helpful. And best to do it when it's still light, I think. We'll arrange it with the morgue staff that someone's there to meet you and walk you through the process. It's not at all frightening. Although it will probably be upsetting,' she felt obliged to add.

'Oh, yes, yes I'm sure,' he said vaguely, still looking around in a sort of helpless way. Spotting a chair, he walked to it stiff-legged and sat in it abruptly. 'I just can't believe … Terry was such a good driver … He wasn't in the Sprite, was he?' he added quickly, his voice rising an octave in panic.

Trudy looked at him blankly. 'I'm sorry, sir?'

'The Frog-eyed Sprite!' Geoffrey said sharply. 'Terry liked to drive the cars. He said it was an advertisement for the business, to show them off. He always chose a car from the showroom, and his current favourite was the Sprite.'

'Oh no, sir. I think it was a Riley. It was rather covered with snow,' she added apologetically.

'Oh, yes, that makes sense, now I come to think of it,' Geoffrey said, suddenly letting out his breath in a sigh of relief. 'What with the conditions …' He waved a hand at the window, and the snow still falling steadily outside. 'We ourselves just went round to our next-door neighbours' for a bit of a drink last night.' He nodded to indicate the house on their immediate left. 'They invited a few of us in the street. It saved anyone having to drive, you see. But Terry was determined to go to this particular "do" and he didn't mind so much driving in tricky conditions, being younger and less of a fuddy-duddy than myself.' He gave a self-deprecating smile. 'Especially if he'd decided to take the Riley. It handles like a tank but it *is* reassuringly heavy.' He rubbed his palms over his knees, and took a shaky breath.

'You knew all about Mrs Vander's party then?' Trudy asked casually.

Geoffrey sighed, smiled wearily, then nodded. 'Oh yes. Terry wasn't one to keep his light under a bushel, Constable. And being invited to such a socially prominent "do" was a bit of a feather in his cap.'

'I see. Was he a heavy drinker?'

'I wouldn't have said so. I mean, no. But at a party …' He shrugged. 'Well, he'd probably have a drink or two. Poor Terry.' He shook his head. 'I just can't believe it. You're sure that he's really dead?'

'Yes, sir. That is, the man in the car is dead.' She again sought out her notebook and recited the number plate of the crashed vehicle.

Geoffrey nodded. 'Yes, I'm pretty sure that's one of ours. I'll have to check the records to be totally sure …' He shrugged vaguely. 'Most of our cars are sports models, you understand, but occasionally we buy more run-of-the-mill makes. Mostly as a favour for friends or—' He suddenly broke off, as if realising that their business practices hardly mattered to the strangers in his front room.

'You say your partner didn't drink excessively,' Trudy began delicately, 'but that he would not hold back at a party. Do you have any reason to suspect that he indulged in more than alcohol?'

'What do you mean?' Geoffrey sounded genuinely puzzled.

'I mean, sir, did he like to take … say, something rather more exotic to raise his spirits? Something other than alcohol, I mean.'

For a second the other man stared blankly at her, and then a flush of colour stained his cheeks. 'Good grief, *drugs*, do you mean? No, definitely not.' He sounded genuinely scandalised at the thought. 'Terry was, well, a bit flash I suppose you'd call it, but nothing like *that*. He had far too much sense to fool around with things like *that*!'

'I'm sorry, sir, but we have to ask. We can see no obvious cause for the accident, you see,' Trudy said mildly.

'Don't you think snow and ice are enough?' Geoffrey asked shortly.

'Perhaps,' Trudy said. She'd grown a thick skin since joining the police force and no longer took it personally when people got angry or upset with her. 'I don't suppose you have any contact details for his next of kin, sir?' she asked, but wasn't all that surprised when Geoffrey slumped a little and then shook his head, his brief burst of anger and indignation now spent.

'I'm not sure he had any,' he admitted wearily. 'Terry certainly never talked about close family anyway – no mention of brothers or sisters, for instance. And I rather got the impression that both his parents are gone.'

At this point, Clement stepped smoothly in. As a coroner, he was used to dealing with the more formal aspects that arose out of death. Whilst he preferred to let Trudy take the lead most of the time, knowing how much she needed to be allowed to learn her trade and gain much-needed experience, there were still certain times when things veered into his territory.

'Someone will need to take on the necessary arrangements, I'm afraid, Mr Thorpe,' he explained mildly. 'Arranging the funeral, sorting out the paperwork, seeing to his will …'

'Oh yes, I'll see to all that,' Geoffrey said at once.

'Thank you, sir,' Trudy said gratefully. 'Well, I'm sorry to be the bearer of such bad news, especially at this time of year. We may have to contact you again, once you've made the formal identification,' she warned.

But the dead man's business partner merely nodded fatalistically, then forced himself to his feet and showed them to the front door.

On the threshold he apologised for not having got around to clearing the path yet, and watched them go all the way to the gate and turn out of sight before closing the door against the bitter chill.

*

Once they were back in the Rover, Clement quickly turned on the engine and they sat, waiting for the heater to kick in.

'Did you get the feeling that he was *sorry* that his friend and business partner was dead?' Trudy asked, little puffs of her warm breath appearing and disappearing in the freezing interior of the car as she talked. She herself hadn't been quite sure that he had. Oh, she was convinced that he'd been genuinely shocked by the news, but there had been something about his manner that didn't quite ring true, given the circumstances; something that didn't quite make sense.

Clement grunted and put his finger on it at once. 'I got the feeling he was more *worried* about it, than saddened.'

Trudy nodded and sighed. Sometimes – not often, but sometimes – her mentor's seemingly infallible perspicacity made her feel distinctly dim. Now that he'd said it, she knew that he was right. That was exactly what she'd meant. Geoffrey Thorpe had become a worried man during their visit. But not, she felt confident, a grief-stricken one.

Which was interesting, but probably not relevant.

After all, she reminded herself firmly, it was almost certain that the inquest, when it was eventually held, would find that Terrence Parker had died as a result of a motor traffic accident.

Chapter 10

Trudy, mindful that she couldn't expect Dr Ryder to spend all of his time helping her with her work, thanked him for what he'd done so far, and said that she had to get back to the office to start on the paperwork. So he duly dropped her off at the station, but she couldn't help but feel relieved when he said that he'd see her tomorrow – unless DI Jennings had found a more senior officer to take over from her.

Although she had been fairly sure that her mentor would want to see things through as much as she did, she had been worried that the presence of his son at home might be enough to curb his usual curiosity.

So with a beaming smile she agreed to telephone him the next day to update him on how things were progressing and arrange when and where to meet.

The communal office was all but deserted, but that didn't surprise her. With weather and illness decimating the number of officers, everyone who had made it in would have been sent straight out again to deal with calls. Which boded well for her being left in charge of the Parker case, she thought happily.

She went straight to her desk and got out her notebook, running her eyes down the list of things she needed to do. On the way from Geoffrey Thorpe's place, Clement had agreed that, as a coroner, he was the obvious person to arrange with the morgue staff about the viewing of the body, and would be sorting that out before going home.

So ticking that item off, she reached for the telephone and got through to a colleague in Birmingham, explaining her predicament and asking if a search could be made of the records to see if her victim had ever lived in the city, or might still have living relations there. It was a big ask, and her colleague didn't sound impressed; Trudy hung up with the profound sense that her request would be buried at the bottom of a pile somewhere on some poor overworked constable's desk. She wouldn't be holding her breath.

Next she went to the records office to see if they had 'anything known' against Regal Cars. Apparently the tax people had no issues with them, nor had they had any run-ins with the various agencies whose job it was to monitor such businesses. Sometimes car dealers weren't always scrupulous about the roadworthiness of some of their vehicles, but it seemed Regal Cars had no major black marks against them in the five years they'd been trading. Nor had their victim come to the attention of the police, with Terry Parker not even having been issued with a parking ticket.

With a sigh, she returned to her desk and set about the laborious process of typing up her notes for DI Jennings, and filling in all the forms that surrounded a fatal road traffic accident.

About halfway through her task, she realised that she hadn't had time to make herself any sandwiches before leaving in such a hurry this morning (let alone have breakfast), and with no shops open, she could hardly go out and buy herself a pork pie or sausage roll.

She resigned herself to ignore her grumbling stomach, and instead worked steadily over her Remington typewriter. At this time of year, it would be getting dark around three o'clock, and she wanted to get the bulk of the work done before then.

She also had to return to the Vander household to pick up that invitation list. She wasn't sure that it was strictly necessary she had it, but she wanted to do a thorough job. She didn't want Inspector Jennings to point out anything that she might have missed, and have grounds to criticise her for slacking!

Hopefully someone would return to the office before the night shift kicked in, and could run her back home in the Land Rover. She didn't fancy trying to have to make her way home in the dark on one of the police bicycles, with no guarantee that the roads had been cleared.

*

Clement dropped into the morgue, where his presence caused a brief scurry of activity from the two people in attendance. He explained about the RTA, filled in forms asserting time of death, and told them to expect a Mr Geoffrey Thorpe to come in and identify one of their (temporary) residents before the day was out.

That done, he went home, hitting an icy patch and almost sliding his car into a lamp-post on the turn-off to his street, making his heart thump in alarm.

Vincent looked up from his chair in the front parlour when Clement walked in, putting aside the book he'd been reading by the fire. 'I didn't know if you were going to be back in time for lunch,' he said, without any obvious censure in his tone. 'So I went ahead and had something. Want me to heat up some soup for you?'

Clement grunted. Why did that question make him feel about a hundred years old? On the other hand, it was the first time in a long time that anyone had been here to care about whether or not he was eating properly, and it felt kind of pleasant. 'Why not? I've just got to make a phone call first.'

He retreated to his study, opened his telephone ledger, and found the number of one of the pathologists who worked under

71

his old friend, Dr Robbins. It rang a number of times and was then finally answered, rather grumpily, by yet another old pal of his, Dr Douglas Carey. 'Hullo? Who the hell's this?'

'Doug, it's Clement.'

'Do you know what day it is?'

'Yes. But unlike you, I haven't spent all day drinking whisky in the comfort of my home, surrounded by doting grandchildren and eating roast beef! I've been up since before it got properly light, attending the scene of a fatal road accident as a favour to help out a certain department which shall remain nameless,' Clement responded cheerfully.

He heard a sigh on the other end and grinned.

'So what do you want from me?' his old friend grumbled. 'A medal?'

'Nothing so useless,' Clement said with a laugh. 'I'm not even ringing to ask you to pull your finger out tomorrow and put my particular cadaver at the top of your list for a post-mortem. I've already had an earful from Robbins about how backlogged and overworked you all are.'

'Well, that's big of you.'

'In fact, you can take all the time you want before you get around to it,' Clement added craftily. 'But ...'

'I knew there'd be a but!'

'But,' Clement repeated patiently, 'I *would* be obliged if you'd run a blood tox screen on my Mr Terrence James Parker first thing, and send it off to the labs, there's a good lad. Look out for one of the barbiturates first, I think,' he advised.

Douglas, who at fifty-two years of age, felt tickled pink to be referred to as a lad, grunted warily. 'What are you up to, you sly old fox? I've heard the rumours about you and that pretty young WPC.'

Clement sat up straighter in his chair. '*You what?*' he yelped indignantly, and after a surprised silence on the other end, heard his old friend laughing.

'No, nothing like *that*,' Douglas reassured him. 'I just meant that you're beginning to get talked about for butting in on cases that should be handled by regular police officers.'

'WPC Loveday *is* a regular police officer,' Clement pointed out with impeccable logic, relaxing back against his chair. 'In fact, *she* was the one who was called out to deal with this fatal car accident.'

'Uh-huh,' Dr Carey said sceptically. 'So why do you want an early tox screen on a simple road traffic fatality? And why are you in no hurry to have a post-mortem done?'

Clement sighed. That was the trouble with asking a favour of old friends – they could be so damned suspicious! Of course, the reason Clement wasn't in any hurry for the post-mortem to be done was because he had a hunch that the findings might not be as straightforward as the circumstances would dictate. And if that was so, DI Jennings would pull Trudy off the case as quick as lightning.

And he was damned if he wanted that to happen just yet. He was having too much fun. Besides, even if his hunch didn't pay off, and it *did* turn out that the cause of death was nothing more than might be expected given the circumstances, it would do her no harm at all to get the experience of handling a case all by herself under her belt. And just as Jennings was determined to hold her back if he could, Clement was as determined to see to it that he wasn't allowed to!

'I thought you'd be pleased I'm giving you an easy ride,' Clement prevaricated. 'I'm willing to bet your schedule is actually as chock-a-block as Robbins was whining about.'

Dr Carey sighed wearily, knowing when he was beaten. 'Yes, you're quite right of course. I've got cadavers coming out of my ears.'

'Lovely image,' Clement said dryly. 'So you'll do as I ask? Run a tox screen right away, then put him at the bottom of your list? And let me know the moment the results are in?'

'What's in it for me?' Douglas asked craftily.

'I'll give you a chance to beat me at golf,' Clement said.

'Hah! Make it a bottle of whisky.'

'Done,' Clement said quickly.

'A good bottle, mind! None of that blended muck!'

'Done,' Clement repeated with a chuckle and hung up, feeling pleased with himself. With a bit of luck, he and Trudy would be able to investigate the little mystery and have it all sewn up in a ribbon before Inspector Jennings knew what hit him!

Of course, if their victim's dilated pupils were caused by a blow to the head, and the tox screen revealed nothing of interest, that wouldn't take long.

On the other hand …

Mentally rubbing his hands together in delight at the thought of investigating another suspicious case with his young friend, Clement went into the kitchen, where, for just a split second, he was surprised to see his son standing over the stove, stirring a boiling saucepan.

He had forgotten all about Vincent being there.

But only for a split second, and only, he reassured himself, because he'd become distracted by the thought of working again with Trudy. That was understandable, wasn't it? His cognitive powers weren't really showing signs of deteriorating that much …

'You all right, Dad?' Vincent said sharply, making Clement focus his attention on his son.

Drawing out a chair from under the kitchen table, he looked at him with a brief smile. 'Of course, why do you ask?' he demanded crisply.

Vincent turned away. 'Oh, nothing,' he said casually. And Clement could only hope that his son hadn't noticed his lapse.

*

Jasper Vander stood on the landing, careful to keep out of sight, but listening avidly to his mother in the hall downstairs. She had gone to answer the front door, and Jasper, who'd left his bedroom to do the same, had recognised the voice of the caller at once, and abruptly halted his descent. It was that rather lovely young WPC who had called earlier, returning no doubt for the bloody party invitation list they'd promised her earlier in the day.

He didn't like that she had come back for it so diligently. At least his mother had the good sense to simply hand over the list and say goodbye, giving the constable no chance to ask any more questions.

Scowling, he made his way to his sister's bedroom and knocked impatiently on the door. It was flung open a moment later by his twin, who scowled right back at him.

'What? Can't a girl listen to Cliff Richard in peace?' she asked, but stood aside to let him pass. She walked over to the record player she kept in her large bed-sitting room and lifted the needle from the 45. 'Bachelor Boy' would just have to wait, though she did think Cliff Richard dreamily good-looking.

'That woman copper's back,' Jasper informed her moodily.

'To pick up the list?'

'Yes. Persistent, isn't she?' Jasper sneered, flinging himself inelegantly into a Queen Anne reproduction chair that creaked under the misuse. 'I don't like it that they're sniffing around, Jules.'

'Why worry? He's dead, isn't he?' Juliet responded airily. She sat down with far more grace in front of the vanity table mirror and regarded her image thoughtfully. 'So we're in clover.'

But her brother was already shaking his head. 'I'm not so sure about that,' he said sullenly. 'And we *definitely* need to do something about Patsy.'

Juliet turned her attention away from her preening, and looked at her twin thoughtfully. She'd long since learned to respect Jasper's brains, along with his ability to get what he wanted. And since she wasn't exactly a slouch in either of those two departments herself, a bond of mutual respect had built up between them over the years.

Although she was also rather fond of her twin, in a detached sort of way, she was even fonder of her own skin. So after a moment's thought, she had to concede that he had a point. 'I agree,' she admitted coolly. 'We'll have to play Patsy very carefully. She's such a dunderhead, and we could be in hot water if she blabs.'

'Oh, she won't blab,' Jasper predicted with a savage smile. 'She might be a bit of a nitwit, but not such a nitwit as that, surely? She'll keep her mouth shut if only to keep her own neck off the chopping block. Won't she? You know her better than I do.'

Juliet considered Patsy Arles thoughtfully. 'Well, she's not particularly bright,' she admitted. Not that that needed to be laboured, really, since she'd been so easily manipulated by them into doing their dirty work for them; her lack of intelligence went without saying. 'But she *is* needy, bless her, and she does so adore me. And she could easily adore you too, if you'd just put some effort into it,' she added meaningfully.

'Oh no, I don't want to have her hanging around my neck like a love-sick calf,' Jasper protested.

'It might be a good idea though,' his sister advised. 'Just until the heat dies down. A woman in love will never snitch on her man, and all that guff,' Juliet added, yawning widely.

Jasper scowled and kicked at one of his sister's shoes that was lying, discarded on the floor near his chair. It skittered across the floor and rolled to a stop near the bed. 'I don't like it that she hasn't called,' he said flatly. 'I would have expected her to call in a bit of a flap by now, wouldn't you?'

For a moment, Juliet thought about that, and sighed. 'Yes, I agree. The silly little chump must have been having kittens afterwards.'

'My feelings exactly,' Jasper agreed. 'So I'd have thought that her first instinct would be to come and unburden herself to you and beg you for help. So why hasn't she?'

Juliet cocked her lovely head to one side, and her lips twisted into a wry smile. 'Well, it *is* New Year's Day,' she pointed out.

'And no doubt her ghastly family have descended on her mother. So she couldn't very well slip away today with ease. Especially in this,' she added, indicating the snow still falling outside. 'Her mummy-dearest wouldn't let her!'

'She could still have telephoned us,' Jasper said.

'I'm not sure they have a telephone,' Juliet said, startling Jasper, who hadn't really given much thought to the fact that the whole world wasn't rich enough and privileged enough to have a telephone in their house. 'Even if they did, she might have been too scared to use it for fear of being overheard. After what must have happened last night …' She trailed off with a frown. 'I wonder what went wrong, exactly? The plan should have been perfect.'

Jasper shrugged. 'Whatever it was, let's just hope the silly cow didn't leave any clues behind her for our pretty little PC Plod to find.'

Juliet glanced at her brother with a wicked smile. 'Fancy her, do you? Our lovely lady in blue?'

'Leave off, I'm not that desperate,' Jasper shot back, but avoiding his sister's knowing eyes. 'Besides, it's not her I'm worried about so much. It's that man she had with her. I didn't like the look of him at all.'

'Ah yes, the yummy Dr Ryder,' Juliet said.

'He's old enough to be your father,' Jasper objected.

'So?' Juliet asked archly.

Jasper stared at her for a moment, then shrugged. 'Your disgusting love life is not my main concern at the moment. We have to face it, there might be sticky times ahead, sister dearest, and we're going to have to come up with something to keep sweet Patsy from flipping out. Either a threat or a bribe, do you think? Or both? Come on, sis, let's put our thinking caps on.'

Chapter 11

The next morning Trudy was just adding the finishing touches to her report when DI Jennings arrived. After giving him time to settle in, she knocked at his door and waited to be summoned.

He listened without any comment as she ran down all the pertinent points about the case, and what she'd done so far. She tried to convince herself that he probably wouldn't be interested in Dr Ryder's thoughts on the state of the victim's pupils, reminding herself of all the times that he'd told her he preferred to have solid facts, not airy-fairy theories. So she helpfully left that bit out. When she'd finished, and he'd had a moment to digest what it all amounted to, he grunted.

'I don't like these marks in the snow around the car that might or might not have been pawprints or footprints,' he grumbled.

Trudy nodded. 'No, sir,' she agreed. 'But they really were too indistinct to draw any conclusions. And with it snowing on and off all through that night and the next morning ...' She gave a graphic shrug.

'Yes. Well, we'll just have to wait and see what the post-mortem brings to light. At this stage it seems most likely that death will have been due to injuries sustained in the crash, or hypothermia – possibly a combination of both – in which case we can get on with putting it all to bed. All right, carry on as you were.'

Trudy bit back a happy smile and left. So it wasn't going to be taken away from her just yet!

She went back to her desk, but her happy smile abruptly disappeared at the sight of the man who was waiting there for her. Around thirty, tall, good-looking with black hair and distinctive green eyes, he grinned widely when she approached.

'If it isn't my favourite constable,' Duncan Gillingham, reporter for the *Oxford Tribune*, greeted her cheerfully. 'What's all this I hear about a dead man in a car in north Oxford?'

Trudy sighed. 'I might have known,' she muttered. How did the press get to hear these things so quickly? Why couldn't they just stay at home in the warm like most sensible people and let everyone else get on with their own business?

Especially this particular specimen!

She cast a quick, worried glance at DI Jennings's door, hoping he hadn't been informed that the press had come sniffing around. Catching the direction of her gaze, Duncan started to walk rapidly towards her boss's office.

'You can't go in there!' Trudy shouted, literally running to put herself between him and his goal, and firmly blocking the doorway. 'Who let you in here anyway?' she demanded.

'Some old bloke or other at the front desk,' he said vaguely. 'Can't interfere with the free press you know,' he added, tutting teasingly. 'And let's face it, there's no one around here to throw me out on my ear, is there?' he said, giving the all-but-deserted room a mocking glance.

'That doesn't mean you can just waltz in …' Trudy was saying hotly when she felt, rather than heard, the door open behind her.

'What the hell's going on?' DI Jennings said, catching first his constable's angry eye, and then the amused eye of the man with her. 'And you are?'

'He's a reporter, sir,' Trudy said quickly. 'He wanted to know about the fatal car accident. I told him—'

'To sling my hook,' Duncan said genially, cutting her off in mid-stride, and (probably unintentionally) earning her bonus points with her superior, who had no time for journalists either. 'But as I was just telling her, the public have a right to know. Care to comment, Inspector?'

Jennings sighed heavily. 'Come on in then. The bare bones only, mind, and you can make yourself useful for once,' he said flatly. 'I want you to put out an appeal for anyone in the vicinity of the accident in the early hours of yesterday morning to get in touch. Or anyone who has any information on the victim, especially any contact details for his next of kin.'

Duncan shot her a triumphant wink as the inspector closed the door behind him, and Trudy, defeated, returned to her desk.

She knew she shouldn't feel unsettled, but she did. Duncan Gillingham and trouble seemed to go hand in hand, and she was feeling defensive of her case. It might not be the most exciting case in the world but, at the moment anyway, it was all hers and she didn't want Duncan butting in.

She brooded all the time the reporter was in her superior's office, and when he came out she was careful not to look at him. Had she done so, she'd have seen the speculative and appreciative look he gave her and so wouldn't have been so surprised when, instead of walking past and heading for the front door, he headed for her again instead.

'So how are things with you?' he asked, casually leaning one hip against her desk. He craned his neck to try and read the piece of paper in her typewriter, and she angrily pulled it out, ripping one corner. Which meant she'd have to fill in the form again.

She swore at him – but only under her breath.

'Things are fine, thank you,' she said shortly.

'Fancy coming out for a drink with me?'

'No.'

'Oh, come on,' he cajoled. 'You know you like me really. And after all that excitement we had over that dead May Queen last year, I thought we'd become friends, at least.'

Trudy sighed and bent her head more industriously over her typewriter, knowing he wouldn't take the hint even as she did so.

She was right – he didn't. 'Why the cold shoulder, Constable Loveday?' she heard him ask, his voice rich with suppressed laughter. 'Isn't it chilly enough as it is, without that?'

'Go away,' Trudy said tiredly.

'After you agree to have a drink with me.'

'Have it with your fiancée,' Trudy said pointedly.

*

Duncan winced at this direct, palpable hit. 'You know, one day …' he began, with some heat, but didn't bother to finish the thought. Instead, he glanced at the telephone on her desk and casually extracted his notebook from his pocket and wrote its number down.

Knowing that he had to make the lunchtime deadline if he wanted to get his piece into the early edition, he reluctantly gave her a jaunty salute and wandered off.

As he walked back to his office, however, fighting his way through the snow and other pedestrians, he began thinking up ways to persuade her to go out for that drink. After all, in his opinion, she owed him that much. Hadn't he all but saved her life not so long ago?

So it was that when his piece appeared in the local paper later that afternoon, the newspaper's readers were asked to contact WPC Trudy Loveday with any information on the case, giving her desk telephone number. Usually he would have given the police station contact details only, and it would have been the job of the desk sergeant to filter out nuisance callers. But this way, she would find herself pestered with interested curiosity seekers for some time to come, and if he knew human nature, (and he prided himself that he did) the vast majority of them wouldn't have any useful information at all. They would simply be calling to try and get more juicy details from her, exasperating her beyond endurance.

That would teach her to play hard to get! It would also, with a bit of luck, prompt her to get in touch with him, if only to vent her spleen. Giving him the perfect opportunity to soothe her ruffled feathers and persuade her to come out with him for that drink.

And who knew where that might lead?

*

But as it happened, one of the first calls Trudy received that afternoon wasn't from one of the newspaper's readers at all, but from her colleague in Birmingham, who not only surprised her by diligently dealing with her request for information on Terrence James Parker, but obviously doing so in double quick time.

In the course of the conversation she learned, however, that the constable given the task had made it a priority only as it involved a trip to a warm records office, as opposed to a call-out to a break-in at a draughty knacker's yard!

Nevertheless, despite such unexpected cooperation, the news from up north turned out to be negative. Wherever their victim had grown up, it appeared that he had not done so in the environs of Birmingham.

Sighing over another dead end, she thanked her colleague warmly and hung up, only for the telephone to ring again immediately.

It was some old lady wanting to know if the dead man in the car had red hair. She had just reassured the old dear that he hadn't, and hung up, when somebody else rang, demanding to know where exactly the crash had occurred.

It didn't take her very long, after questioning her callers as to why they had contacted her, to find out exactly what Duncan Gillingham had done.

Damn the man!

When her telephone rang for about the tenth time in so many minutes, she almost snarled her name into the instrument.

'Is that Constable Loveday?' a cultured male voice asked politely.

Trudy composed herself and sighed. 'Yes, sir,' she agreed, expecting the usual prurient demand for information that she couldn't give out.

'I've just read the article about Terrence Parker.'

'Yes, sir,' Trudy said again, forcing herself to remain calm. It was no good letting thoughts of Duncan rile her like this – especially since her own boss had put him up to it. 'But I'm afraid I can't give out any information other than that which has already appeared in the newspapers.'

There was a moment's puzzled silence, and then the voice said, somewhat amused, 'Yes, I'm sure that's so. I'm calling, however, to give *you* some information. The article has asked for anyone who knew Mr Terrence Parker to contact you?'

Trudy sat up a little straighter in her chair. She turned to a fresh page on her notebook. 'You know Mr Parker, sir?'

'Yes. But it's rather … well, let's just say that I prefer to be discreet about this. What I have to tell you, I wouldn't like to discuss over an open telephone line. Can you possibly call on me? Normally I'd be happy to come to you at the police station, but with the roads being like they are, I'm afraid of ending up in a snowdrift.'

Trudy did just wonder, momentarily, if this could possibly be another time-waster, maybe somewhat bolder than the rest, but something about his tone of voice made her think that he was not.

'That's all right, I understand perfectly. Where do you live, sir?'

'I'm at my office in Aldates at the moment.'

Even better, Trudy thought. She wouldn't even have to try and find a ride – she could walk it easily. She took a note of his address, listened to his directions on how to find the office, and promised to be there as soon as possible.

It was just as she was shrugging into her coat that she remembered she'd promised to call Dr Ryder sometime today, and had so far been remiss.

She quickly rang his home number and was rather frostily told by his son that his father had gone into his office to check on things, so she thanked him and hung up.

She rang the coroner's office, relieved to be told by his secretary that the coroner was free. Due to the weather, court wasn't sitting, since witnesses and office staff were finding it hard to get about, just like the rest of the country at the moment.

When she was put through, she asked him if he wanted to meet her outside Christ Church to go and talk to a mysterious man who had some very discreet information about their dead man. He couldn't say yes fast enough.

*

'Brrrr … it's perishing,' Trudy said in greeting, the moment she spotted the coroner walking towards her down the pavement. A path had been cleared with just enough room for people to walk single file through the snowdrifts. 'Luckily, we don't have far to go. The address is just down here somewhere.'

They walked carefully down the hill, slipping and sliding a little where the compacted snow had turned almost into ice. Trudy checked the numbers on the shops and office entrances for the one she wanted. Her caller had been clear in his directions, however, and she found the place a few minutes later.

She paused, looking at the gold lettering on the pane of glass in the door. 'Prescott, Watts and Cummings.'

'Solicitors?' Clement guessed, reading it over her shoulder.

'Close. I looked them up in the phone book before I left. They're accountants.'

Clement raised an eyebrow. 'And where there are accountants, there's usually money involved.'

Trudy nodded happily. 'Interesting, isn't it? "Follow the money" was one of my old training sergeant's favourite maxims! So let's see what he has to tell us.'

Chapter 12

Philip Prescott was a small man in every way. Shorter than Trudy by some inches, he had small feet, small hands, and a small, neat face. He could have been aged anywhere between forty and sixty, for although his face was unlined it did not seem particularly young. His hair was a nondescript brown, as were his eyes.

He was dressed in a neat three-piece suit of charcoal-grey with a plain white shirt and black tie. His office was small, like the man, but the view from his window was impressive – a view of Christ Church college itself, and its sweeping gardens, now, of course, obliterated by a seemingly habitual white blanket of snow.

'I must say, I'll be glad when all this white stuff disappears,' the accountant said, by way of an opening gambit once Trudy and Clement had introduced themselves and were sitting opposite his desk.

'Yes, I think we're all getting rather tired of it,' Clement agreed with a brief smile.

Preliminary courtesies over, Prescott nodded, leaned forward and put both bent elbows on the top of his desk. He then neatly placed both hands, palm-to-palm in front of him, making his fingers into a steeple. Throughout the course of the following interview, he would periodically and gently butt the underside of his chin with these steepled fingertips. It was almost certainly a subconscious habit, Clement mused. He wondered idly how he had acquired it and if he was aware he was even doing it.

Trudy, a little surprised at first by the eccentricity, quickly became used to it.

'Thank you for getting in touch with us, sir. I take it you knew Mr Parker?' she began conventionally.

'Yes, but in a professional capacity only. We were not friends, I must make that perfectly clear,' the accountant said. He had a precise way of speaking, which matched his general demeanour and probably boded well for his professional skills. Nobody, after all, liked a sloppy accountant.

'I see. Then I take it you called us in because you dealt with the books for his business?' Trudy sought clarification, her pen poised over her notebook.

'For Regal Cars, yes,' Philip Prescott corrected her. 'He was a partner of the company.'

'Yes, we've already spoken to Mr Geoffrey Thorpe,' Trudy admitted cautiously. 'I got the feeling that they were the only two people concerned with the car dealership? That is, that they didn't answer to anyone else?'

'That is correct. It is a private enterprise, not a public company,' the accountant confirmed. He stirred in his chair, his fingers butting his chin for a moment or two, before he sighed.

Trudy recognised all the signs of a naturally very cautious man, who was also a law-abiding and responsible citizen, trying to work out what he felt it was his duty to say, whilst not compromising his professional ethics.

Trying to help him out – and push the interview along – she spoke tentatively. 'I found Mr Thorpe a very pleasant man. Very straightforward, I think,' she offered.

'Yes, so do I,' Philip Prescott said at once.

'Did you deal mostly with Mr Thorpe or Mr Parker?' she tried next.

'Oh, Mr Parker I suppose, slightly more than Mr Thorpe.' The accountant paused to examine these words, clearly found them inadequate, and added, 'That is to say, it was more often than not Mr Parker who delivered the accounts here, rather than his partner.'

'I see. I take it they both worked on the books?'

'Yes, they did. I haven't found any pattern to their methods – I think they both made entries as and when they had the time, in between selling automobiles, I suppose.' He shook his head over this outlandish practice.

'I see.' Trudy tried to look scandalised too. 'And how often did they bring the books here for you to work on?' she asked next.

'Oh, every quarter.'

'And you say it was more often Mr Parker who did this?' Trudy reiterated, unsure why she was being so pedantic about this – unless the accountant's manner was catching! Perhaps it was because she was beginning to get the distinct impression that this man was going to be tricky to interview. He obviously didn't like making bold statements of fact, so she was going to have to be careful not to miss any inferences. Or worse still, misread any of them.

Clement, watching benevolently as Trudy's interview technique came on in leaps and bounds right in front of his eyes, repressed a small smile of satisfaction, and was happy to just watch and listen. He knew he could always jump in if he spotted any opportunity that she seemed to miss.

'Yes. And it was certainly Mr Parker who preferred to deal with any queries that I might have had arising from them.' There was something portentous in his emphasis on this sentence that nudged Trudy's curiosity – as of course, it was meant to.

Obligingly, she went where she was led. 'And did you have many queries rising from their accounts?'

At this direct assault, however, Philip Prescott again shifted uncomfortably on his chair. He opened his mouth, closed it again, thought for a moment, and then sighed. His fingers, during this hiatus, gently but rapidly tapped the underside of his chin.

'I wouldn't say …' he began, then checked himself and sighed again. 'There was nothing …' Realising that his visitors were looking at him with impatience, he forced himself to take the plunge. 'All right, let me put it this way. In the three years that I have been working with Regal Cars, I have never felt worried that an investigation by the Inland Revenue would turn up anything … actionable. From *their* point of view.'

Prescott looked at her carefully, then turned to look at the mostly silent man by her side. Seeing that the coroner seemed disinclined to comment, he turned his attention back to the policewoman. Trudy looked back at him just as carefully.

'I see,' she said slowly, thinking it through. 'But, putting aside Her Majesty's revenue men, would you say that there were occasions …' This time it was she who had to pause to find just the right word; something innocuous enough not to spook him into reticence, but enough to get him to reveal the meat of the matter. 'Let's say, when something in their books … surprised you, or struck you as … odd perhaps?'

'I would, yes, most definitely,' Philip Prescott said quickly and with some relief. In fact, he even managed a near-smile. He seemed pleased by her intelligence, and pleasantly surprised by her willingness to approach everything at a suitably oblique angle.

Trudy, who was rapidly getting the hang of how to handle this particular witness, hoped they could now start making some real progress.

'And was it Mr Parker's, er, entries in the books that surprised you, more than those of Mr Thorpe?' she asked, watching his face for signs that she'd either blundered or scored a hit.

'Oh yes indeed. We accountants very quickly learn how to "read" our customers' work, as it were. And I must say that Mr Thorpe had a very neat and tidy way of doing things. A bit over-meticulous sometimes, so he does not always find the most effective way of doing things, but his entries had the saving grace of at least being … unambiguous.'

Clement, who was both entertained by, and very interested in the small man in front of him, took a moment or two to appreciate his latest, very careful, offering.

'Unambiguous,' Trudy, too, savoured the word thoughtfully and nodded. 'But Mr Parker's work, by comparison, tended to be rather more, should we say, a little slipshod?' she probed delicately.

The accountant's fingertips did rapid overtime under his chin, but this time his prim lips almost twitched into a smile. 'I think that would be a generous interpretation of it, yes.'

Trudy nodded. 'I see. Would you say that Regal Cars are a successful enterprise, as a whole, Mr Prescott?'

Again, the man thought that over very carefully before replying, checking for hidden pitfalls and mantraps.

'I would say,' Philip Prescott finally said with his usual precision, 'that it was solvent. That its turnover was appreciable and that its income seemed to be quite adequate for the two men concerned. But rather more, I think, for Mr Parker than for Mr Thorpe.'

Trudy, for the first time, wasn't quite certain that she'd read between the lines correctly this time. Knowing that a direct question would probably not be received well by her witness, she sought ways to get clarification.

'Is Regal Cars a straight partnership, Mr Prescott? By that I mean do they equally own one half of the company?'

'They do,' Mr Prescott said, a gleam of approval in his eye. 'They each own equal equity, and they do not draw their respective salaries on the basis of who sells the most cars. That is to say – no bonuses.'

Trudy, feeling on surer ground now, nodded. 'So it didn't matter if one of them sold more cars one week than the other one did. The profits would be shared equally between them.'

'Yes.'

'Was Mr Parker, on the whole, a better salesman than Mr Thorpe?'

'No, I would say they were more or less on a par. I noticed that Mr Thorpe's sales tended to be more regular and – well, not predictable, exactly, but shall we say, tended to follow the same pattern. Mr Parker told me that his partner tended to sell the less high-end range of sports cars, mostly to younger men. Whilst he sold fewer cars, but more of the higher-priced items, and usually to older men.'

Trudy nodded. This made sense to her. She was beginning to get a feel for their car crash victim now. A young, handsome man, who appealed to wealthy widows, was probably the same kind of man who found it easier to sell very flashy and expensive sports cars to middle-aged men who, perhaps, should have known better.

'I can see, from a business perspective, that that would make sense,' Trudy said, mindful that she was talking to an accountant. 'Two partners, each specialising in a different customer base, would optimise their sales considerably.'

Now Philip Prescott actually did manage to smile, clearly finding this young police officer very intelligent and accommodating indeed.

'To be clear then, both men took exactly the same amount of money in salary from the company each month?' she asked cautiously.

At this, Philip Prescott's finger-bumping stopped abruptly.

She had become so used to it, that Trudy found its cessation almost shocking.

'Ah. Now,' Mr Prescott said, sitting up even more rigidly in his chair. 'That's what the Regal Car books *showed*. That is, the books that were shown to me when *Mr Parker* brought them over.'

Jackpot! Trudy felt herself tensing and deliberately made herself relax again. She must not lose her witness's confidence at this point. 'And when Mr Thorpe brought them over?' she asked, very casually.

Philip Prescott finally separated his hands, laid them flat on the top of the desk and leaned back slightly in his chair. 'Yes. The thing is, Mr Thorpe brought the entire set of books to me last November – that is, all the years of their trading, up until a month before the latest quarter ended. He asked me to audit them thoroughly. I have to say that I got the impression – nothing but an *impression* mind you,' he stressed primly, 'that Mr Thorpe had done so without the knowledge of his partner.'

'And what did …' Trudy caught herself just in time from asking a direct question. Quickly, she corrected herself. 'And did the books shown to you at that time indicate that Mr Thorpe had always received his *equal* share of the profits every quarter?'

The accountant gave her a congratulatory smile. Trudy had a mental picture of him patting her on the head, rather like a dog owner pleased with the antics of his favourite Labrador.

'No, Constable, they did not,' Mr Philip Prescott said, with immense satisfaction.

*

'So our dead man was cooking the books,' Clement said, the moment they were back outside on the pavement.

It had become almost dark during their time in the office, and the Christmas lights, yet to be taken down, cast a cheerful glow over the shops. Trudy shivered at the sudden drop in temperature from warm office to freezing outdoors.

'Stealing from his partner,' Trudy acknowledged. 'Which was, presumably, less dangerous than stealing from the tax man!' Trudging automatically back up the hill, she wondered aloud where this took them, exactly. 'Presumably he'd been pilfering more than his fair share since they set up the business. He strikes me as the kind of man who would have liked to have money to splash around.'

Clement nodded, then realising that Trudy couldn't see him

do so – since they'd been forced to walk one behind the other due to the snowbanks crowding in on either side of them – said loudly, 'Yes, I agree. Unluckily for our dead man though, Geoffrey Thorpe had finally got wise and caught him out.'

'Which might explain why Geoffrey Thorpe looked more *worried* when we talked to him, as opposed to being actually sad.' Trudy nodded. 'He must have been hoping he could keep all their business problems a secret, to avoid loss of confidence in their firm. He couldn't have been feeling very friendly towards Terry for some time – certainly not enough to really mourn his passing. I'm only surprised they kept on trading! Mr Thorpe must have faced him with it as soon as he'd found out and demanded that Terry pay him back every penny, wouldn't he?'

'I would think that's a fair bet,' Clement agreed dryly.

Chapter 13

The news that her car crash victim was turning out to have feet of clay did not sit well with Inspector Jennings. At the top of the hill, Trudy and Clement had separated to go back to their respective workplaces, and on entering the police station, Trudy had immediately made her report to her superior officer.

'So he was a wrong 'un,' the inspector grunted after she finished speaking. 'I don't see how it's relevant in the circumstances though.' *If* the car crash was purely accidental, he added to himself silently. But what if it wasn't?

Damn it, he didn't have the men for this sort of complication! They were stretched so tight with the few staff that he *did* have, that he couldn't possibly justify allocating another officer to what was almost certainly still going to turn out to be a simple road traffic fatality.

And had it been anyone other than WPC Loveday and that bloody interfering coroner who were currently looking into the matter, he might have felt sure enough that the odds were in his favour, to simply let it drop. But that pair had the knack of summoning very real mountains out of apparent molehills. It was enough to give a man indigestion.

What he needed were more facts to go on. But with everything backlogged like it was, the facts weren't going to be arriving on his desk any time soon. If it did turn out after all that there was something iffy about Parker's death though, his superiors would come down on him like a ton of bricks for letting so much time pass before he pulled his finger out!

'Damn it, I suppose you'll just have to keep digging,' he capitulated, pretending not to notice the look of delight that crossed her face. 'Only until we get the autopsy report, mind,' he admonished, scowling at her. 'Or the mechanic's report on the car. That'll tell us whether there was some hanky-panky done on his vehicle. You did set that in motion?' He shot her a hard look.

'Yes, sir,' she confirmed, knowing that he would have been delighted to catch her out in failing to do something so obvious. 'But they say it's going to take some time. They couldn't even find a breakdown recovery vehicle until—'

'Yes, yes,' Jennings interrupted her impatiently. 'Well, what are you waiting for? Isn't it the end of your shift?' he demanded testily.

'Yes, sir,' Trudy said, and wisely scarpered before he could change his mind.

Once outside the door, she realised that she hadn't asked him if she could continue to use the services of Dr Ryder. Which meant that he hadn't said she couldn't, didn't it?

*

The early edition of the *Oxford Tribune* was delivered later than usual (due to the inconvenient snow) at Raven's Rest B&B in Summertown that afternoon.

The woman who was currently occupying Room 4, a corner room on the top floor, read the article about the death of Terry Parker, a car crash victim, as she sat on the edge of her bed.

She felt like crying. Or maybe laughing. Because when life played dirty tricks on you, you had to have a sense of humour, didn't you? But mostly, she felt like raging. Like stomping about and throwing things, and stamping her feet and ripping something – anything – into tiny little bits.

But of course, she did none of these things. Instead, she forced herself to read the article through twice, meticulously, before closing her eyes for a few moments and breathing deeply.

She was twenty-eight years old, although she believed – with good cause – that she looked several years younger than that. Her thick dark-brown hair was cut in a modern, youthful style, and she wore clothes that she had made herself, copied from the latest fashion magazines. Since she was a good seamstress, she was often admired for her outfits. She walked and sat well, and she was very careful to keep her speaking voice low and clear.

Consequently, very few people would have pegged her as the daughter of a man who made his living driving a lorry and delivering coal in Tunbridge Wells. A girl from a bleak council housing estate, who'd left school at fourteen and had fallen pregnant at the age of eighteen after being far too naïve and trusting.

Phyllis Raynor had worked very hard and very diligently to expunge both of these latter faults from her personality over the years. She had also taken several correspondence courses in order to prepare herself for a career as a secretary, as well as reading widely and well, to educate herself in the more social graces.

She'd been careful to cultivate friends who had no idea of her humble origins, learning from them the many tricks of the middle-class trade that came so naturally to them. She'd also listened and learned from the bosses in the many business offices she'd worked in, where office politics could be as vicious as any practised in Whitehall. And one of the many things she'd learned from her unknowingly helpful teachers was that people who succeeded in life didn't indulge in theatrics, or allow any obstacle to deter them from their chosen path.

So she did not indulge in self-pity, as her younger self might have done. And she now had far more self-control than to let her anger have free rein. Instead, she sat on the bed, coolly and calmly, and forced herself to think. Just where had this latest turn of events left her? And how could she turn it to her advantage?

When she'd come to Oxford on New Year's Eve she'd had a definite plan in mind. It had been a simple plan, but she didn't think that she'd been overly optimistic in having great expectations that it would prove to be effective. It wasn't as if she'd rushed things, or gone at things half-cocked. It had taken her a long time to finally track down her prey, and she hadn't been about to let all that hard work come to nothing by letting impatience get the better of her. No, she'd watched, and waited, and made sure of the lie of the land before making her move. What's more, she'd chosen her moment to strike for the optimum psychological advantage.

But no matter how well you checked out all the angles, and thought you'd set up everything perfectly, accounting for every possible permutation you could think of, there was just no accounting for bad luck, was there?

Dirty, rotten luck. She seemed to have had so much of it, all her life.

So was she going to go home with her tail between her legs, no better off than when she'd arrived? All because of Terrence bloody Parker?

No, she told herself firmly. She was not.

All right then, she thought flatly. So where and how could she get the money that she was determined to have? She'd invested too much of her time, energy and emotion on things to let this latest farce come between her and the cash she had set her mind on. She needed a new start, damn it. In her mind's eye, she was already spending the money, maybe even living abroad. Buying expensive French perfume, lying in the sun on a beach in the Med somewhere, with no more worries about having to scrimp and save.

She got up and paced about a bit, her brown eyes flicking impatiently around the room. She had paid upfront for three more days here, and her mum didn't mind having Vicky over the holidays, so she didn't have to rush back.

So she might have enough time to come up with a Plan B.

On the other hand, she had to consider any possible risks. It was one thing to reach for the jackpot when you knew what you were doing and were confident that you weren't taking too many chances. It was another thing altogether to wing it and hope for the best.

Did she cut and run?

Or hold out and find another angle?

She read the newspaper article for a third time, but the facts were still scanty. Which meant she was probably safe enough for the moment. Terry would hardly have been likely to talk to anyone else about her, would he? And certainly not to that silly cow he'd thought he was going to marry.

Abruptly, Phyllis Raynor stopped pacing and thought about Millicent Vander for a bit. The last time she'd seen her had been at the New Year's Eve party Millie had hosted; a party that she'd been only too happy to gate-crash with such high spirits and high hopes.

Millie Vander, so proud of her red hair and 'pocket Venus' glamour. The hostess with the mostest, so well brought-up and pampered for all her life.

Oh yes, Phyllis knew a fair bit about Millie. Widow of a rich husband who'd given her all that she'd ever wanted. And before that, born to well-heeled, very respectable parents who'd also indulged her every whim.

Women like that grew up never knowing what it was to have to claw and fight for everything they wanted. Women like that just expected their every desire to be served up to them on a silver platter. Like a younger, handsome man, for instance.

My, my, hadn't Terry hit the jackpot with *that* lady bountiful?

The look on his face when he'd spotted her, Phyllis, at the party had been priceless!

Phyllis felt a snarl of a smile on her face, and quickly rearranged her features into their usual, placid, slightly bored expression. It didn't do to let the mask slip; she'd learned that the hard way. The image she presented to the world was her armour, and an attractive young 'lady' could always expect certain things from men and society in general that a working-class guttersnipe never could. *Always keep the harridan hidden*, she reminded herself.

She walked to the window and looked out over the B&B's small town garden, which lay buried under a layer of snow.

Bloody snow – when would it go? she wondered resentfully. It was really getting on her wick! Every time you went out, it froze your bloody nose and fingers and toes into icicles.

She sighed and turned away from the window. She was still thinking about Millie Vander – only now she was smiling a very different kind of smile.

All right, so things with Terry had turned into a busted flush, but that didn't mean all was necessarily lost, did it?

A woman who didn't like to question an obvious interloper at her own party simply because she didn't want to make a fuss or cause an embarrassment, was almost certainly the same sort of woman who would pay handsomely not to have her dirty linen aired in public, wasn't she?

And a woman without a backbone but with plenty of money was just what Phyllis needed right now. In fact, it was almost poetic irony, when you came to think about it. To think – Terry had planned to marry into money, and now that money was going to find its way to her.

She'd just have to think about the best way of going about things; that was all. Attractive middle-aged widows with plenty of money might seem an easy target, but sometimes … Well, you just never knew.

And she'd seen the look in Millicent Vander's eye when she'd caught Phyllis and Terry having their little 'chat' in the deserted hallway just before midnight. Of course, he'd been furious with her, and the hold he'd had on her arm had been anything but lover-like, but Millicent hadn't realised that. And she certainly hadn't been close enough to hear that the words he'd been hissing in her ear were threats, and not sweet nothings!

No, their hostess had seen only two flush-faced people, locked together in a close and electrically charged embrace, and had jumped to the most likely conclusion. The sort of conclusion that most women, worried about their fading looks and their advancing age, would jump to on seeing 'their' man with a younger woman.

And the look in the society matron's eye had been wild, hot and venomous.

Phyllis would not make the mistake of underestimating her. A woman scorned, as she knew better than anyone, was a force to be reckoned with.

She'd have to be careful. But one thing was for sure: one way or another, she wasn't going to leave Oxford without a substantial amount of money.

Chapter 14

At the same time that Phyllis Raynor was pacing her room and contemplating Millie Vander with such relish, Millie's twin children were out and about in the city on business of their own.

They'd purposely waited until it was fully dark before venturing out. As that obligingly occurred at barely five o'clock in the afternoon, not too much patience had been required on their part. Which was a good thing, since neither of them had ever been blessed with that particular commodity.

They had each dressed in their winter skiing clothes, usually only worn at Gstaad in season, and thus all but guaranteed to keep them well insulated. Even so, they were both glad when they finally turned down a side road just off Hythe Bridge Street, and approached the address they were looking for.

'Patsy's place is just down here,' Juliet said to her twin, her voice muffled by the mink lining around her hooded jacket. 'You'd better stay here,' she added, as they reached the front gate. 'Her mother can be a bit protective of her, and if she sees you, she might invite us in and make sure we don't slope off to Patsy's bedroom for a private chat. If she sees just me, I should be able to come up with something to make sure Patsy comes out on her own.'

Jasper sighed heavily. 'Fine, but hurry up, if you can. I might just freeze to death out here otherwise.'

Juliet hurried to the door and rapped hard. For once, their luck seemed to be in, for it was Patsy herself who opened the door. Quick as a flash, she glanced behind her, checked the coast was clear, then reached up to grab a coat from the rack in the hall and stepped out through the door.

She shut the door very quietly behind her. 'Come on, let's get down the path and behind the hedge out of sight, just in case!' Patsy hissed, shrugging into the coat quickly, already shivering violently. 'I don't *think* Mum heard the door go. She and Granddad have been on the sherry all day,' she added with a nervous giggle.

It wasn't until they got near the gate that Patsy was able to see Jasper standing in the light of the streetlamp across the road, and her steps slowed automatically.

'It's all right,' Juliet said bracingly, when she saw that the younger girl was about to balk. 'Jasper won't bite.'

In the glow of the same streetlamp, Patsy's curly ginger hair became bright orange, making her stand out in the mono-chrome landscape. By mutual consent, they tucked themselves as close as they could in the shadow of a large privet hedge, which not only provided them with shelter from the icy wind, but from any prying eyes that might be looking out of neigh-bouring windows.

'I'm ever so glad you came, Juliet,' Patsy said, clutching the sleeve of Juliet's luxurious coat with gloveless, icy hands. 'I've been that worried, I can't tell you! I thought I was going to just die!'

Juliet ignored the dramatic language thinking that, for once, Patsy had probably earned a few histrionics. 'What the hell happened?' she hissed instead, glancing around nervously at the deserted streets. 'Were you in his car when it crashed?'

'Of *course* I was in the car,' Patsy squeaked, aggrieved. 'That was the plan, wasn't it? Hang around until he came out then beg a lift to my auntie's place in Wolvercote? And then … you know …'

Juliet nodded impatiently. 'Yes, yes, that was the plan. So you were actually with him when the smash happened?' she repeated.

'I was. And I was never so scared in all my life,' Patsy said, putting her spare hand on her chest and patting it comfortingly.

She probably meant it too, Juliet mused, but it came out with so much gasping and eye rolling that Patsy sounded like a third-rate actress in a trite thriller, killing any genuine sympathy she might have felt stone-dead.

Not that Juliet was known in her peer group for her sympathetic personality.

'Just tell us what happened,' Jasper, impatient and unimpressed by all this girlish chatter, demanded harshly. His voice had a flat, ugly lash to it that made Patsy's hand on his sister's arm tighten instinctively in reaction.

'Jasper, don't be a pig,' Juliet admonished him. It was not that she didn't agree with him, but rather that she knew the best way to deal with Patsy was to let her indulge herself. 'Can't you see the poor girl's been through an ordeal?' Juliet speared her brother with a speaking look and he sighed and held up both hands in surrender.

'Pats,' Juliet said, letting her voice turn sugary. 'You managed to waylay him in the driveway, like we hoped, and you told him about spending the night in Wolvercote. Right so far?'

'Yes, and he said that was right close to where he lived, and he could give me a lift if I wanted, just like you said he would.' Patsy nodded. 'Wasn't that clever of you both? That you knew he'd do that!' She spoke to appease, her eyes still darting nervously from Jasper to Juliet.

Jasper again sighed impatiently at this blatant flattery, but Juliet spoke over him firmly. 'Yes, well, that's because he's such a total lech. We know him, you see – *knew* him, I suppose I should say – very well indeed,' she confirmed bitterly. 'He never could resist a pretty face.'

Patsy blushed. That *Juliet Vander*, of all people, should call *her*

103

pretty! When everyone knew that Juliet was the most beautiful and glamorous girl in all of Oxford.

'Nobody's mourning him, I promise you, so you can save any pity you might be feeling,' Juliet said sourly.

'So, you got in the car,' Jasper tried to chivvy both of the women along. 'Did anyone see you?' he demanded. This was one of the most crucial things they needed to know, and they had discussed, before setting out, how vital it was to find out just how much danger they were in. Now he noticed that his twin, too, was holding her breath, waiting for the verdict.

'Oh no, I don't think so,' Patsy said annoyingly.

'You don't *think* so?' Jasper echoed savagely, making her visibly jump.

'No, I can't see how they could have done,' she amended quickly. 'There was nobody else in the driveway right then. It was dark away from the house lights too, where he'd drawn up under those big bushes you've got in your garden,' Patsy said, a slightly tearful edge to her voice now.

Catching it, Juliet hastily took over. The last thing they needed was for the silly little cow to start sobbing and getting all upset. Not when it was vital that they all behaved normally.

Patsy's mother would be onto it in a flash if her little darling started moping.

'You did fine, Patsy, really you did. I couldn't have done it better myself,' Juliet said, shooting her twin another 'keep quiet' glare. 'OK, you got in the car and he started off up the main road. The road was passable then?'

'Yes, the main road was,' Patsy said, still preening over her idol's latest praise. 'But it was still slippery, mind, and the wheels did slide sometimes, but he was a good driver. At least, he was at first, but the further we got away from the house, the more he sort of kept … I don't know. Slumping over the wheel a bit.'

'Drunk, was he?' Jasper sneered.

'Yes. I suppose he must have been,' Patsy agreed hesitantly.

'What happened, exactly? When the car crashed,' Juliet said, keeping her voice calm and patient.

'Well, it was when we turned off the main road into the side ones. The snowploughs hadn't gone through there for some time, and the back end of the car just seemed to slide right out from under us as we turned. I thought he'd correct the wheel, like he'd been doing, but he just didn't. His chin was on his chest, and he wasn't even holding the wheel, I don't think, because I noticed the steering wheel was sliding through his hands. And then we just skidded into this snow and the tree beyond it. I was so frightened I couldn't even scream!'

Just as well, Jasper thought callously to himself. If she had let rip, it would have brought somebody running for sure. And then they would all have been in the soup. They wouldn't have been able to rely on this nitwit to keep her head in an emergency.

'It was good thinking on your part not to make a sound,' Juliet said, forcing herself to smile in admiration. 'You kept a cool head. You must have been really up against it, but you were clever enough to keep quiet.'

At this, Patsy positively beamed, conveniently forgetting that it had been fright and shock that had kept her paralysed in her seat for several seconds after the collision.

'You obviously weren't hurt yourself?' Juliet pressed on. 'You got out of the car and walked away all right?'

'Yes, I did.' Patsy gulped. 'We didn't hit the tree that hard, to be honest. He'd already slowed right down to make the turn, and since I had time enough to guess what was going to happen, I braced myself with my hands on the dash. It was more of a jolt than anything else. But I couldn't get the door to open very wide. I don't know if it got dented, or if it was because of the snow pressing against us, but I managed to wiggle out of the gap anyway. Then I just ran off to my auntie's place. It was only a quarter of a mile or so, but it was so dark, and my ears were ringing, and it was so cold, I thought I might die! Really I did.'

She looked hopefully from one to the other, but this time there were no congratulatory comments on her bravery.

'But you didn't let on anything to your aunt, right?' Jasper demanded instead. 'She didn't realise anything out of the ordinary had happened?'

Again, the twins held their breath for the all-important answer.

'Oh no, I told her not to wait up for me before I left for your party. She was so pleased I'd been invited, and that Mum had let me spend the night away from home. She's always been a better sport than Mum! She even gave me the key to her house so I wouldn't have to wake her. Mum would have waited up, counting down the minutes,' Patsy predicted bitterly. 'I just let myself in and helped myself to her gin.'

Juliet couldn't help but grin at this matter-of-fact piece of pragmatism. 'Good for you,' she said approvingly.

'And then what?' Jasper pressed.

'Nothing,' Patsy said, sounding confused. 'My dad picked me up from my auntie's place about eleven the next morning and brought me home, and I've been home ever since. And then I read in the papers today that he died!'

She took a deep, shaky breath. 'I thought someone would come! I thought he'd be found. I didn't know he was dead … I wouldn't have left him, if I'd known.' Her voice was beginning to rise into a hysterical wail again, and Juliet quickly grabbed her arm and squeezed it tight.

'You didn't do anything wrong! And you've nothing to feel guilty about. Listen to me,' Juliet said forcefully. 'It wasn't your fault. None of it was – how could it be? He was driving. The accident had nothing to do with you.'

Patsy sniffed. 'Yes, that's true,' she agreed, feeling a little better.

'And you could hardly be found alone with a man in his car, could you? Not someone with *his* reputation,' Juliet put all the scorn she could into her voice. 'Your dad would have scalped you.'

'That's right, he would,' Patsy admitted nervously. He still would, she thought uneasily, if he ever found out.

'OK, you *had* to run off. And anybody would have thought the same thing – that someone would have heard the smash and come to investigate it. It wasn't your fault that they didn't. If the collision was as gentle as you said, and the snow muffled the sound … Well, you weren't to know that, were you? You did the right thing,' Juliet reiterated firmly. 'You just remember that. All right? You looked after yourself, and we girls have to do that in this wicked, rotten old world. Right?' She knew this last bit of bravura would appeal to the drama queen in Patsy, and sure enough, she saw the other girl's head come up.

'That's so true,' she said, so solemnly that Jasper had to turn his head away and bite back the snort of laughter that threatened to erupt from his throat.

Patsy nodded and sniffed. 'All right, Juliet, I just won't think about it,' she said meekly.

'That's the spirit! Now, we just wanted to come to explain that there's nothing to worry about. You don't say anything, to anybody, ever, all right? If you really have to – if push comes to shove, say, and the police start asking questions, you just say that you left the party, and Jasper here drove you to your aunt's place and left you at the doorstep.'

Patsy eyed Jasper warily. 'All right,' she agreed reluctantly. 'But the police won't ask, will they?' she asked in real alarm.

'I don't see why they should,' Juliet said crisply. 'Why would they? It was just a road smash. It's sad and tragic and all that, but nothing they'll be interested in. Just keep your head down, don't volunteer information, and don't talk about it to anybody. Not your mum or granddad or anyone, OK?'

Jasper, taking his cue, reached into his jacket and pulled out his wallet. He extracted all the paper money he had and thrust it at Patsy.

'What's this for?' Patsy asked, shying away from it, and him, like a nervous horse.

'It's just for your trouble,' Juliet said soothingly. 'We know things haven't worked out as we hoped, but that doesn't mean you should lose by it. And we're grateful you were willing to try and help us out in the first place. And we feel a bit guilty you had to go through all that you did. Take it and buy yourself something nice – but be careful not to let your mum find it. She'll wonder where you got so much cash.'

Patsy reached out a half-frozen hand and accepted the money wonderingly. There was so much there, she could buy herself a whole new wardrobe! And some make-up, and perfume, and that new handbag she'd spotted in …

'Don't spend it all at once,' Jasper snarled, and she blinked, then nodded wisely.

'Of course I won't,' she said. 'I'm not stupid, you know!'

'Of course you're not,' Juliet agreed, giving her a pat on the back. 'You take care now. And remember – say absolutely nothing about this, or what we were going to do, to anyone.'

'I won't,' Patsy promised.

She turned and hurried back up the path. When she got to the door and looked back, she was relieved to see that they'd already disappeared into the darkness.

She carefully tucked the money deep into the pocket of her coat and slipped inside. She then went straight upstairs to her bedroom and hid the money in her secret hiding place, before she sat on her bed, rocking slightly back and forth.

'No, I'm not stupid,' she muttered resentfully to herself. 'No matter what people might think.'

She glanced out of the window, seeing only her own tight and unhappy face reflected back at her.

She would keep quiet all right, and tell no one about being in the car that night. But only because she just knew Jasper Vander must have done something bad. Really bad. There had been something very wrong with Terry Parker just before he crashed that car; she was sure. He might have had a few drinks, but she didn't believe he'd been so drunk that he couldn't drive properly.

She thought about the dead man, and felt sorry for him, but not enough to do anything about it.

Juliet and Jasper had hated him. And now Terry Parker was dead.

And she definitely didn't want to do anything that would make the twins angry with *her*.

She might just end up the same way.

Chapter 15

The next day, Trudy rose in darkness and made her way down-stairs. Her father, a bus driver, was unusually still abed, but only because his bosses were having trouble getting the bus routes cleared. Every fresh snowfall or freezing overnight spell turned roads that had once been passable into an ice rink. And nobody wanted to be driving a double-decker on an ice rink. Or riding on one, presumably.

She boiled an egg and ate some toast, careful not to wake her parents, then let herself out the house. The same Land Rover that had been doing the rounds, shuttling police staff from their homes in the city to their stations, was waiting, and she greeted the driver – a rather glum-faced PC from Headington – with a weary smile.

They discussed the snow that seemed to have brought the whole country to a standstill, and the PC's little girl, who had been delighted with her Christmas present of coloured plasticine, but not so enamoured of a doll.

Once at the station, she was delighted to find that DI Jennings wasn't in yet. Since he'd left no word ordering her otherwise, she decided that that meant that the Terry Parker case was still her top priority, and immediately set off walking to the coroner's house. And if that made her difficult to contact any time soon, that was really a shame, wasn't it?

Once again, it was Vincent who answered her knock at the door, and for a moment she actually wondered if he was going to let her in. He hesitated so very visibly in the doorway, looking her up and down, that she began to feel distinctly uncomfortable. Eventually he moved to one side.

'Dad, it's your policewoman again,' he called over his shoulder as Trudy edged around him.

He was dressed in warm woollen black trousers with a black shirt, and a knitted cable-stitch pullover in stone-coloured wool over the top. His light brown, almost fair hair shone with golden highlights under the hall light, and she could still smell his after-shave. Obviously, he had not long risen.

She was very aware of how attractive he was, and felt more uncomfortable still. She wondered why he didn't like her, though she knew that she was taking it too personally. Which was silly. Once he went back to wherever he lived, she'd never see him again.

'Hello, Trudy, come on through, I'm in the kitchen,' she heard Clement call, and with a smile of relief at the sound of her mentor's voice, hurried out of the hallway.

Vincent noted her pleased reaction, and his lips tightened. He followed close on her heels as she walked into the room.

'I didn't know if you'd be free today,' Trudy said amiably, slinging her satchel and the accoutrements it contained onto the seat of a drawn-out table chair, and taking off her police officer's cap.

Vincent's eyes widened at the mass of glossy, sable curls that had been hidden underneath, and couldn't help but wonder what they would look like, tumbling down around her face and shoulders. He turned abruptly to the kettle and switched it on. 'Another cup of tea, Dad?' he asked flatly.

'Please. And one for Trudy – she probably needs defrosting!'

Clement grinned. He was sitting at the table, a plate of bread-crumbs in front of him, smeared with a tell-tale orange trail of marmalade. 'You walked from the station?' He looked up at her.

Vincent, watching the exchange, was relieved to note that his father seemed friendly, but not effusive. He was showing no obvious signs of being over-pleased to see her, and neither did he follow the girl with his eyes as she set about shrugging off her coat and sitting down. Rather, he folded up the newspaper he'd been reading, and pushed aside his plate, looking totally relaxed.

He was, in fact, showing none of the tell-tale signs of an infatu-ated older male in the presence of a pretty younger woman, and Vincent told himself to relax. He'd been letting his imagination get the better of him, which was not like him.

'So what's on the agenda for today?' Clement asked.

'I thought we'd tackle Geoffrey Thorpe again,' Trudy said. 'See what he's got to say for himself?'

'Hmmm.' Clement nodded. 'I agree. It's tricky though, isn't it? Not being sure what we're dealing with exactly? Until we get cause of death, we're groping about in the dark – and maybe for no good reason.'

'What's this?' Vincent asked, intrigued, pulling out a chair and sitting at the table. 'It all sounds rather convoluted.'

Clement cast an amused smile at his son. 'I thought you weren't interested in my work?' he accused amiably.

'I'm not.' Vincent smiled back. 'But this sounds interesting. Why is "it" tricky? And what is "it" anyway?'

Clement cast Trudy a questioning look, seemingly wondering if she would object to his son knowing the bare details, but she shrugged back, letting him decide. This display of tacit under-standing again annoyed Vincent. It was as if they were speaking a language known only to themselves – and he just didn't like it.

'A man was found dead in his car on New Year's Day. He'd been to a party the night before. Cause of death was probably due to injuries or maybe hypothermia,' Clement said briskly. 'But there are a few inconsistencies.'

'Such as?' Vincent sipped his tea, his golden-flecked hazel eyes darting from his father to the pretty young woman opposite him.

'Possible footprints, which might be indicative of a second person at the scene, who maybe just checked out the crash site and for some reason failed to report it – or maybe not,' Clement listed. 'The trouble is, with all the snowfall and wind, it's not easy to say for certain what the marks might mean. The victim had pinprick pupils, which may have been caused by a concussive head injury – or maybe not. Certain irregularities in the victim's business life – which might be relevant, or ...'

'Maybe not,' Vincent obligingly finished for him, nodding. 'I get it. But most likely he had a bit too much to drink and crashed the car? Knocked himself out and froze to death?'

'That's the most likely outcome, yes,' Clement said and smiled. 'But Trudy and I would both like to be sure there's not more to it than that.'

Vincent grunted, unconsciously echoing one of his father's habits. 'Well, you're clearly having a lot of fun playing sleuths. I'll have to start reading more murder mysteries. Agatha Christie, here I come.'

Trudy smiled at him, relieved to see him finally smile back at her.

Clement regarded his son thoughtfully.

*

Geoffrey Thorpe was not a man at ease. That much was very clear from the moment he ushered them into a small snug off the main living room in his house.

A quick telephone call by Clement had confirmed that the car showroom was not open that day. It was not surprising – who was going to fight their way along treacherous, near-impassable

113

roads in order to look at a car? It was not even as if they could take one for a test drive.

'I wish this weather would clear,' Geoffrey complained with a forced smile as Trudy and Clement took matching armchair seats opposite a small fireplace. 'January is always a slow time to sell cars at the best of times but what with this …' He indicated the white stuff outside the window and shook his head grimly. He was standing in front of the unlit fire, resting one elbow on the high marble mantelpiece, but he did not look all that casual. His eyes kept darting from them to the window and back again.

'We'd like to thank you for officially identifying Mr Parker's body, sir,' Trudy began crisply. 'It can't have been easy.'

'No, it certainly wasn't,' he agreed flatly.

'You may have seen a piece in the local papers, asking anyone with any knowledge of Mr Parker or the accident, to contact us?' she went on. She was still annoyed with Duncan Gillingham for giving out her phone number. Luckily, the nuisance calls were dwindling away now.

'Er, yes, I did see it,' Geoffrey said, abruptly deciding to sit down on a two-seater settee at right angles to them. That done, he diligently set about straightening a non-existent crease in his trousers, thus continuing to avoid meeting her eye.

'One of the people who contacted us was Mr Philip Prescott,' Trudy said, and saw him wince.

'Oh?'

'Yes. He's an accountant for your firm?'

'Yes.'

'Is there anything you care to tell us now that you forgot to mention before, Mr Thorpe?' she asked mildly. But she was holding her breath as she did so. She was very aware that, without having any definite suspicions to go on about the cause of Terrence Parker's death, this man had every right to turn on them and demand to know what all the questions were about. And what business was it of theirs what state their company finances were in?

Luckily for her though, the vast majority of the British public were anxious to be seen to cooperate with the police and this man proved no exception. His shoulders slumped and he sighed, eventually lifting his eyes as far as the empty fireplace.

'I suppose you mean the … loan … Terry had taken out of the firm's accounts?'

'A loan?' Trudy echoed delicately.

'Yes. Well …' Geoffrey smiled wanly, finally meeting her gaze. 'That was how he described it to me when I tackled him about it.'

'I see. It was a rather … convoluted way for him to arrange a loan, wasn't it?' she said, careful to keep her tone neutral.

With a sigh, the other man got up again and paced restlessly to look out the window, turning his back firmly on his visitors. 'Look, it was clear that he'd been skimming,' he told the view out the window. 'He knew it, and I knew it. But it would have been a hell of a mess if I'd kicked up a fuss about it. I could have, of course. But imagine the scandal! Besides, in spite of, well … the money thing, we actually worked very well together. And the business is successful. Terry is a … *was*, a great salesman, and I knew if I kicked him out of the business, well, sales would drop off. Instead we got our heads together, and worked something out.'

'He was paying you back, in other words,' Clement put in.

'Yes. And I was watching him like a hawk, to make sure that he did,' Terry Parker's business partner said bitterly, still determinedly addressing the snowy scene that lay beyond his home. 'And, of course, part of the deal we worked out was that, from now on, I'd be in sole charge of the books and payments, and so on.'

'How much did he still have left to pay you back?' Trudy asked.

'A little more than half of what he took – or borrowed, as he preferred to call it.'

Money, Trudy thought, that now would not be paid back. Unless … 'Do you know what happens to his side of the business now he's gone, Mr Thorpe?'

115

'Yes, it comes to me,' Geoffrey Thorpe said, without a flicker. Either he hadn't yet registered the significance of that, or he was a very fine actor, Trudy thought, glancing at Clement. Did he really have no idea that this gave him an ideal motive for getting rid of an unreliable, thieving, business partner?

'Why do you think he "borrowed" the money, sir?' Trudy asked next.

Geoffrey Thorpe gave a wry laugh and finally turned back from the window, wearily slumping back down into his chair. 'Oh, that was typical of Terry,' he said tiredly, running a hand across his face. 'He was always living beyond his means. He liked to think he was the sort of man who should *own* and *drive* fancy sports cars, rather than sell them. You know the type I mean? He always had to buy the best wine and spirits. Order the most expensive meal at a restaurant. Dress in tailored suits rather than buy them off the rack. I have no doubt the money went through his fingers like water. He liked to entertain women too – play the wealthy bachelor.'

'I see,' Trudy said, wondering what Millicent Vander would have thought of this description of Terry. Somehow, she didn't think it would have pleased her. 'We're still having trouble tracing his next of kin; we had thought he might have come from Birmingham originally, but—'

'Birmingham?' Geoffrey interrupted with a frown. 'Why Birmingham? I got the impression … what was it now … Something he said to me once. Oh, some offhand remark about … why am I thinking about tiles?' he suddenly asked, making Trudy blink in surprise.

'Tiles, sir?' she echoed blankly.

'Yes, tiles …' The other man rubbed a hand more vigorously over his forehead. 'The curse of a fading memory. I know Terry said something once in passing that made me think he came from … oh, I know, I've got it now. Not tiles. The Pantiles!'

Trudy was still no further forward, and it was Clement who

came to her rescue. 'The Pantiles, as in the rather nice shopping district in Tunbridge Wells?' he asked smoothly.

'Yes. Exactly,' Geoffrey said with a small smile. 'I remember now – it was last summer – or the summer before. We had a garden party here at the house – Terry came, obviously, and my wife mentioned that she was having difficulty getting something specific she wanted. Can't remember now what it was, something continental, I think … Anyway, Terry said something about how she'd get just what she wanted if the Pantiles were around the corner. As it happened, we'd shopped there not long after our honeymoon, when we were holidaying not far from the town, so we both knew where he meant.'

'And he might have come from Tunbridge Wells?' Trudy nodded, making a rapid note in her notebook.

'Perhaps,' Geoffrey said, with a shrug. 'It's a little odd, now that I come to think of it. The moment he mentioned it, Terry seemed to get flustered. Well, not flustered so much, but he gave a start, as if annoyed at himself for speaking without thinking, and then he quickly rushed on to say something else, as if he regretted it, and wanted to take our minds off it.'

'He acted as if he'd made a slip,' Clement clarified quietly.

'Yes. You know, I rather think that's exactly how he acted,' Geoffrey admitted thoughtfully. Then his eyes glazed over. 'Terry never *did* like to talk about himself and his past, now that I come to think of it. He always became evasive whenever talk turned more personal, about families and childhood memories and things like that. I wonder now …'

And so did Trudy. Why, she asked herself, would someone not like to talk about themselves and their families or the past? Usually you couldn't stop someone – people loved talking about themselves as a rule. So why had Terry Parker been so reticent?

He didn't have a police record; it was one of the first things she'd checked.

Although they talked a little more, nothing else of significance seemed to come out of it, and Trudy and Clement left ten minutes later.

One of the first things Trudy did on leaving the Thorpe residence was to get Clement to pull over at the next telephone box they found, and she used some of her pennies to place a call through to the local station in Royal Tunbridge Wells. There she spoke to the desk sergeant at the police station. Given that the bad weather conditions were rife everywhere, the sergeant took a note of her request for someone to search the records for any mention of their dead man, but warned her it might take them some time. This didn't surprise her – she hardly expected her inquiry would be put at the top of their to-do list. If they were to make any progress with the case before Inspector Jennings pulled her off it, she mused wearily, it would be a belated Christmas miracle!

Trudy nevertheless thanked him and hung up, feeling frustrated.

She got back in the car, glad that the heater was working, and rubbed her hands together briskly.

'So, where do you want to go next?' she asked determinedly. She was not going to allow setback after setback to get the better of her.

'You have that party list of Millicent Vander's?' Clement asked after a moment's thought.

Trudy nodded and brought it out. 'Plus telephone numbers and addresses. At least she was thorough,' Trudy said, unfolding the piece of paper from her satchel.

'Any of them live close by?' Clement asked, looking out at the dull, leaden white sky that was clearly threatening yet more snow. 'I don't want to have to criss-cross the city if I can help it. I'm not sure where the ploughs have been – and haven't.'

Trudy saw the sense in that, and checked the list, running her eye down the neat handwriting. 'Oh, here's someone I haven't got around to yet.' She had, whenever she'd had the time, been systematically going through the list and talking to people she'd been able to make contact with on the telephone. 'He lives just around the corner and down the next turning on the left.'

'Perfect.' Clement grinned.

*

It was when they were walking up the recently shovelled path to the door of No. 11 Cleeves Road, that it happened.

Clement felt his left leg drag, pitching him forward slightly. Before he could stop himself, he took a tumble, falling full-length onto the ground. Luckily, his heavy overcoat saved him from serious injury, and his thick gloves protected his hands when he thrust them out instinctively in front of him to take the worst of his fall.

'Dr Ryder!' Trudy, who was in front of him, rushed back. 'Are you all right? It's so icy everywhere!'

Clement, who knew the weather conditions had nothing to do with it, forced himself to his knees, and gave her a rueful smile. 'I never was any good at ice skating,' he said gruffly.

He gingerly got to his feet, feeling embarrassed to have to lean – even for a second or two – on the helping arm that Trudy had hooked underneath one armpit.

He took a tentative step forward, relieved to feel his legs hold him. 'No harm done – except to my pride,' he said cheerfully, brushing the ice and snow off the front of his coat, and from the knees of his trousers.

'Are you sure?' Trudy asked anxiously.

'Of course. My bones aren't that brittle yet, young lady,' he said, giving her a flat stare, and hoping that she'd take the hint. Like most men, he didn't like to make a fuss.

He was still feeling shaken though, as he stood behind her after she'd rung the doorbell. Not because of the fall – which probably hadn't even caused him more than a few bruises. But because of the reason for it.

For there was no longer any getting around it.

He was becoming unsteady on his feet.

He was so lost in anxiety over this thought, that it wasn't until he heard the sound of voices that he realised the doorbell's summons had been answered, and he forced himself to concentrate on the matter in hand.

But at some point in the not too distant future, he knew there would have to be a reckoning, and that hard choices awaited him.

Chapter 16

David O'Connor looked surprised but not displeased to see a policewoman and an attractive if unknown man on his doorstep, and invited them in out of the cold immediately. He began to look really animated, however, when it became clear that they wanted to discuss the New Year's Eve party he'd attended, and the fatal car accident that had subsequently followed it.

In his mid-fifties, plump, balding, with deep-set dark-blue eyes, he was meticulously dressed in trousers and silk waistcoat, with a dark-red smoking jacket unbuttoned over the ensemble. He happily admitted to being a perennial bachelor, and thus was often invited to many parties to 'make up' the male numbers.

He showed them into a very warm, very cosy snug in his small, but very well decorated home, and bustled about settling them down in chairs and offering them mulled wine and mince pies that he promised them earnestly he'd baked himself.

It took Trudy a little while to break through all the bonhomie and chatter, and steer the flow of talk onto more lucrative topics.

'So you and Mrs Vander are old friends?' she offered as an opening gambit.

'Oh my, yes! Well, I was friends first with her late husband, of course, but Millie is such a dear too. Such a shame George went so suddenly like he did. He was a real gentleman. Not too many of us around nowadays, let me tell you. Would you like some brandy butter with the pies? I have some in the pantry.'

'No thank you, these are delicious just as they are,' Trudy assured him, and took another obliging bite out of the pastry offering, which was, in fact, very nice indeed. Clement, seated by the fire, was already absently munching on his second pie, and looked, to Trudy's eye, just a little distracted.

Although he sometimes took charge if their witness was a man around his own age – since they often responded more fully to him than to herself – this time he seemed happy enough for her to take the lead in the questioning. Perhaps he just didn't care for their witness's over-effusive ways?

'What time would you say you arrived at the party?' she pressed on somewhat indistinctly around a mouthful of mincemeat. It flashed into her mind that her mother would scold her for talking with her mouth full, then she instantly dismissed it. Building a rapport with a witness was far more important than good manners.

'Oh, not *too* early, naturally,' David O'Connor assured her coyly. 'Guests should know when to arrive and when to leave, don't you think? So, it must have been around nine or so. I was in time to see the golden boy arrive anyway – the dear departed Terrence. Poor dear Millie thinks she has a poker face, but, my dear, let me tell you, that woman should never be allowed anywhere *near* a pack of cards!'

Trudy rapidly interpreted this and nodded. 'Yes, I thought I detected a fondness in Mrs Vander's voice when she mentioned Mr Parker,' she said, rather more discreetly.

'Fondness? My dear girl, it's the talk of the town! Well of *our* circle anyway,' he felt impelled to modify, before rushing on, 'that she was absolutely smitten with him.' The cherubic-faced bachelor nodded solemnly. 'One could see why, of course. He was rather a fine-looking specimen. But, oh dear, one just couldn't overlook the age gap, could one? Really, I think it most remiss of her friends not to, well, steer her clear of such an impending disaster, don't you?'

'Disaster?' Trudy repeated. 'Was it that serious then, between them?'

'Oh my, yes!' David gave a small theatrical grasp. 'It was no mere harmless flirtation, believe me. Everyone was expecting an announcement any day. We were all positively agog waiting for the other shoe to drop.'

'Wait, you're saying that Mrs Vander and Mr Parker were actually *engaged to be married*?' Trudy asked, wanting to make sure she'd got that clear.

She saw, out of the corner of her eye, Clement perk up a bit and start taking proper notice.

'Well, as good as,' David said, hedging now. 'Everyone knew that the gentleman in question was just waiting for the right signal to get down on one knee. And Millie, the little minx, had been humming and hawing, but showed certain signs to those of us in the know that she was working up her courage to give him the nod, as it were. In fact, I rather thought things might have ended with an announcement that night.' David nodded emphatically once more, his plump cheeks all but aquiver with glee. 'Millie did seem to be buzzing with excitement at the beginning of the night. You know, like you do when you're hugging a secret to yourself? I took it to mean she was going to finally throw caution to the winds and say "be damned to you all" and make it official.' He paused to smile and take a sip from his mug of mulled wine. 'And I wasn't the only one who thought something was in the air either, you mark my words! Those ghastly children of hers were going around with faces like something out of a Shakespearean tragedy.'

He gave a gleeful little titter of remembrance, then tried to look contrite.

He failed.

'I see,' Trudy said, taking it all in. She couldn't help but wonder how reliable their voluble witness was, and glanced at Clement. He too was frowning slightly in concentration as he considered the possible ramifications of this latest information. Did it, in fact, get them any further forward?

Trudy could, she supposed, understand why Millicent Vander had been in no great hurry to mention the fact that she was rather closer to the victim than she'd implied. Worry, grief, shock, the need to save face or a combination of any of these things might have contributed to her silence. She was too intelligent – and socially sensitive – not to have been aware that her so-called friends were probably gossiping and laughing about her behind her back. Challenging the social mores of her peers wouldn't have been easy for a woman like her. Was this gossipy, fussy little man really reliable in what he was saying?

'She must have been very fond of him to consider marrying a man quite a number of years younger than herself,' she mused delicately. 'And if she was in love with him, his death will have been a real tragedy for her.'

David O'Connor looked, to his credit, genuinely upset now. 'Oh yes, I think she did love him, poor thing. And you're right – it's so sad. Terry too, dying so young! Such a good-looking man. What a shame. Mind you …' The sympathy seemed to vanish with astonishing quickness and a much more sly, thoughtful, perhaps even slightly spiteful look came to his eyes. 'I got the feeling there might have been a serpent in paradise, for all that.'

'Oh? What makes you think that?' It was Clement, finished with the excellent mince pies, who prodded their witness into further disclosures.

'Well,' the other man eagerly turned his attention to the coroner, his eyes twinkling in excitement. 'I do believe there was a bit of a contretemps at the party involving a rather nice-looking young woman – who, incidentally, didn't seem to know anyone else at the party apart from the young Lochinvar – and our hostess.'

Trudy again had to take a moment to decipher this. 'Sorry, are you saying he was flirting with someone else? *At Mrs Vander's own party?*' She tried not to sound shocked, but couldn't help but feeling indignant on the hostess's behalf.

'Oh no, quite the reverse,' David said hastily, turning avidly in his chair towards her now, the intensely white daylight streaming through the windows and gleaming off his silk-lined smoking jacket collar as he did so. 'Far from Terry and the mystery woman being all cosy, I do believe a nasty little spat was taking place between them, behind all the fake smiles and lowered voices.'

'You're saying Mr Parker was seen arguing at the party with another guest?' Again it was Clement who asked the deliberately straightforward question. He, like Trudy, was finding all the gushing rather trying.

'Well, it certainly *looked* like it to me,' David, pressed to be exact, again hedged a little. 'I was too far away to really be able to *hear* anything, mind,' he said, with such obvious regret and chagrin that Trudy had to stop herself from smiling. 'But I thought their body language was positively *screaming* hostility. On both their parts – his and hers,' he added unnecessarily, nodding his head emphatically, his eyes wide and solemn.

'So who was she? The woman, I mean?' Trudy asked.

'My dear, I told you, I don't know!' David spread his pink, well-manicured hands about in a helpless gesture. 'I don't think any of us did! I certainly didn't know her from Adam – or I suppose I should say Eve! And that in itself was odd, since dear Millie does tend to play it rather safe when it comes to her little soirees, and invites the same old people over and over again. Mind you, this time she played a bit of a blinder, snagging our local celebrity,' he added, eyes beaming in approbation.

'Who? Sorry, who are you talking about?' Trudy asked patiently.

'Oh my dear, our divine Katherine Morton, our "Lady of the Easel" no less. Exhibits at the Royal Academy with monotonous regularity and all that,' David gushed with just a hint of sarcasm.

Trudy nodded, suddenly remembering that someone else had mentioned her before. But she was far more interested in less high-flying partygoers right now.

'To get back to the woman you saw Mr Parker having words with,' she said firmly. 'Presumably Mrs Vander must have known who she was? If she'd invited her?'

'Not on your Nellie she didn't then!' David said robustly. 'I know dear Millie very well, and although she was very polite and the perfect hostess, I could tell she had no idea who she was either!'

'Oh, she was a gate-crasher?' Trudy asked, not sure why she was so surprised by this turn of events.

'I don't see what else she could have been.' David nodded happily. 'I had a discreet word here and there, and none of the regular gang were in any hurry to claim her! Of course, Millie refused to be flustered, and simply acted as if everything was fine. But I could tell she wasn't happy. Especially when the mystery lady monopolised the golden boy.'

'I know you said they later argued, but at first, did Mr Parker seem pleased to see her – this mystery woman?' Clement asked next.

'Not he!' David bubbled gleefully. 'He had a face like thunder right from the off! She didn't stay very long, I'll give her that. Her brass neck didn't extend *that* far. She just had a bit of a drinkie and a few nibbles. Then they sort of circled around each other for a bit, and eventually she approached him, and, like I said, they had this whispery sort of spat and then took it out into the hall for some privacy. I really wish I could have heard what it was they were talking about!' he added gloomily. Then he suddenly snapped his fingers. 'Mind you, you might ask our Lady of the Easel – she had a much better vantage point than yours truly. She was sitting quaffing champagne like there was no tomorrow on the sofa, and they were arguing right behind her. If anyone managed to catch anything they said, then Katherine did.'

Trudy nodded, making a note of that. 'So what happened after the, er, spat?'

'Oh, they parted again and circulated a bit, pretending nothing had happened, but I noticed them slip off into the hall together not long after, like I said before. I then got a bit distracted by this rather fetching young man who's up at Wadham, reading English, and when I looked around again, she seemed to have left altogether. *He* was still there though. Terry didn't leave until after we'd chanted in the new year and sung dear old Robbie Burns' little piece.'

Trudy frowned, not getting the reference, and Clement made a mental note to tell her about the origins of 'Auld Lang Syne' some time.

'Did you see Mr Parker actually leave?' Trudy asked next, without much hope, and was therefore delighted when this seemingly endless font of knowledge once again came up trumps.

'Actually, I did then!' David O'Connor said triumphantly. 'I was just having one last little drinkie on the sofa by the window and saw him walking down the drive towards the cars.'

'Did he seem intoxicated?' Trudy asked quickly.

Her witness looked at her, eyeing her uniform, and then gave a pixie-like smile of pure impish mischief. 'Oh no, officer, I can't say that he did. Oh, he'd had one or two drinkies I'm sure, but he was hardly *staggering*! Scout's honour. He was perfectly fit to drive, as I was myself,' he swore piously.

'And you didn't notice anything unusual about him then?'

'No. Oh, wait a minute … But that might be nothing. I wasn't sure …' Clearly he wanted her to tease the titbit out of him, and Trudy, smothering a slightly irritated sigh, obliged him.

'I really would be happy to hear anything you may have noticed, sir. We are dealing with a fatality,' she reminded him, further massaging his ego and sense of self-importance by adding solemnly, 'and you may have been the last person to actually see Mr Parker alive.'

127

David O'Connor's plump lips formed a perfect 'O' at this, and he nodded, going perhaps just a little pale. 'Oh my! Yes … Well, like I said, I may have been mistaken. It was dark, you must remember, and I only caught a flash, as he backed the car out and swept it around in readiness to go through the Vanders' double gates … But I thought I saw a flash of brightness in the car with him.'

Whatever either Trudy or Clement had thought he might say, it certainly hadn't been that.

'A brightness?' Trudy echoed flatly. 'Do you mean … someone had a torch on inside?'

'Oh no, sorry, I'm not being clear, am I? Dear me! No, I meant that I thought I saw, for a moment or two, a paler, brighter colour in the car with him, where there shouldn't have been any such thing. As if someone with light hair was sitting beside him – perhaps a blonde, or an older woman with white hair, maybe. The young Lochinvar had dark hair, you see,' he said helpfully, looking from one to the other of them, delighted with himself and the stir this latest revelation was having on his visitors.

'*He had a passenger with him?*' Trudy gasped.

'As I said, I couldn't be sure,' David hedged carefully once again. 'But if I were a betting man, I'd have said he wasn't alone when he drove away that night.'

Chapter 17

'What sort of things does she paint?' Trudy asked warily some twenty minutes later, as they pulled up outside the home of the feted artist Katherine Amy Morton. She didn't understand 'art' but she knew that the coroner did, and often purchased new canvases for his home.

They'd discussed the garrulous David's testimony on the (thankfully) incident-free drive to the famous artist's Oxford residence, and had come to no set opinions on his reliability. But they had both agreed that *if* Terrence Parker had left the party with a passenger, then that passenger needed to be found and asked to account for their actions that night. As Clement had pointed out, it was perfectly possible that Terry had given someone a lift home and then gone on and had the accident when he was alone. But if so, why had no one answered the newspaper's appeal for information?

Trudy had instantly responded to this by pointing out that no matter what the cocky Duncan Gillingham thought, not everyone read the *Oxford Tribune*, or hung on his every word even if they did! Perhaps the possible passenger had not seen the appeal for information?

Now, as they sat outside a street that consisted mostly of elegant terraced Georgian houses that had long since been converted into spacious flats, she listened as the coroner gave her a brief history on the artistic credentials of their next witness.

'She was influenced by Laura Knight in her early works, but then became more surrealist,' he began, leaving her no further forward, although she nodded wisely. 'She made her name early and was a bit of a "wild child" in London in her twenties and thirties. Had affairs with revolutionaries in Mexico and that sort of thing,' he added casually.

Trudy, sitting in a fast-freezing car in a quiet street in Oxford, thought about hot-blooded rebellious men and tequilas and baking desert temperatures, and blinked. 'Oh,' she managed.

'Then she married some upper-class twit named Fairweather with a receding chin but a large bank balance, had a child, and then divorced him. She kept using her maiden name for her career, obviously, so she's always been known simply as Katherine Morton. After ditching the spouse, she moved here and began painting her more "clever" stuff,' he swept on.

Trudy sighed heavily. She knew what that meant. 'I'm not going to understand her stuff then,' she predicted tiredly. She liked a tree to look like a tree.

'She'd probably be disappointed if you did. The Americans currently love her and pay silly money for her canvases, but she's on record as saying that no American ever had a true artistic taste.'

'She sounds like a "character" all right,' Trudy agreed without enthusiasm. She could tell that the coroner was looking forward to meeting her, however, and she only hoped the woman met his expectations.

'Hmmm.' Clement made a non-committal sound and reached out to open the car door. 'Let's just hope she's a good witness,' he said prosaically. 'Artists are supposed to be observant; now we'll see if they actually are.'

He didn't, to Trudy's mind, sound particularly optimistic though.

They made their way carefully up the slippery, frozen-slush steps of the pale stone building, noted that 'Miss Morton' had a flat on the top floor, and pressed the bell.

Nothing happened.

Clement pressed it again.

Still nothing happened.

'She must be out,' Trudy said. Perhaps, she mused nervously, she should get back to the station now and report the latest interesting findings to Inspector Jennings, before he became too annoyed at her prolonged absence?

Clement smiled grimly. 'Perhaps. More likely she's still in bed and can't be bothered to get out of it.' He pressed the bell again, and this time left his finger on it for nearly a minute. Eventually the door to the main hall clicked open and they stepped inside.

Trudy was surprised to find the communal area actually quite warm; they tended to be freezing in places such as this. She said as much to the coroner, who began to climb the stairs with a firm grip on the handrail and carefully lifting his feet.

'Ah, you're forgetting,' he chided amiably. 'This is an upmarket building. No caretaker would dare let the radiators stay cold in this weather. He'd have half a dozen toffs biting his ears off if he did.'

Trudy was still smiling over this image when the door to No. 8 was flung open just before they reached it.

The woman who stood in the doorway scowled at them with the ferocity of a Valkyrie that had just had a juicy steak snatched from under its nose. She was, perhaps, forty-five or so, but had the well-preserved look that meant she could have been as much as fifty. She had curves, a lot of messy brunette hair and narrow but sparrow-bright hazel eyes. She was also free of make-up, which left her face looking strangely naked.

She was dressed in a pair of silk grey trousers with a wide flare at the feet (which were bare) and a huge white knitted polo-neck sweater, the neck of which came up almost to her ears.

'Was it you who was leaning on my bell?' she demanded. Her

voice had a definite 'smoker's rasp' to it, and her eyes widened just a little as they took in Trudy's uniform, but then her gaze stopped and stayed on Clement.

'Guilty,' Clement said with a slight bow. He had never looked or sounded more imperious and Trudy saw the artist quickly readjust her attitude. Instead of belligerence, a sort of grudging amusement spread across her features. Her face was pale and a pinched, triangular shape, that seemed at odds with the curves of her figure. She reminded Trudy of a peculiar sort of cat – one that had the fluffy, comfortably body of a round tabby cat, but the startling head of a Siamese.

'You'd better have a bloody good reason for disturbing me, no matter if you do look and sound like James Mason,' she warned him flatly, standing aside to let them pass.

Clement seemed to take the compliment in his stride, and Trudy briefly wondered if the coroner even knew who James Mason was. Did he ever watch films? Would he be flattered at being compared to a movie star?

'Is death and disaster, mystery and the pursuit of prurient gossip a good enough reason?' he asked her mildly.

The artist again gave him another approving glance.

Realising that this was going to be one of those 'sophisticated' affairs that she could never quite get the hang of, Trudy was happy to settle down and play second fiddle this time. Let Clement flirt and enjoy himself – she was no spoilsport!

'Hmph,' the artist said, but her lips twitched in a grudging smile. 'You've intrigued me. Well, you might as well sit down,' she said gracelessly, indicating the chairs that were littered haphazardly around the large, white living room into which she'd shown them. A window overlooking the street and a large weeping silver birch tree that was growing in the garden of the house opposite, lent a suitably 'artistic' view of the city and some of the 'dreaming spires' in that part of town.

Their hostess literally threw herself into a rather scruffy-looking black leather wingback chair that creaked at the mistreatment. In front of the chair was a low coffee table all but overflowing with stuff: a poinsettia (bright red and already wilting due to lack of water), magazines, empty coffee cups, and a large leather handbag that looked stuffed to the gills with items. There were also three packets of cigarettes, all of them open, a large table lighter in the shape of an eagle, and a large onyx ashtray brimming over with ash and stubbed-out cigarettes. There was one slipper in pink satin scuffed at the toe, some nutcrackers and a bowl of walnuts and various pens with their tops off. There was even, Trudy noticed with a grimace, a copy of the *Oxford Tribune*, opened at the crossword page.

'Well – where do we start?' Katherine Morton demanded, reaching for one of the cigarette packets and lighting one up. She vaguely offered the packet to them, shrugging when they both declined. 'Is it to be death, mystery, gossip or what-have-you first?' She lifted her head slightly to blow the smoke towards the ceiling. Her fingertips were yellow and nicotine-stained and she tapped one bare foot on the floor in a vigorous tempo without, apparently, having any idea that she did so.

Clement noticed that the walls were conspicuously bare of any paintings at all – either her own creations or anyone else's. Obviously, the painter liked to be free of artistry when she was relaxing in her own private living room.

'First of all, I'm Dr Clement Ryder, city coroner, and this is WPC Loveday,' Clement said. Trudy could tell he was enjoying himself. He liked people who challenged him, and something about the way the artist notorious for her free spirit was regarding him, told her that Katherine Morton felt the same way.

'Dr Death no less? Now I *am* impressed,' Katherine drawled.

'Let's start with gossip, shall we?' Clement said, magnificently ignoring the jibe. 'You attended a New Year's Eve party at Mrs Millicent Vander's house recently.'

'I did, but don't hold that against me,' the artist begged

133

mockingly, taking another ferocious draw of her cigarette. Trudy noticed that she sucked on it so hard that it made the sides of her cheeks pull in. Clearly, the woman lived on her nerves and cigarettes. And maybe alcohol, for there was a distinct smell of spirits in the air.

Trudy let her eye wander briefly around the room, surprised to find it bare of almost any personal touches. No books, no paintings, just a photo of a lovely young girl of about twenty or so, that was perched in isolated splendour on top of a sideboard. She looked a bit like Katherine, but Trudy didn't think it was a photograph of the artist as a younger woman. Her daughter maybe, a younger sister or perhaps a favourite niece?

'You're not a fan of Millicent, I take it?' Clement deduced with a twinkle in his eye, and Trudy hastily drew her attention back to the matter in hand.

Katherine shuddered. 'Don't be nasty,' she admonished.

'So why *did* you go to her party? I did think, when I was told you were on the guest list, that it wasn't the sort of … event … that would be likely to appeal to you,' Clement admitted.

The artist broke off her concentrated smoking to give a great guffaw of genuine laughter. 'Not only a James Mason lookalike, but a true gentleman as well. My, my,' she said admiringly, and reaching forward to extract another cigarette, lit it straight from the one that she'd almost finished.

She regarded the glowing tip of this latest cigarette with a vague look. 'Why did I go? Yes … Why *did* I go? Because I was feeling masochistic? Or was I lonely?' She seemed to be having a genuine debate with herself. 'Or was it because nobody else had invited me out? No, that can't be right, the sycophants never let up. So they must have, but because of the weather maybe I couldn't … Oh. I know. I simply found myself at seven o'clock on New Year's Eve in Oxford, on my own, and panicked. Yes, that must have been it. In those circumstances, I think one can be forgiven for attending even a Millie Vander party, don't you?'

Her eyes opened wide in a challenging smile. 'Also, of course, I wanted to be with people who would be so in awe of my talent and fame that they'd fawn on me like …' She took a drag of her cigarette, tried to come up with some words, but shrugged instead.

Seeming to tire of the game, she sighed heavily. 'Most likely I could see I was running out of booze and knew dear old Millie could be trusted at least to have ordered much, much champagne.'

She cocked her head to one side and regarded Trudy, quietly taking notes, then looked back at Clement. 'Now I'm becoming intrigued. Let's get on to the mystery, do,' she appealed.

'All right,' Clement agreed amiably. 'What can you tell us about the mysterious gate-crasher at the party?'

'*Oh her*!' the artist said, nodding her head admiringly. 'Now we're talking! Yes, she certainly had some nerve, that one,' Katherine agreed, getting up and walking to the sideboard, where she reached inside and drew out a decanter of something pale and golden, still talking all the while. 'She could have sold herself out as an artist's model, even if she wasn't exactly a teenage rose anymore. Good bone structure, and she had style, you know? Held herself well, walked well, and had a look in her eyes that would make you think twice. I can think of several men who'd have been panting to paint her. Malt?' She jiggled the spirit bottle temptingly, but Clement merely smiled and shook his head.

She shrugged and poured herself a hefty slug into a chunky, cut-glass tumbler and brought the nearly full glass back to the chair. She then flung herself down in it again, without – miraculously – spilling a drop. 'Of course, her clothes were handmade, but she made them *look* as if they'd come straight from Paris. It was clear as day that dear Millie had no idea who she was, and neither had anybody else.'

So David O'Connor had been right about that, at least, Clement mused. Millie *had* had an uninvited guest in her house that night.

'Did you speak to her?' he asked curiously.

'Not I,' the artist shot back at once. 'I was too busy making inroads into the champagne and being outrageous. Which is the unspoken agreement, isn't it?' The artist opened her eyes wide in mock innocence. 'Staid society matrons provide a bit of scandalous company at their parties, and the said scandalous company doesn't disappoint. I flirted with some very married men just enough to upset their wives, and said one or two libellous things to the more stick-in-the-mud-types, then settled down with a bottle of Moët's best efforts and commenced to get decently plastered. Besides, I was not on the mystery woman's radar. Which stands to reason,' Katherine Morton said, taking a swig of whisky. 'Lions in the jungle tend to avoid one another. It's a courtesy thing.'

Trudy turned a page on her notebook, but privately wondered if you got lions in jungles. Didn't they tend to roam about on the plains? Her lips twisted into a smile as she scribbled assiduously. Whimsy, it seemed, was infectious.

'So who *was* on her agenda?' Clement interposed smoothly.

'Oh, Millie's fancy man, I rather think,' Katherine said, sounding bored. 'I didn't realise, until that night, that dear old Millie had it in her! A younger swain, no less! I can tell you she went up several notches in my estimation when I finally figured it out.'

'One of the guests rather thinks Terrence Parker and the gate-crasher were having a discreet spat. And that you might have overheard it,' Clement said, watching Katherine yawn mightily. She opened her jaw so wide he fancied he could almost hear the delicate bone in her lower mandible crack.

'Sorry? Oh, yes, you're quite right. At one point in the night they were hissing at each other like a pair of kettles, behind me – I was on the sofa ...'

She reached into her handbag suddenly, which was so full that items instantly began to tumble out as she rummaged around inside it. More pens, a notebook, a bottle of aspirin, a hairbrush, a set of what looked like crayons, a packet of tissues ... It all tumbled onto the already full table, until with a cry of triumph,

Katherine pounced on the required object, which turned out to be a tube of lipstick.

'Ah,' she said with satisfaction, twisting the bottom, revealing a deep red tube of colour.

'What was the argument about, could you hear?' Clement asked, watching, fascinated, as the woman, still holding the glass of whisky in one hand, and utterly without benefit of a mirror, very neatly and effectively outlined her mouth with the vibrant red.

'Yes I did, as a matter of fact. Oh, you've no reason to look so pleased, I assure you. It's disappointing – very,' Katherine warned him. 'In fact, it was downright sordid. They were arguing about another woman.'

Chapter 18

'Infidelity? You're right, that *is* dreary,' Clement drawled, not batting an eyelid. 'Which one of them was being accused of it?'

'Oh he was, definitely,' the artist said, gurgling with laughter around the glass, which had been pressed to her lips. 'I heard the name Vicky mentioned, I believe. And he wasn't happy about it, I can assure you. Millie's charmer wanted nothing more than to get her out of there before she could spill the beans good and proper. Kept hissing at her that they'd discuss things tomorrow.'

'What things?'

'Alas, *that* I can't tell you,' she apologised vaguely. 'They didn't actually say. That is, our gate-crasher intimated, hinted, suggested and downright threatened, but never actually came out with specifics.'

'But Terry Parker understood the threat?'

'I'd say so!' the artist said with another delighted gurgle. 'If I hadn't already been three sheets to the wind, I'd have been more appreciative. The last thing I'd have expected at a Millie Vander party would be actual entertainment! So, what's next? You promised me – what was it … tragedy or death and something-or-other? We've done the gossip and the mystery, so let's get on to the tragedy,' she said with relish.

138

Clement reached forward and picked up the *Oxford Tribune*. 'Read the papers lately?'

'Hah! Not I!' Katherine snorted. 'I go straight to the "funnies" then the crossword. So-called news is hardly ever that, is it – news, I mean?'

'Ah, then you missed the death bit. Millie's charmer, to be precise.'

For a second Katherine Morton went very still and then she tossed off her drink and said flatly, 'So he died?'

'You don't sound surprised,' Clement said quietly.

The artist shrugged. 'Dying *isn't* really so surprising, is it? People do it all the time,' she stated dully. The sparkle had definitely gone now, and it seemed to Clement that she reached forward and lit yet another cigarette more out of habit than anything else.

'We found his body in his crashed car early on New Year's Day,' Clement informed her. 'We believe he died shortly after leaving Millie's house that night. Or early morning, I should say.'

Trudy, watching her, saw the artist turn her head and stare at the sideboard. Was she going to pour herself another large whisky? How much did the woman drink during the day? But perhaps she was doing the older woman a disservice, for the artist made no effort to rise.

'Poor old Millie,' Katherine Morton said quietly instead. 'To have your grand affair, your gloriously defiant pie-in-life's-face moment end before it had even properly begun … What a damned shame. The woman will probably never work up the courage to actually "live" again.'

She sighed heavily.

'Did you see Terry leave the party?' Clement asked next. It wasn't that he didn't agree with Katherine's sentiments, just that, at that moment, Millie Vander's troubles were not his priority.

'Nope.'

'There's some debate over whether or not he had a passenger with him in the car.'

139

'Did he?' Katherine asked quickly – if a little indistinctly – around a mouthful of whisky.

'We don't know,' Clement admitted briskly. 'Certainly nobody other than himself was found in the car. Is there anything else you care to tell us – about Millie or the mystery woman? Did you know Mr Parker?'

'Never met him before that night,' Katherine said, and gave yet another huge yawn. 'Millie's too boring to mention, and the only thing I know about the mystery woman is that she has the same taste in negligees as myself.'

'Sorry?' Clement said, put off his stride for the first time since he'd entered the artist's lair.

'Oh, didn't I say? I saw her in town,' Katherine said, dragging her gaze away from the sideboard and turning to Clement, giving him a lazy, cat-like smile. 'In Beatrice's in the High.' She named a boutique clothes shop that was out of Trudy's budget, but she knew which shop she meant.

'It was the day before the party, I think,' Katherine swept on. 'I was in the shop looking for a Hermès scarf I wanted. I was just browsing, as you do, and noticed this apricot silk dressing gown and negligee. I was just about to go in for a closer look, but this woman beat me to it.' She shrugged. 'I let her have it.' She grinned magnanimously. 'Not that I wouldn't have fought her for it if I'd really wanted it, mind.' The artist frowned thoughtfully. 'Now that I come to think of it, I never did find that Hermès I wanted,' she mused, staring down into her nearly depleted glass.

'And you're sure this woman was the same woman who gate-crashed the party?' Clement asked, glancing at Trudy, who was looking at him with an excited gleam in her eye. No doubt they were both thinking the same thing. If the woman had bought the nightwear, she might have paid by cheque. Or better yet, asked to have it delivered. Either way, they might, with a bit of luck, have a lead on the mystery woman!

'Oh yes, it was her all right,' Katherine said, sounding, once more, thoroughly bored. 'I'm an artist – I don't forget visual things. Names, dates, yes. Not what people look like. So that's everything covered,' she said sadly. 'Death, tragedy, mystery and gossip. Now I need another drink. Sure I can't get you one?'

*

'Let's hope they've cleared the pavements on the High Street and Beatrice's is open!' Trudy said eagerly, once they were back in the car.

They were in luck, on both counts, and Clement even managed to leave the car where it didn't obstruct too much of the High Street.

The shop assistant in the underwear section was highly amused by the distinctive gentleman's obvious unease as the nice police lady and herself talked about ladies' lingerie. By tacit consent, they both chose to spare his blushes by ignoring him. Within moments they were deep in discussion.

'Oh, you *do* remember the lady, and the set she bought?' Trudy was able to get down to business very quickly.

Again they were in luck, for it turned out that not only had the shop assistant recognised the famous local artist immediately she'd walked in, but she'd also been the one to handle the sale of the items in question to the other customer as well.

'Oh yes indeed, er, madam,' the shop assistant said, for a moment wondering if she should more properly address Trudy as 'Constable'. She was clearly not a customer, and therefore a sale was out of the question, but habit won over the day. 'It was just as you described it – a peignoir and negligee set in apricot silk with ecru lace. Very nice, but not quite our top, *top* range you understand.' In other words, affordable, Trudy surmised.

'And the woman who bought it, can you describe her?' Trudy asked eagerly.

'Yes madam, I believe so. She was wearing a nice two-piece in powder blue, that almost looked as if it was a genuine Balmain. Let's see, she was several inches shorter than madam, and her hair was almost exactly your shade, but cut short. She had dark-brown eyes, just like madam too, and I should have said she was in her late twenties. Possibly very early thirties.'

Trudy, who couldn't remember anybody ever calling her 'madam' nodded happily. This matched, more or less exactly, the description they'd got from Katherine Morton before leaving her to her cigarettes and whisky.

'Can you remember how she paid?' Trudy asked next. But here, it seemed, her run of good luck had run out.

'Madam paid by cash,' the assistant said firmly.

'Oh. I don't suppose she took advantage of your delivery service?' Trudy asked, deflated.

'I believe she may have, madam. Give me one moment to check the register,' the shop assistant said, reaching down behind the glass-topped counter (displaying the latest French cami-knickers, from which Clement kept his gaze firmly averted) and withdrew a large red flock velvet-covered account's journal.

She ran a bony, perfectly manicured finger down the lists on first one page, then the next. 'Let me see, this would be December the 30th … Ah yes! I thought she had. The purchases were sent to the Raven's Rest later that day.'

'The what?' Trudy asked, startled.

'I do believe it is a rather nice bed and breakfast in Summertown, madam,' the assistant proffered helpfully.

Trudy thanked her with real gratitude. Clement tipped his hat to her and beat a thankful retreat.

Chapter 19

The Raven's Rest, alas, lay off a small side street somewhere between the Banbury and Woodstock roads, which had last seen a snowplough many days ago.

Forced to abandon the car on the main road, they were relieved to find a path of sorts, which had been forged by the street's residents, hacking a narrow corridor through the three-foot-high snowbanks. They had to walk in single file, and by the time they reached the bed and breakfast – a nice-looking Victorian house in pale stone – they were both shivering.

The house had probably once belonged to a respectable merchant and his extended family over a hundred years ago, but now boasted 'vacancies', a 'television lounge' and a telephone in the lobby.

The owner didn't look happy to see a police uniform cross her doorstep, and listened, stony-faced, as Trudy described the guest she wished to see. The landlady, about fifty, round and looking like a disapproving pouter pigeon, reluctantly agreed that she did indeed at present have a guest staying in her establishment, such as the one described. With a haughty sniff, she gave them the guest's name – Mrs Phyllis Raynor – and her room number.

After being very careful (under the owner's gimlet eye) to

knock their boots free of any lingering snow on the sisal mat in the small reception hall, they walked up the carpeted steps to the top floor.

The woman who answered the summons looked at them blankly for a moment, then slowly turned her head a little to one side.

'Yes?' she said uncompromisingly.

'Mrs Raynor? Phyllis Raynor?' Trudy asked. She was aware her voice sounded portentous and wished it didn't. But she'd reacted instinctively. Perhaps it was the way the woman's face became instantly shuttered when she saw her uniform. Or perhaps she was gaining enough experience to know when a witness was going to be uncooperative. But she just knew that there was going to be no cosy or revealing chat with *this* witness, and it brought out the officialdom in her.

'Yes,' Phyllis said again. Her tone wasn't aggressive but it wasn't neutral either, and made it very clear that she wasn't interested in whatever it was they were selling.

'I would like to ask you a few questions. It's in connection with a police inquiry,' Trudy said firmly.

The woman, who stood uncompromisingly foursquare in the doorway, blocking any view of the room beyond, cocked her head slightly to the other side. She didn't look intimidated, angry or worried.

'Yes? What it is you want to know?'

'Did you attend a New Year's Eve party a few nights ago?' Trudy began.

'I did not.'

Trudy blinked. That had been flat, clear and unequivocal. She took a breath and girded her loins for a tussle.

'Do you know a Mrs Millicent Vander?' she tried again.

'I do not.'

'Are you sure you weren't at her party, here in Oxford, on New Year's Eve?'

'I'm very sure,' Phyllis Raynor said flatly.

'What would you say if we had witnesses who could put you at that party?' Trudy said, feeling on surer ground now. Surely Mrs Vander would recognise her, and probably several other party guests, if it came to that?

'I would say they were mistaken,' Phyllis said calmly. 'Is there anything else you need?'

Trudy wanted to say yes. Her back was up, and she wanted to throw Terry Parker's name at Phyllis and see how she reacted to it. But caution held her back. For a start, she was on very shaky ground already. They didn't know, yet, that there was anything criminal in his death, and her remit to investigate the case probably didn't include aggressive questioning. Besides, something told her that she would need more ammunition before seriously tackling this woman in earnest.

'Thank you, Mrs Raynor, that's all,' Trudy forced herself to say, and gave a tight smile.

The door shut instantly in her face.

Clement, who hadn't said a word, backed up to let his young friend pass him, then followed her equally silently down the stairs. There, the landlady – who hadn't budged from the reception hall – watched in silence as they left.

Once outside in the frigid, deeply unpleasant air, Trudy pulled her coat tighter around herself and sighed. 'I didn't like Mrs Raynor,' she admitted with a wry laugh. 'She *was* lying, wasn't she?'

'Oh yes, I think so,' Clement agreed at once.

Trudy sighed. 'Well, I wasn't in any position to really question her properly, and Inspector Jennings would have had a fit if she lodged a complaint against me. And speaking of the inspector, I'd better get back to the station and report on everything we've found out,' she said without enthusiasm. The day was wearing on and he'd no doubt have any number of other duties to allot her that had nothing to do with the fatal car crash.

'Yes, and I should get back to Vincent,' Clement said. 'I promised to beat him at nine-card brag. I'll just pop into the office first and see if anything urgent has come in.'

And so it was that Clement dropped her off at the station to face the music, and then set out for his place of work, where he found his secretary had failed to arrive, and admin had all but ground to a halt.

He went back to his house, grumpily wishing that the snow would clear so that everything could get back to normal. Surely this blasted arctic spell wouldn't last much longer?

*

Jennings listened to his WPC's findings with a scowl. He'd been hoping by now that he could put this blasted case to bed, but the more his constable discovered about the victim, the less he liked it. Reluctantly agreeing to allow her one more day, he then tossed a hundred-weight of paperwork at her and told her to get on with it, and commented that if she expected to be paid overtime, she wasn't as bright as she thought she was.

Trudy retreated to her desk with a respectful, 'yes, sir,' and rejoiced that the case was still hers.

*

That night Dr Douglas Carey rang Clement with news about the toxicology report he'd been asked to perform on the coroner's road traffic fatality.

'You were right about the barbiturates,' he said jovially, once the preliminary hellos and mutually unflattering insults had been swapped. 'Nothing exotic – just an ordinary, run-of-the-mill sleeping concoction prescribed by GPs and quacks the country over,' he added unhelpfully.

'Was the dose fatal?' Clement asked, reaching for a pen and

jotting down notes as the two medical men swapped facts and theories.

'I wouldn't have said so, no,' Douglas said cautiously, giving him the technical details. 'I think you'll agree, if our chap was otherwise fit and healthy enough, that wouldn't have polished him off. Can't say for certain, of course, without the full autopsy – which I've now had to bump up as a priority,' he warned his old pal, his tone now apologetic. 'If our cadaver turns out to have a hitherto unsuspected heart condition or underlying asthma or any other number of nasty conditions – well, you know as well as I do, all bets are off.'

Clement grunted. 'It's all right, old man, you don't have to protect your rear end with me. I think, on the whole, he's likely to turn out to have been as fit as a flea, but you never can tell,' he admitted. 'All things being equal though – you don't think the drug killed him – even with a fair bit of alcohol in his system?'

'Unlikely, I'd say. But it would have made him woozy, and he'd have dropped off to sleep fairly soon after taking it. Maybe within fifteen to twenty minutes or so – depending on his constitution.'

'Not ideal, that, if you're behind the wheel of the car after a snowstorm,' Clement said wryly.

His friend concurred.

'So, he either took it by accident,' Douglas said, 'took it deliberately, the fool, or …' He trailed off, leaving Clement to pick up the thread.

The coroner duly obliged. 'Or it was slipped to him shortly before he left the party he'd been attending,' Clement said with satisfaction. 'I doubt he took it deliberately since he knew he would soon be driving. And people intending suicide, as you well know, tend to do so tucked up in bed or in a chair, with a large dose of some alcohol or other of their choice at hand,' he theorised out loud. 'Taking a sleeping dose and then driving is a pretty haphazard way of going about it too. There would be no way you could be sure of dying, even if you did bury your car in a brick wall. Not to mention the possibility that you might crash into another car and take some poor innocent soul with you.'

Clement leaned back in his chair, aware that he was feeling pleasantly excited. Oh, not because a man had died, but because it was beginning to look more and more likely that someone had thought they'd got away with murder.

And they hadn't.

But he shouldn't rush things. 'How likely is it he could have taken it by accident?' Clement asked, then realising he wasn't being clear enough, he added, 'I mean, could you tell in what form the barbiturate had been administered? Because if he had to be injected with it …'

'No, not by needle,' Dr Carey said at once. 'I think it was prob-ably taken orally – and more likely than not in a regular sleeping draught form. We're running more tests now to be sure, but I think it's almost certain that a powder was dissolved in water or some other liquid. So it's possible he didn't know what he was drinking. I think when we've got it narrowed down, it'll turn out to be a fairly bog-standard sleeping powder. You know – the kind that millions of sleepless souls and insomniacs toss back every night with their Horlicks.'

'Over-the-counter stuff even?' Clement asked, with a sigh. If that was the case, they would not catch their killer by being able to track down an incriminating purchase of some obscure poison. Or from a GP's prescription.

'Probably,' Dr Carey said cheerfully.

Clement called him something distinctly slanderous. His friend responded by informing him even more cheerfully that Clement, as coroner, now needed to inform the constabulary of the fact that they had – at the very least – an 'interesting' death on their hands.

Clement had to agree. 'Send the reports directly to me, and I'll pass it on to WPC Loveday,' he said. At least, that way, they could keep Jennings out of the loop for a while longer, giving them a bit more time to gather conclusive evidence. It was inevitable, of course, that the case would be taken away from them sooner or later, but he was sure that Trudy would agree with him that they were still the best people for the job.

'I'll do that, old sport,' his friend said. 'Happy hunting.'

Clement grunted and hung up.

It wasn't until he looked up that he saw his son was watching him from the doorway of his study, a gentle smile on his face.

'That sounded all very promising and cloak-and-dagger,' Vincent said with a grin. 'You look disgustingly like the proverbial cat that just ate the canary. Is it something to do with the case?' he added eagerly.

Clement regarded his only son with a grin of his own. 'You've changed your tune,' he accused amiably. 'I thought I was overworking?'

Vincent shrugged. 'Yes, well, since you've been telling me all about this Terry Parker fellow, I admit, I've become intrigued.'

Clement leaned back in his chair, his eyes impish. 'Fancy lending a helping hand?' he offered magnanimously. He was sure Trudy wouldn't mind if he brought Vincent in on things, just as an added pair of hands.

Chapter 20

Trudy was surprised to hear a knock at her door just before eight o'clock the next morning. Her Land Rover taxi wasn't due for another half-hour, and she hoped that there wasn't an emergency call-out somewhere. She quickly picked up her piece of half-eaten toast and trotted to the front door, where she found Clement Ryder standing on her doorstep.

'Dr Ryder! Please, come in,' she said, backing away. Upstairs, she heard a creak, and realised that her voice had carried to her parents upstairs, who were, she was sure, about to get dressed and make a hasty appearance. They both liked and approved of the professional man, and were secretly proud that he thought so highly of their daughter that he insisted she act as his police liaison.

'Do you want a cup of tea?' She led him to the small kitchen, where the electric bars on the fire had chased away the worst of the freezing temperatures.

'Thank you,' Clement accepted, sitting at the table.

By the time her parents came quickly down the stairs, he'd given her both the good news and the bad news about the toxicology results. Good, because at least now they could be reasonably certain Terry Parker's car crash had not been due to the bad weather or drunken driving. Bad, because once DI Jennings knew about it, they both understood that the case would quickly be yanked out from under them.

'Dr Carey had these sent over from his office this morning,' he was saying, tapping a slim buff folder he'd brought in with him. He looked up as first Barbara Loveday, and then her husband Frank, pushed into the kitchen. He rose with a smile and greeted them in order.

'Mrs Loveday, Mr Loveday, I hope you don't mind me dragging your daughter off to work early. There have been developments in the fatality we're looking into.'

Trudy's mother wanted to know if he'd had breakfast, and in spite of the fact that he had, still asked if he'd like some scrambled eggs on toast. Frank Loveday cast him a knowing smile as he fended her off, and headed for the kettle. This he refilled and set to boiling.

It took a while, but eventually Trudy was able to extract herself and Dr Ryder from her parents' understandable but rather persistent questioning about their latest investigation, and once they were out of Botley, she was able to relax a little.

She read the toxicology report as Clement drove very slowly and in fits and starts to accommodate other drivers who were finding their brakes all but useless. By the time they were approaching the police station – the Rover slipping and sliding a bit more than either one of them would have liked – she had finished absorbing them and had tucked the papers neatly back into the file.

'As you said, once the inspector reads this, he's going to assign it to someone else,' she told him gloomily. 'Probably Sergeant O'Grady, when he's back from sick leave.'

'Hmmm. I've had a thought about that,' Clement said, pulling the car to a very slow and tentative halt. The front bumper nosed its way rather too deeply into a snowbank, but he didn't think it would be enough to prevent him from being able to reverse back out of it.

He turned to look at his young friend, knowing he was going to have to be rather canny about this. Trudy might want to go on investigating what they now regarded as 'their' case as much as he did, but she was duty-bound to keep her superior officer informed. And her strong sense of loyalty would have to be handled tactfully if he was to squeeze any more wriggle room out of the situation. 'I promised Dr Carey, my contact in pathology, that I would inform the police about this right away.' He nodded at the folder she still held. 'And so I have. You're the police, right?'

Trudy looked at him and began to smile as she understood what he was intimating. Then she sighed heavily, the smile falling from her face as fast as it had arrived. 'It's no good,' she said glumly. 'I've got to tell the inspector.'

'Of course you do,' Clement said robustly, privately wishing the inspector a million miles away – preferably somewhere without transport. 'But he won't be in quite yet, will he? We're still too early for him?' Clement sincerely hoped that this was the case – it was the primary reason, of course, for his early-bird attitude to the day.

He was relieved when she confirmed this by nodding, albeit a little uncertainly.

'And you can always leave the pathology report on his desk, can't you? You don't *have* to hand it over in person, telling him what it is?' he prompted, careful to keep his voice mild and matter of fact.

'Well, no, I suppose not,' Trudy said, again tentatively. She could see where Dr Ryder was going with this but … did she dare risk it?

'And if you left the report on his desk, say under a pile of other paperwork …' Clement mused casually out loud. 'He'd probably not find it until the end of the day, or maybe not even until tomorrow if luck were on our—'

'He'd have a hissy fit!' Trudy predicted glumly, interrupting him before she could become even more tempted. 'And I'd be hauled over the coals faster than you can say Jack Robinson!' she added bitterly.

'But you wouldn't have done anything *wrong*, would you?' Clement wasn't about to give up yet. 'He *did* give you another day on the case, yes? And you have been presenting him with your findings as and when they've come in? You could argue that you'd done the same now, right? You called in to work early, found him out, left the report on his desk?' he cajoled temptingly. 'He wouldn't actually know, not for *sure*, that he wasn't the one who'd "lost it" in the pile? You did tell me a while ago his desk was always chock-a-block with paperwork and files, right?' Although he wouldn't normally stoop to such underhanded tactics, prefer-ring instead to simply demand that he get his own way, right now he didn't want to rile the inspector too much. He might just pull Trudy off the case.

'Yes, that's true enough – he's not the tidiest of men,' Trudy admitted. 'And right now, with the weather, and being short-staffed, he's been more rushed and careless than ever.' She knew she was allowing herself to be talked into something she'd almost certainly be reprimanded for later, but right at that moment, she thought it would be worth it.

'All right. I'll go in and see if he's there. But if he is, mind,' she warned sternly, as the coroner began to grin in relief at having successfully suborned her, 'I'll have to hand the folder to him and tell him what's in it.'

Clement sighed, but reluctantly agreed. He could only ask so much of her, after all. He sat in the car for an anxious few minutes as his friend went inside the station, and it wasn't until he saw her emerge, smiling, that he felt himself relax.

'He wasn't in,' she said needlessly and happily, as she got back into the car beside him. 'But we'd better make the most of our time. What do we do first?'

'Well, first we go to my place, and discuss things. We've a lot to do, as you said, and not much time left to do it in. But we're in luck there,' he added, turning the ignition on the car, and cautiously backing his car's nose out of the snowdrift.

'Oh?' Trudy said.

'Yes. Vincent has offered to help,' Clement said brightly.

Trudy's heart fell a bit as she contemplated that mixed blessing. 'Oh,' she said faintly.

*

But any fears that she might have had that Vincent Ryder would turn out to be a bit of a wet blanket fell by the wayside the moment they started to discuss the case.

In the coroner's warm and cosy study, with chairs gathered around the roaring fire as they had their council of war, it quickly became apparent that the younger Ryder was definitely going to be an enthusiastic part of the team.

On the drive to the house, however, Trudy had had to insist that any contribution Vincent might make had to be kept a total secret from Inspector Jennings, who really would have apoplexy if he learned that a member of the public had been given intelligence into an ongoing investigation. Which meant, unfair or not, it would be left to Trudy to claim any credit for anything Vincent might contribute. And if, deep inside, she doubted that Clement's son would be of any viable use at all, she was tactful enough to keep her opinion from Dr Ryder.

Now, as they sat in front of the fire, Clement spoke first.

'All right. So, what do we know?' he began briskly. 'We know Terry Parker is a bit of a ladies' man. We know he's very reticent about his past. We know he's a thief, who quite happily stole from his business partner. We know – or at least can reasonably surmise – that he was planning on marrying Millie Vander for her money. We know he attended Millie's party, where he must have, somehow, ingested a commonplace sleeping draught. I did some preliminary research on the barbiturate used, which would probably have started to take effect within fifteen minutes of consumption, depending on a person's individual physical tolerance to such drugs. Some patients can start to feel drowsy very quickly, whilst with others it can take longer.'

'So he must have been given the dose at the party,' Trudy said, nodding her head. 'At least that gives us a set list of suspects, which is something.'

'Right, anybody who was at the party,' Vincent chimed in, looking and sounding excited. It was certainly an improvement, Trudy mused, to his earlier frowning appearances! She had been able to tell, originally, that he hadn't been too keen on his father doing what he considered to be strictly police work. But both she and Clement knew only too well how infectious 'detective fever' could be, and she was happy that he'd now become intrigued by the case. 'Which lets off the business partner – what's-his-name?'

'Geoffrey Thorpe,' Clement helped out.

'Yes, because he wasn't at the party. We can be sure of that, yes?' his son shot back.

'He wasn't on the invitation list supplied by the hostess,' Trudy corrected him cautiously. She had learned the hard way never to take anything for granted. 'And when we interviewed him, he claimed to be elsewhere at the time – at a neighbour's house for a small party. But we'd better check on that,' she said, starting a fresh page in her notebook, under the heading 'Things to do'.

'Who at the Vanders' party would have a motive to kill him?' Vincent asked eagerly.

'Well, the hostess for a start, if she found out her lover wasn't the golden boy she thought,' Trudy said at once. 'And I think there's a reasonable chance that Millie might have begun to suspect that, given all that seems to have been going on at the party that night.'

'Right, the gate-crasher,' Vincent put in. 'She denied being there, you said?'

'Yes, but we both think she was lying, don't we Dr Ryder?' Trudy said, looking at the coroner.

Clement, who'd been watching and listening to the two young people with a small, indulgent smile, nodded obligingly.

'We don't know exactly what her motive was,' Trudy added cautiously, 'but Katherine Morton thought they were arguing about some love affair or other.'

'What, the triangle going on between herself, Millicent and the dead man you mean?' Vincent sought clarification.

'Maybe,' Trudy said.

'But not necessarily,' Clement felt compelled to caution them. 'Whilst it's possible the victim and our gate-crasher had been having an affair, an accusation of infidelity cast against the victim might *not* have been about Millicent. From what we know of our victim, Terry Parker might have been cheating on his wealthy lover, and the gate-crasher both!'

'It's beginning to get complicated,' Vincent said, sounding not a whit put out.

'And let's not forget the horrible twins,' Trudy said darkly. 'Both of them had a reason for getting rid of Terrence. I can't see either one of them being thrilled at the idea of having him foisted on them as a stepfather.'

'That's a bit drastic though, isn't it?' Vincent put in doubtfully.

Trudy snorted inelegantly. 'Huh! You weren't there. Believe me, those two are a right poisonous pair. When it comes to hanging on to their own creature comforts, I think they'd be willing to do almost anything. Dr Ryder, don't you agree?' she again appealed to Clement to back her assessment.

'Yes, they're used to being the apple of their mother's eye all right,' Clement agreed at once. 'And Millie struck me as being a very indulgent mother,' he added for his son's benefit.

'Got it – they were worried she might start spending her money on the fancy man and not on them. Is that the lot?' Vincent asked.

'There's the possible passenger in the car,' Trudy added, a shade uncertainly, and explained about the unsatisfactory sighting of a passenger in Terry's car, which might tie in to the indistinct footprints that were found leading away from the crash scene.

'But presumably the passenger can't be the killer,' Vincent objected after a moment's thought. 'You don't give someone a sleeping dose then get in the car with them, do you? You might end up wrapped around a tree yourself.'

Clement and Trudy, who'd both already considered this, nodded in agreement. 'Unless he or she wanted to make certain Terry died,' Clement felt obliged to play devil's advocate. 'He or she gave him the dose then got in the car, just to make sure he didn't make it home in time to stumble into bed, safe and sound.'

'Yes. It is, when you think about it, a rather iffy way of trying to kill someone, isn't it?' Trudy mused out loud. 'Presumably the killer knew the dose itself wouldn't be fatal, so would have been counting on Terry crashing the car and dying as a result, or freezing to death afterwards. Hold on!' She sat forward suddenly as something occurred to her. '*So he or she would have had to have got the timing just right!*' she pointed out, her voice rising with excitement.

'Yes!' Vincent cried, her excitement catching. 'If they'd given it to him too soon, he'd just have got sleepy and fallen asleep on the couch or something. And Mrs Vander would have been sure to let him just sleep it off.'

'How was it done?' Trudy asked, momentarily stumped. 'How could the killer have known just when to give him a doctored drink?' she asked, looking and sounding baffled.

'I'm not so sure it would be as hard as you might think,' Clement interposed, feeling like a bit of a spoilsport. He hated to ruin their fun. 'Don't forget, it was a New Year's Eve party. At midnight, or just before, I imagine Mrs Vander topped up the champagne glasses for the traditional toast. After which, I think the killer could be fairly sure that most of the guests, given the snow and conditions, would all leave pretty soon. Including our victim. Hence … an ideal time to slip the dose into his champagne glass. The bubbles would also have helped to disperse the drug quickly.'

'Oh yes, that makes sense,' Vincent said, a little deflated.

'I still say it sounds a bit risky to me,' Trudy said mutinously. 'What if they'd been seen? Or if Terry had simply decided to stay longer?'

'Hmmm, you're right of course,' Clement said. 'It sounds as if we're dealing with an opportunistic killer, rather than a meticulous planner.'

'So, we're saying then,' Trudy summarised, 'that Terry was killed by someone at the party. This someone put a dose of sleeping powder in his glass sometime around midnight and … what … just hoped that he'd crash the car and either die of his injuries or freeze to death before he managed to get himself home?'

'Putting it like that, it does sound a bit half-hearted, doesn't it?' Vincent asked. 'Are you sure we haven't got that wrong, and it was all very carefully thought out and planned after all? And we're just not seeing it?'

'You've been reading too many Sexton Blake or Sherlock Holmes novels, my boy,' Clement reproved, grinning at him. 'You want us to be up against a veritable Moriarty or a criminal mastermind. The truth is bound to be a lot more prosaic, and probably sad and pathetic than that. Real life often is.'

'There is the question of the sleeping dose though,' Trudy said. 'I mean, if it *wasn't* premeditated, why did the killer bring the drug to the party in the first place?'

Clement sighed and rubbed a hand across his forehead. 'Yes. It's a bit of a puzzler, either way you look at it, isn't it?' he admitted, and grinned widely. He couldn't help it. As much as he might like to be the voice of reason and adult caution, he was as intrigued and gung-ho as the youngsters.

Trudy and Vincent glanced at each other, similar smiles on their own faces.

He looks a lot more handsome now that's he stopped being so disagreeable, Trudy thought.

She's really quite something, this police constable. I can see why Dad likes her so much, Vincent thought.

'OK what's our first move?' Trudy asked, turning back to the coroner.

'I think we have to go back to the beginning,' Clement said. 'We need to talk to Millicent Vander again.'

Chapter 21

Trudy and Clement left the disgruntled Vincent with the far less interesting task of ruling out Geoffrey Thorpe once and for all. Although he'd agreed to be a 'silent' partner given Trudy's superior officer's likely reaction to his interference, it didn't mean he had to like it. Besides, although they'd given him Thorpe's address, he wasn't all that sure how, exactly, he was supposed to find out if the dead man's business partner really *had* been at his neighbour's house on New Year's Eve.

It was all right for his father and Trudy – they had experience of this sort of thing.

Did he just go to the houses either side of the Thorpe address, ring the bell, and ask them straight out? Or was he supposed to come up with some ruse or other? Either way, he knew he had to figure it out, as he was due to meet Trudy at a café near her police station at twelve-thirty, to give her an update over lunch.

*

Oblivious to Vincent's predicament, Clement and Trudy drove cautiously along St Giles, and on up the Woodstock Road, having to stop on the way to help the driver of a black Austin 35 dig his car out of a snowbank. They weren't the only good Samaritans out on the road, however, and all together they made quick work out of hauling the water-beetle-shaped car out of its difficulties and allowing it and its driver to get back on their merry way.

Millie Vander hadn't yet risen when they knocked on her door ten minutes later, and it was left to Juliet to go and rouse her, whilst Jasper reluctantly 'entertained' them in the drawing room until his mother could put in an appearance.

Trudy and Clement both took a seat at opposite ends of a large, four-seat sofa whilst Jasper lounged against the mantelpiece of an unlit fire. Since the whole house was toasty warm from the central heating, the inhabitants of the house didn't have to worry about lighting real fires.

'So, Mr Vander,' Trudy said, not about to miss an opportunity to question a witness for a second time. 'We've heard that Mr Parker may have had a passenger in his car when he left your house the other night,' she began, rather surprised to find her opening gambit got an instant reaction. For there was no doubting Jasper jerked visibly, and a flash of alarm shot across his handsome, petulant face, before he could prevent it.

'Did *you* see who it was, sir?' she asked quickly, not wanting to give him time to recover.

'Me? No, why should I?' he instantly blustered. He was dressed today in black woollen trousers that fitted him tightly and a plain white sweater, which made the most of his black hair and muscular, if small, stature. He really *was* good-looking, Trudy acknowledged grudgingly, but his tendency to play the spoilt brat was, in contrast, totally off-putting.

'Besides, I can't imagine that you've got that right, you know,' he said now, succeeding only in sounding more condescending than persuasive. He folded his arms protectively across his chest. 'I can't think offhand of any guests we had here that night who might have been a candidate for a lift. Most of them either walked here, or lived on the other side of town. I can't think of

161

anyone who lived that far north.' He studied his fingernails with feigned boredom.

Trudy knew he was protesting too much. But why should this pampered prince care about Terry Parker's driving arrangements?

'Our witness seems sure that they saw someone with light or bright hair sitting beside Mr Parker when he drove away,' she said firmly, stretching the truth just a bit. Luckily, Jasper wasn't to know that their witness had been vague and unsure, at best.

At this, Jasper merely shrugged and refused to be drawn. 'Really?' he said, in his best bored voice and then yawned. There was something slightly overdone in his insouciance that made her wonder if he was trying too hard. Was he desperate not to give something away? 'Sorry, late night,' he added, with a brief smile.

'I'm so sorry to keep you waiting, er …?' Millie, arriving in lounging pyjamas and a wrap-around housecoat, looked even more flustered when it became apparent that she couldn't recall either of their names.

'WPC Loveday, Mrs Vander, and this is Dr Ryder,' Trudy said obligingly, as they both rose politely to their feet. 'We just have one or two more questions about Mr Parker and your party.'

'Really! Surely you don't need to keep pestering Mumsy with this stuff.' It was Juliet who spoke as she entered and came to stand at her mother's side.

'We've learned one or two more things since speaking to you last that need clearing up,' Trudy said firmly, not about to be bested by someone who called their parent 'Mumsy'.

'Why don't you go and make me some tea and toast, darling,' Millie said, sensing perhaps that a potentially embarrassing scene needed to be nipped in the bud. 'You too, Jasper. Go and help your sister with breakfast,' she ordered.

Both Trudy and Clement were surprised by the hint of steel behind the pleasant tones, and they shot each other a quick, questioning glance.

Jasper sighed elaborately, but moved from the fireplace. Juliet looked about to object to being ejected from the action, but then her twin shot her a grim warning look, and Juliet clearly thought twice about it. 'Oh, all right,' she muttered gracelessly.

Once they were gone, and the door shut behind them, Millie sighed wearily. 'Please, sit down,' she said, slipping automatically into hostess mode. She chose for herself a comfortable-looking armchair set at a ninety-degree angle to the sofa. It was, Trudy mused, an astute way to prevent them from being able to watch her face full-on, as they talked.

'So, how can I help you?' Millie asked politely.

'Is it true that you and Mr Parker had ... Shall we say, an understanding?' Trudy began gently.

'An understanding?' Millicent repeated questioningly. She opened her big green eyes very wide, and seemed to become somehow even more petite and fragile before their very eyes.

It was, Clement thought, a very neat trick, which he presumed this pocket Venus had often used in the past – probably to good effect. It was certainly designed to bring out the protective instincts in the male heart. Pity his own pump was far too cynical to be fooled.

'Yes,' Trudy said firmly. 'Several people have intimated that they expected an announcement to be made shortly.'

'I'm awfully sorry, but I'm still all at sea, Constable,' Millicent said, cocking her head slightly to one side and allowing a small frown to appear between her brows. 'What sort of announcement do you mean?'

'An engagement,' Trudy ploughed determinedly on, getting annoyed with the other woman's fencing. 'Isn't it true that you and Mr Parker were a couple?'

'Of course not!' Millie said, sounding and looking genuinely shocked. It was only then that Trudy realised what a truly wonderful actress she was. 'Mr Parker is – was, I mean – a friend of mine, nothing more,' she insisted, sounding wounded to the core that anybody could possibly think anything else.

So that was how she was going to play it, Trudy thought. She couldn't help but admire the older woman, really. After all, how could anyone prove anything different now? With Terry Parker dead, nobody could gainsay her, could they?

'You really shouldn't listen to prurient gossip, Constable,' Millie continued, managing a small, forgiving smile. 'I'm afraid, as you grow older, you'll realise that so-called friends can really be rather spiteful. People do so love to imagine scandals where none exist, don't you find, Dr Ryder?' Millicent turned to give him a gracious smile.

'Oh, I'm afraid so,' Clement agreed mildly, for there was no point in antagonising the woman by insisting that she was a bare-faced liar.

'I think they get bored,' she turned back to Trudy, and shrugged.

'Mr Parker hadn't proposed to you?' Like a terrier with a bone, Trudy was not prepared to let it go.

For a moment, it seemed to her that the older woman's eyes flickered in what she would have sworn was genuine pain, and the younger girl began to feel guilty for being so brusque.

'No, he had not,' Millicent said, and for once her voice had the ring of stark truth.

'Had you any reason to suppose he might?' Trudy tried again, her voice gentler now, as she sensed that, beneath the theatrics being played out in front of her, she might have touched on a real vulnerability in her witness. After all, this woman had lost a man she loved, and Trudy knew that she mustn't lose sight of that.

Millicent Vander managed to smile. 'I certainly expected no such thing,' she said firmly.

'What can you tell us about the woman who was at your party that nobody seemed to know?' Trudy went on to describe Phyllis Raynor, but here again, Millicent wouldn't be drawn.

'I have no idea who she was,' the older woman said with a sophisticated smile. 'But you don't like to make a fuss, do you? She didn't stay long. I did wonder if she had the wrong address.

Or perhaps one of my naughty male friends had brought her as his plus-one and didn't like to own up to it. Men can be so silly sometimes, can't they?' she said, opening those big green eyes of hers innocently.

And with that, Trudy and Clement had to be content.

*

They left the house, if not with a flea in their ear, then certainly feeling a little chagrined and put out. 'She made me feel like I was being a right brute,' Trudy said ruefully. 'And a boor. And naïve and who knows what else.'

'Yes, she is rather good at that, isn't she?' Clement agreed mildly. 'Playing the misunderstood, mistreated poor little woman.'

'She *was* head over heels in love with our victim though, I'm sure of it.'

'I agree,' Clement concurred. 'But she'll never admit it in a month of Sundays.'

'It gives her a motive though, doesn't it? The woman scorned, and all that,' Trudy mused out loud. 'If she found out that he'd been having an affair with Phyllis Raynor, the lovely gate-crasher?'

'Yes. And it also occurs to me that she's got to be our number-one suspect when it comes to being the one most likely to have delivered the sleeping dose to our victim *if* it was a spur-of-the-moment thing.' He paused by the entrance to the gate as Trudy looked questioningly at him. 'Think about it,' he encouraged. 'If our killer acted on impulse, then she's really the only one who'd have access to the murder weapon, isn't she? Who takes their sleeping pills to a party? No one, that's who. But a hostess in her own home …'

'Of course!' Trudy said, wanting to kick herself for not thinking of this herself. 'She can simply go upstairs to the bathroom or her bedroom or whatever, and hey presto! She had a murder weapon right there at her disposal.'

Liking this scenario more and more, Trudy stopped walking down the pavement towards the car and turned to face him, her breath pluming out like gusts of steam between them in the frigid air. 'Say she sees or hears something compromising going on between the love of her life and the mystery woman, and in a fit of sudden rage or despair or what-have-you, she wants revenge. She's hardly the type to go and get a kitchen knife, is she? But she's only got to think things through for a bit and she's bound to think of her sleeping pills.'

'*If* she takes them,' Clement said. 'Don't lose sight of the fact that, as of now, this is speculation of the wildest kind. For all we know, she might sleep like a baby quite naturally, and there's nothing more compromising in her medicine cabinet than aspirin and corn plasters.'

Trudy giggled at the thought of the elegant Mrs Vander with corns on her tiny toes. Then she sighed. 'You're right, of course. Still … It does make you wonder, doesn't it?' she said.

'Oh, it does indeed,' Clement agreed dryly.

Chapter 22

Geoffrey Thorpe stood just inside Terrence Parker's small garden shed and glanced nervously around. He'd known that his business partner kept a spare key to his house hidden inside a galvanised tin watering can, ever since Terry had had to use it last summer. Circumstances had dictated that they needed to hold an impromptu meeting at the dead man's house and Terry had discovered that he'd left his main keys back in the office. Geoffrey remembered chiding him about leaving a spare key so accessible, but was glad now that his business partner had been so lackadaisical.

He breathed a sigh of relief to see that the watering can was still there. He looked around again, reassured by the blank windows and still curtains on either side of his late partner's house. Even so, he felt hideously exposed, and – not for the first time since his death – cursed Terry Parker long and hard for being such a damned nuisance. He quickly retrieved the key and ploughed somewhat awkwardly across the lawn, with its thick layer of virgin snow, towards the back kitchen door. There he used the key and very gingerly pushed the door open.

Since he hadn't spotted any police presence in the front of the house, or now at the back, he felt reasonably sure that it was safe to proceed.

He began his search in the most obvious place – the small, book-lined snug-cum-study at the front of the house, that Terry had always liked to refer to as his library. In the walnut writing bureau he certainly found a lot of papers – bills, bank statements, even Terry's passport. But not what he was looking for.

Trying to quell a sense of mounting panic, he went through the bookcases, but found nothing hidden either between or behind the books.

Next he went upstairs, where he found the second, spare bedroom empty of everything except a bed and a wardrobe. He commenced searching the main bedroom. In the bedside cabinet, however, he only found an old Edgar Wallace paperback that Terry had been reading, along with an electric torch and a bottle of aspirin. On top of the cabinet there was only a small portable alarm clock – the kind that folded away into a small, hard, square leather-bound case when not in use, or when you needed it if you were travelling away from home.

In the bathroom cabinet there was nothing but the usual toothpaste, toothbrush and shaving gear.

He searched under the mattress. He lifted the Axminster rug at all four corners and peered underneath. He went to the wardrobe and searched through the pockets of any garment that happened to possess them.

With a growing sense of panic he went to the kitchen – a last resort – but found nothing but tins of this and that in the cupboards, a half-empty box of cornflakes standing beside the draining board, and only the usual array of cutlery in the cutlery drawer.

Of the piece of paper he was looking for, there was not one sign.

For a moment he leaned despairingly over the sink, his hands shaking a little as he tried to think. It wasn't at his office, for he'd already searched it from top to bottom, and now it didn't seem to be in Terry's home. Where else hadn't he looked?

He could only hope the police hadn't already found it. But

would they have any reason to search the belongings of the victim of a motor car smash? He hoped not. Because if they had found it, he'd be …

Motor crash! Of course! Geoffrey Thorpe let out a breath of relief. Terry's car! He could have kept it there. Not that Terry owned a car as such, choosing instead to drive around for weeks at a time in one or other of their sports cars. But he had his favourites.

He drove to the car showroom, cursing every weather-related delay, even though he was glad (for once) that the atrocious weather had kept the salesrooms closed. He certainly didn't want curious staff watching what he was doing. He made his way to the large, freezing and deserted showroom and searched all the cars that Terry favoured. But their glove compartments and side-door pockets were bare.

That only left the car Terry had died in. He used the more commonplace car often, when he didn't need to impress anyone. Had he left it in the Riley somewhere?

And once again, Geoffrey Thorpe began to despair. He just *had* to get that damning, incriminating piece of paper back and destroy it.

What the hell was he going to do?

*

Duncan Gillingham couldn't believe his luck when he passed the Port Meadow café not far from Trudy's police station, and saw her sitting inside. Why it was called Port Meadow when it was nowhere near that famous open vista, he had no idea, nor did he care. He was only pleased to see that it was open for business, and there, sitting at one of the tables near the window, was Trudy Loveday herself.

He felt his heart thump, as it always seemed to, whenever he caught sight of her. He was never quite sure why it persisted in doing so. Perhaps it was the uniform! Or perhaps it was because she was so spiky, she challenged him as few women in his life ever had.

He pushed into the café, happy to breathe warm air for a change. All the sub-zero air just lately was making him cough.

*

Trudy, sensing a male presence looming down on her, looked up, expecting to see Vincent. They had arranged that morning at Dr Ryder's house that they'd meet, so that he could either confirm or blow a hole in Geoffrey Thorpe's alibi.

Clement had had to leave her for the day to go to his office in order to catch up on anything urgent and make sure nothing had come in that required his attention. He'd been reluctant to go but Trudy had promised to fill him in on anything. And since tomorrow was Saturday, and not a working day for him, they could only hope they'd have one last full day before the axe fell, and Inspector Jennings assigned the case elsewhere.

A smile was already forming on her face before she realised that it wasn't Vincent slipping into the seat opposite her after all. She blinked at Duncan, the smile dropping off her face, and then she scowled instead.

Her cap was lying beside her place setting at the table, and she raised a hand automatically to check that the pins holding her bun in place were all secure. She had a lot of thick brown, curling hair, which she could sometimes be a bit vain about, but it could also be a nuisance and hard to control at times. Just like the man opposite her now! Relieved to feel that her mop of hair was suitably tidy, she felt reassured.

'And to what do I owe this dubious honour?' she asked glumly.

Duncan smiled at her winningly. 'Now is that any way to greet a man who tried to help you out?' he admonished. 'Did you or did you not get lots of helpful calls from the public after my

170

piece asking for anyone with information on your dead driver to come forward?' he asked, opening his green eyes innocently.

It gave her an uncomfortable flash of déjà vu, for hadn't Millie Vander done just the same thing not so long ago?

'You should have given out the station's front desk number,' she said snappily.

She saw Duncan's smile widen even further and held on to her temper with difficulty. She knew that he liked to get under her skin, so why oh why did she let him?

'So, what's good here?' he asked, loudly enough to catch the attention of the waitress who moved forward to stand beside him, little notebook and pen poised patiently. She was a pleasant-faced, plump, middle-aged woman who looked as if she'd been doing the job for so long that her feet now forgot to feel tired.

Realising that it was pointless crossing swords with him, Trudy sighed over her own cup of tea. She'd decided to wait until Vincent arrived to order any food, and now she was glad that she had. With any luck he'd be late, and this annoying snoop would have already left her in peace.

Selecting the Welsh Rarebit, Duncan asked the waitress (with a wink) to renew Trudy's teapot, and Trudy sighed again.

'So, anything new for me on our dead motorist?' he asked blandly when the waitress had moved off.

'Isn't that old news by now?' Trudy shot back. 'Surely you've got more interesting stories to write?' So far, the press had got not one whiff that the fatality had been caused by anything out of the ordinary, and she wasn't going to reveal, by so much as a flicker of an eyelash, that that wasn't in fact the case.

She only hoped she could make sure that Vincent didn't let the cat out of the bag if he arrived on time.

'Everything's about the weather,' Duncan complained morosely. 'It's all over the television, the radio, the front pages. We're all getting sick of it. Come on, haven't you got anything interesting for me at all?' he wheedled.

171

Trudy ignored the appeal. 'With this bug going around, I'm being run off my feet doing the work of at least three,' she said, not totally exaggerating. When not working on the Parker case, the inspector had her working overtime every day. 'Why not run a piece praising our heroic public service workers in the face of illness and snow?'

Duncan blew her a raspberry. 'I can just see my editor going for that.' He laughed.

'Well, don't you normally make stuff up when there's no real news?' she taunted him. 'Go find a half-frozen cat up a tree and call out the fire brigade or some …' This time, when the door opened, she saw that it was actually Vincent. So much for her hope that he'd be delayed.

He drew off his knitted hat as he stepped inside, and the interior café lights shone on his head, bringing out the fairer highlights in his hair. He looked around, spotted her, then glanced, puzzled, at her companion.

Realising he'd lost Trudy's focus, Duncan turned sharply in his chair, following her line of vision. He didn't look at all pleased to see a good-looking, well set-up chap making his way towards them.

'Vincent, this is Duncan Gillingham, a reporter for the *Oxford Tribune*,' Trudy said at once, before either man could speak. 'He was just importuning me, as always, for a story,' she added, although she could see, with relief, that he needed no second warning.

Vincent gave a barely perceptible nod of understanding, and then smiled at Duncan. 'Hello.'

Duncan, for his part, lounged more firmly in his chair and made no attempt to tuck his seat further under the table, giving the newcomer a bit more room to squeeze between their table and the empty neighbouring one.

'It's good to get out of this perishing cold,' Vincent said amiably, shrugging off his heavy overcoat and hanging it on the back of a chair, revealing his brown corduroy trousers and cable-stitched sweater in dark cream. It set off his good looks too well for Duncan's liking, and he shot a quick, suspicious glance at Trudy.

'OK who's this? A witness? A perpetrator? A narc?' he drawled provocatively, and not surprisingly, Vincent's hackles begin to rise.

'Nothing so interesting, I'm afraid,' he said, forcing himself to sound wryly amused. 'Just a friend,' he added mildly, and smiled across at Trudy. 'I'm not late, am I?'

'No,' Trudy said, and shot a significant – and speaking – glance at Duncan. Unluckily, at that point the waitress arrived with his lunch, and Trudy became resigned to the inevitable.

'Shall we order?' she said to Vincent with a weary sigh.

She opted for the tomato soup, with Vincent going with scrambled egg on toast. Duncan, damn him, kept up an amusing line of patter all through lunch, ranging from some of his more outlandish newspaper articles, to scurrilous gossip about the current mayor, and the names of likely horses for when the racecourses were finally open that Vincent pretended to make a note of.

It was clear though – even to the waitress – that the two men couldn't stand each other and the older woman gave Trudy an approving and friendly wink when she caught her eye. It did her good, on a slow and miserable day, to see a pretty young girl (in a policewoman's uniform no less!) being fought over by two good-looking young chaps. Which, in her opinion, was just as it should be.

Trudy, for her part, simply let the two men spar and patiently waited her time. Sooner or later even Duncan would have to tire of the game and leave.

He did so eventually, but only after their plates were cleared and their teacups empty. 'Well, I'd best be off,' he finally informed them, standing up and buttoning his coat. 'WPC Loveday, can I have just a quick word outside? I need a quote for the evening edition.'

Trudy wanted to tell him what he could do with his quote, but discretion got the better part of her. If she didn't say what he wanted, she knew that he was perfectly capable of saying something truly outrageous in front of Vincent.

'Fine,' she sighed. To Vincent she smiled and said, 'Would you mind ordering us some teacakes or something? I don't know when I'm going to get the chance to eat again.'

*

Duncan only felt how tight his shoulders had become once he was walking to the door, and cursed himself for being such a fool. Allowing his nose to be put out of joint by some second-rate Adonis. He deserved a good kicking!

Once outside in the grey, bitter air, he turned to her and smiled breezily. 'Scraping the barrel a bit with him, aren't you?' he said, jerking his head towards the café window.

'Sorry?' Trudy said, her tone about on a par with the ambient temperature.

'Lover boy back there. He must be thirty if he's a day. Bit old for you, isn't he?'

Trudy opened her mouth to tell him that it was none of his business, then changed her mind. Instead she looked him straight in the eye and said, 'And how old are you, Duncan?'

He paled slightly, drew in a sharp breath, and then he was laughing. 'Oh, touché, my dear constable. Touché!' But inside he felt definitely riled. Why did he let this girl, of all girls, get to him?

'And how is your fiancée?' Trudy, not content with one victory, added sweetly. 'You *are* still engaged to be married to the daughter of the owner of the newspaper, aren't you?' She saw his jaw clench, but was in no mood to let him off lightly. 'How long must it be now? Getting on for more than two years, at least, by my calculation.' But even as she heard herself say it, she sensed that she'd made a mistake.

174

First of all, what business was it of hers? More worrying still, why had she even thought of it? It implied that her subconscious mind, at least, had been keeping score. But before she could even begin to explore the reasons behind that unnerving thought, Duncan was already leaning in towards her, his green eyes flashing fire.

'Yes, it *has* been a long engagement, hasn't it?' he gritted. 'And have you really never asked yourself why I'm in no damned hurry to walk down the aisle?'

This time, when Trudy opened her mouth, no sound came out. For a moment she simply stared at him, feeling totally nonplussed. Then, as she saw him smile with real satisfaction at the way he'd flummoxed her, she struggled to rally.

'It's really none of my business,' she managed to snap. And turning away from him, she put her hand on the door handle of the café's front door.

'Isn't it, Trudy?' Duncan snarled, just before she slipped inside.

Chapter 23

Once back inside the warm café, Trudy became aware of just how fast her heart was beating. She suspected her face was also flushed, and she hoped that Vincent Ryder would put her high colour down to the rapid change of temperature from freezing to warm.

She made her way back to the table, firmly keeping her gaze averted from the window and the world outside. But she had no need to worry, Duncan Gillingham had stomped away the moment he'd shot his last bolt.

It might have comforted her to know that he was as angry with himself as with her – or it might not. Right then, she was feeling distinctly flustered.

She thanked Vincent mildly for the slices of buttered malt loaf that were already being brought to the table by their attentive waitress, and sat down with a sigh.

'So,' she said briskly, forcing her mind to the matter at hand. 'Was Geoffrey Thorpe where he said he was, New Year's Eve?'

'Yes, he was,' Vincent said flatly. He had been looking forward to regaling her with how clever he'd been to get that information, but right now, he couldn't care less. 'That man, Gillingham,' he said, very casually instead. 'Known him long, have you?'

'Too long,' Trudy said wryly. 'As a police officer we have to put up with pains in the bum like him all the time.'

Although she sounded genuinely put out, Vincent hadn't liked the intensity of that little scene he'd just witnessed outside, nor the flush on her cheeks and the sparkle in her eye when she'd come back to the table.

Did his father know about this reporter bloke, he wondered? One thing was for sure – as soon as Clement got back from his office, Vincent was going to find out all he could about him.

'OK, what now?' he asked. He tried to sound just as normal, but Trudy could sense that his old wariness around her had come back.

For a moment she wanted to curse all men for being far more trouble than they were worth. What did it matter, after all, what either one of them thought of her?

'Now we go to the library,' she said firmly.

'The library?' Vincent asked, sounding surprised and slightly disappointed. 'Why the library?'

*

The library was situated in the town hall close to the High (as all Oxford-dwellers called the High Street) and Carfax, and not surprisingly was almost empty on a near-dark Friday afternoon in the dead of a vicious winter. Most of the city's population was very sensibly staying indoors in such weather, and those few that had decided to venture out tended to select their reading material quickly and leave just as rapidly.

So, settled into the reference section in glorious isolation, Trudy and Vincent were able to set about their task in peaceful silence.

Trudy had explained to Vincent how vital it was that they found out more about their victim. Having questioned all the main witnesses, and with their time running out before the case was taken from them, the life and times of the dead man were becoming more important than ever. Someone had wanted to kill him, and they needed to try and get an angle on who and why.

'And if we can find the connection between him and Phyllis Raynor, that'll be a major breakthrough,' Trudy had told Vincent as they left the café.

Of course, the problem with that, Trudy realised very quickly once they set to work, was Phyllis Raynor might not be a local girl, since nobody at the party seemed to know her. Indeed, if she had any past connection with the dead man, it was just as likely to have been in Tunbridge Wells (or wherever their victim was from originally). And it was unlikely that she would have done anything noteworthy enough to have earned her any recognition even within her own backyard, let alone in Oxford.

And so it proved. They could find no trace of Phyllis Raynor anywhere – not in the census, not on the voting register, and not in the newspaper archives. Trudy had deliberately given Vincent the task of trawling through the *Oxford Tribune*'s press cuttings for mention of any of the main players, whilst hoarding the *Oxford Mail* and *Oxford Times* to herself. She wanted no further reminders of Duncan Gillingham! But after two hours of diligent searching, the only snippets they found – not surprisingly – related to the triumphs of Katherine Morton's artistic career, and a single mention of David O'Connor who'd won a prestigious flower arranging competition back in 1959! (Trudy's imagination had no difficulty in supplying her with a mental image of the happy, gossiping, dapper 'confirmed bachelor' delivering a perfect posy to the impressed judges.)

'The library will be closing soon,' Trudy whispered to Vincent gloomily. 'We'll have to come back and finish this tomorrow. I haven't managed to get through all the *Mail* and *Times* stuff yet.'

'I'll do it,' Vincent heard himself volunteer, and felt slightly surprised. He had no idea why he'd done it. Sitting in a mausoleum of a library, going cross-eyed skim-reading newsprint on the off-chance that a name might spring out at him wasn't his idea of fun, but something stubborn inside him wouldn't allow himself to admit defeat.

'Oh, thanks,' Trudy said, and meant it. 'Be sure to make a complete note of anything you might find, no matter how innocuous it seems. And no matter how tenuous a link it might be.'

'I'll be sure to do that,' Vincent promised, mollified by the genuineness of the smile of gratitude she gave him. 'Wouldn't it be wonderful, though, if we could just type a name into some super-computer somewhere and have the answers printed out for us a few seconds later?' he added, stretching his arms and loosening his aching shoulders.

Trudy rolled her eyes. 'It would be my idea of Shangri-La,' she whispered back. 'You have no idea how many records I have to …' She stopped abruptly as one of the librarians leaned back in their seat and sent a stern look their way.

Shame-faced, and taking the hint, they gathered up their belongings and stole away like naughty children.

Once outside, Vincent nodded at her awkwardly, and said, 'Well, I'd best be off. Dad will be home soon, and I was going to make something for supper …' He heard himself wittering on and abruptly stopped. 'Goodnight,' he added firmly, and strode determinedly away.

Trudy watched him go, slightly puzzled by his abrupt departure, then shrugged, and turned in the opposite direction to head to St Aldates, and the police station. Once there, she pushed open the door to the office gingerly and looked around, but there was no commotion. No grinning PC Rodney Broadstairs warning her that the inspector was on the warpath and wanting her to report to him the moment she showed her face. No notes from the inspector saying the same left on her desk. No sign, in fact, that Inspector Jennings had found the submerged toxicology report yet and was thus out for blood (namely hers!).

With a sigh of relief and a weary eye on the clock, which was already saying that her shift was officially over, she reached for the pile of paperwork that had been left next to her typewriter and set about sorting out other people's messes and responsibilities.

Chapter 24

But as WPC Trudy Loveday diligently set to and started tackling her workload, Phyllis Raynor left the Raven's Rest Bed and Breakfast and set out to do some work of her own. Work that her very respectable, working-class parents would no doubt have described as 'dirty' had they known about it.

Navigating the pavements, which had become little more than tunnels in the snow after so many days of unrelenting snowfall, she pulled her coat and scarf closer around her. The streetlights revealed very few people out and about in the premature darkness of a winter's afternoon, but she was glad of the anonymity her bulky winter clothing gave her nonetheless.

When she had finally battled her way to reach the entrance of the large, impressive house where Terry Parker had spent his last hours on earth, she regarded it thoughtfully. She'd seen it before on New Year's Eve, obviously, but then she had been too tense to really give it its due. Now she could admire the solid, Cotswold stone bastion that screamed secure, understated wealth and upper-class respectability. She had to hand it to Terry – when he went digging for gold he didn't mess about.

She took a last look around the deserted, dark, freezing road behind her, then stepped onto private property and made her way to the door. There, after taking a long, slow breath, she straightened her shoulders and rang the bell.

She was almost as tense now as she had been on the occasion of her previous visit. As then, a lot was riding on the outcome of the next hour or so. Would it be easier or harder for her to gain an advantage now? Was Millie Vander a better bet? True, she didn't have as much on Millie as she did on Terry. But on the other hand, Millie had, possibly, far more to lose – depending on what sort of woman she was.

Phyllis had been careful to avoid her at the party naturally (which had taken some doing, since the older woman had been – technically anyway – her hostess!) But from what she remembered of the attractive redhead, Millie had seemed very much the darling of society that Phyllis had assumed her to be.

Not the sort, surely, to relish scandal or ridicule? Phyllis very much hoped not. She was going to have to play this by ear, of course, but on the whole, she rated her chances of success pretty highly.

The door was suddenly jerked open, snapping her abruptly out of her nervous reverie. A young, rather lovely girl with a sulky face regarded her with narrowed eyes.

'Yes?' the girl demanded peremptorily.

'I'd like to speak to Mrs Vander please,' Phyllis responded amiably, totally ignoring the youngster's rudeness. She recognised the girl as someone who'd been at the party, and assumed her now to be Millicent Vander's daughter. She was well aware that Terry's latest meal ticket was the mother of twins.

She was also a complication that Phyllis could do without right now, and she only hoped she'd be able to get rid of the little madam quickly. She wanted no witnesses to her upcoming chat with Terry's latest amour, or the negotiations that were sure to follow.

'Who shall I say is calling?' Juliet asked, a shade less insolently. Just as Phyllis had remembered her from the party, so too had Juliet placed Phyllis. When she'd asked Jasper at the time who the stranger was, she'd been surprised and amused to discover that he didn't know. She could usually rely on her twin to make the acquaintance of anyone who looked pretty in a skirt – no matter what her age. And the woman on the doorstep must be approaching thirty, if she was a day.

'A friend of Terrence Parker's,' Phyllis said with another amiable smile, showing no annoyance at Juliet's flat stare.

'Mother isn't seeing anyone,' Juliet said stiffly, beginning to close the door. For some reason she didn't like the look of this visitor, and besides, any friend of Parker's was hardly a friend of theirs.

'Oh, but she'll want to see me,' Phyllis said firmly, her hand shooting out to prevent the closure of the door.

Juliet looked mulish. 'You were at the party here, on New Year's Eve,' she said, her voice accusing.

'Was I?' Phyllis asked blandly. 'Are you a maid? If so, you need to ...' Juliet wasn't able to let this insult pass, and it totally distracted her, just as Phyllis had hoped it would.

'No, I'm not the bloody maid!' Juliet fumed. 'And like I said, Mother's not seeing anyone. She's not well.' She added the lie as a distinct afterthought.

'Oh dear. I understand that Terry's death must have upset her dreadfully,' Phyllis said blandly. 'But she really will want to see me, you know,' she added firmly.

And again, Juliet felt unsettled. There was something about the woman's tone – something knowing in her voice – that made the hackles rise on her back. She also seemed so confident of herself. No doubt about it, this attractive woman was beginning to make her skin crawl. And why exactly was she so set on talking to her mother? She knew for a fact that her mother didn't know this woman; she'd said as much at the party. They'd laughed about it in fact, with Jasper assuring their slightly put-out mother that no real party could be considered a success nowadays without at least one gate-crasher.

183

Whilst part of Juliet wanted to shut the door in her face – sensing as she did that here was danger of some kind – another, perhaps more sensible part of her, was arguing that it might be a good idea to find out what this woman wanted.

Especially since the police were still snooping around about Terry Parker's death. Although she was fairly sure Jasper and herself were safe enough, still … This woman had been at the party, after all. Was it possible she had seen or heard something that could come back to haunt them?

'Fine.' She made her decision and stepped back, allowing Phyllis to pass by her and stand in the hallway. 'Wait here a minute,' Juliet demanded rudely, heading into the drawing room whilst Phyllis calmly pulled off her gloves and unwrapped the scarf from around her neck.

*

It amused Phyllis to look around the anteroom. It was here that Terry had finally dragged her for their last private tête-à-tête, all but hauling her out of the party by physical force. It was also here, just in front of the grandfather clock, that he'd stuck his face so close to hers, his expression contorted by anger and hate, and hissed at her to go before she ruined everything. He'd looked so furious that she couldn't help but kiss him hard and passionately. She'd known it would only enrage him further, knowing that he was helpless and in no position to either retaliate or make a scene.

After that contemptuous gesture, he'd literally man-handled her out the door, promising that they'd talk money later.

Yet another in a long line of promises that he'd broken, she mused grimly.

*

184

In the drawing room, Juliet saw at a glance that Jasper was lounging by the wireless listening to a pop programme, whilst her mother sat at her favourite table, playing a complicated game of solitaire. Mucking about with cards was one of Millie's favourite pastimes, but Juliet couldn't see the appeal herself.

'Mumsy, there's an odd woman here to see you,' she said, but she was watching her brother as she spoke. At this provocative statement, she saw his head shoot up and swivel around to look at her and she grimaced a warning at him.

Slowly, he reached out and turned off the radio, watching her with a puzzled and questioning frown tugging at his brows.

'What do you mean – an odd woman?' Millie asked. Tonight she was wearing a long, warm woollen gown in various shades of purples and pinks. It had cost a good deal of money, and looked like it had. On her feet were high-heeled mule-slippers – with layers of pink feathers – that tapped annoyingly on any wooden flooring whenever she moved.

'Juliet, I really do wish you would speak properly. What's her name, darling?' her mother admonished lightly.

'I've no idea – she was very careful not to give it,' Juliet drawled. 'But I recognise her. She was the gate-crasher at *the* party.' It was how they all described that event now – as *the* party. The Vander family could hold as many celebrations in the coming years as it liked, but New Year's Eve 1962 was always going to be *the* party.

Again, Juliet was watching her twin rather than her mother. So intent was she on sending him a silent warning that all was not well, that she missed entirely the way Millie went pale as milk and swallowed hard.

'Well, then, ask her to come in,' Millie said, a little faintly. 'Goodness gracious, she must think we have the manners of Neanderthals!' She forced a light laugh.

Millie rose from behind the table, her knees feeling unsteady, and walked to the mirror hanging over the fireplace, quickly checking that her red locks were perfectly arranged and her make-up still adequate. Her heart rate was climbing and she forced herself to take long, slow breaths.

She needed to be calm and clear-headed right now. If she could just take control of things, and turn this meeting into another inconvenient social occasion, everything would be all right, she reassured herself.

'Fine,' Juliet said sarcastically, leaving and returning a moment later with Phyllis.

'Mrs Vander, thank you so much for seeing me,' Phyllis said at once, going towards her quarry and holding out her hand, leaving the other woman no other option than to take it. 'I have debated long and hard about whether or not I should come, but given the … er … circumstances, with Terry I mean …' She allowed a small shrug to lift her shoulders and spread out her hands in the universal gesture of helplessness. 'I thought it best that I should.'

Jasper moved forward at that point, and Phyllis's eyes flickered towards him with renewed annoyance. Damn it, both brats were in attendance! She needed Millicent Vander feeling undermined, uneasy and upset – and thus vulnerable to pressure. The bolstering presence of two members of her family was not something Phyllis could tolerate.

'I think it best if we talk in private,' Phyllis said, lowering her voice, and looking Millicent firmly in the eye.

Millicent blinked once, her mind flashing back to the last time she'd seen Terry with this woman. And their emotionally charged embrace in the hall outside. This woman kissing Terry so hard …

With the memory of that betrayal, back came the same rushing tide of emotions that she'd felt back then; that moment of stunning shock, quickly followed by despair, jealousy, hurt pride and finally a wave of anger so strong it had almost seemed to lift her off her feet.

It had been enough to send her scurrying back into the gaiety and noise of the packed living room before she had to watch a moment more of it. She'd never felt humiliation like it before in her life, and it had been both shocking and all-consuming.

As she had done then, she now firmly squashed her feelings into a tight hard ball and hid them firmly behind a smiling face and a hardening heart.

'Very well, Mrs, er ...?'

But Phyllis was far too wily for that. Instead she stepped forward and indicated a chair. 'Do you mind if I sit?'

'Of course not,' Millicent responded with instant and instinctive good manners. No matter what the circumstances, it wouldn't do to be inhospitable. She could almost hear her nanny's voice in the back of her head lecturing on the responsibilities befitting the mistress in her own home. 'Children, why don't you run along and let ... my guest and myself have a little chat.'

'We're not ten years old, Mother,' Jasper snorted, annoyed. He eyed the newcomer with a mixture of hostility and admiration. She was, after all, very good-looking and his interest was fully aroused.

'Oh come on, Jasper, let's leave them to it,' Juliet said, shooting daggers at him. Her twin opened his mouth to argue, then caught the quick, furtive shake of Juliet's head and sighed. He was used to paying attention to Juliet at times like this. His sister was rarely wrong when it came to judging her own sex.

'Fine. As if I want to listen to gossip anyway,' he drawled, going for rude sophistication and, shoving his hands deeply in his trouser pockets, slouched out of the room behind his twin.

But Juliet turned instantly they were out in the hall. Putting a finger to her lips to quieten him, she reached for the door handle and made a great show of shutting it firmly. But she didn't remove her hand from the handle and after a few moments, very carefully began to lower it, then nudge the door open, just an inch.

It wasn't much, but it was enough. As children they'd often eavesdropped on the grown-ups' conversations, (you learned all sorts of eye-opening things that way) and it didn't take Jasper but

187

a second to catch on. Just as when they were little, Juliet dropped to one knee, turned her face to one side and stuck her ear to the gap. Jasper, standing over her and upright, did likewise, his own ear pressed against a spot higher up on the doorframe.

Neither attempted to whisper to each other, knowing that was a sure way of getting caught. Instead they just listened intently, saving any discussions for later, when they were alone in one or the other's bedroom.

Chapter 25

'I'm sorry, but I really don't recall your name.' Millicent opened the proceedings, and reached down to the coffee table that separated her from her unexpected guest, groping for the table lighter and an ornately engraved solid silver box. 'Cigarette?' she offered, opening the trinket, which would have paid Phyllis's bills for a number of years.

Phyllis coolly accepted one and allowed it to be lit. In the past, she'd once used the end of a lighted cigarette to inflict a burn on someone, giving her the chance to run for it, and thus getting her out of a potentially tricky jam. She didn't expect to have to resort to anything so uncouth this time, but having the cigarette gave her something to do with her hands. For in spite of being confident of having the upper hand, she was not totally without nerves.

'You can call me Irene,' Phyllis said. It was, in fact, her second name, but she'd never liked it and only used it on occasions when she preferred to remain elusive.

'And what can I do for you, Irene?' Millie asked, perching carefully in the armchair facing her. Like her daughter before her, she sensed a threat here, and like her daughter, she wanted to know more.

Although she'd had what most people would have called an easy life, Millie had always known how to fight her corner to get what she wanted. True, this had usually involved using her looks to manipulate the men in her life. But she'd also been to a posh public girls' school where she'd learned tricks from her fellow pupils that would make sewer rats hesitate – along with proper deportment and French, of course.

And if there was one thing life's experiences had taught her, it was this. Knowledge was power. And knowing your enemy could be especially useful.

Phyllis, watching the other woman closely, saw the moment the cat-green eyes hardened and realised, with a droop of her spirits, that she might not have things her own way as much – or as easily – as she'd previously hoped. *Oh well*, she thought, with a wry twist of her lips. *Very few things in life that are worthwhile come easy.*

'It's about Terry,' Phyllis began mildly.

Millicent slowly nodded. 'Of course it is,' she agreed just as mildly.

'He was mine,' Phyllis said conversationally, drawing casually on her cigarette and idly watching the smoke ascend to the ceiling as she blew it out.

'I beg your pardon?' Millie asked, genuinely startled.

'Mine,' Phyllis reiterated mildly, still regarding the glowing end of her cigarette with calm contemplation. 'You should have kept your hands off him,' she added.

'I think you're confused,' Millie said, her voice just as calm as that of the woman seated opposite her. 'I never had my hands "on" him, I assure you.'

Phyllis gave a sudden bark of laughter. 'That's not what he told me. And from what I've been hearing on the grapevine, that's not what your friends think either. You were to all intents and purposes practically engaged already.'

Millie's eyes flickered. 'I have no idea what Terry may or may not have said to you,' she responded mildly. 'And you really shouldn't listen to gossip either. He was a friend of mine, that's all. He could be ... unreliable at times – or rather I should say that he had an odd sense of humour. I think you'll find that he was simply pulling your leg, you know, if he intimated there was anything serious going on between us.'

Cool green eyes met and held dark amused brown eyes. Both women smiled.

'Oh yes, he was very unreliable, I agree with you there,' Phyllis concurred. She let the moment hang portentously for just the right amount of time, and then added deliberately, 'As both a husband and a father.'

Outside, in the hall, Juliet felt her twin's hand fall to her shoulder and squeeze hard in reaction.

Inside the drawing room, Millie froze for a moment, then slowly leaned back in her chair. She'd gone distinctly pale, which was hardly surprising. She felt, in fact, rather sick, and a little punch drunk.

But she knew better than to allow it to show – or to acknowledge it.

'I'm sorry to hear that,' she forced herself to say mildly. 'But, clearly, I didn't know Terry that well. I had no idea that he was a divorced man. I'm so sorry for your loss,' she added politely. 'I'm a widow myself, so I know how it feels to lose a loved one.'

Phyllis's eyes flashed. She was certainly a cool one, this rich society matron. And whilst one part of her admired the other woman's backbone – respected it, even – another part of her knew that it simply wouldn't do.

'Yes. I know,' Phyllis said. 'A very *respectable* widow,' she allowed a light but distinct emphasis to fall on the world 'respectable'.

Millie felt her heartbeat rise as the nature of the threat now became all too clear.

So that was the name of the game, she thought wearily. *Blackmail.*

She sighed and elegantly cast one leg over the other. 'It must have been a shock to you to hear about your ex-husband's death,' Millie said casually. 'He never told me he'd invited you to the party,' she added sweetly, 'otherwise I'd have introduced myself.'

A little reminder to this upstart that she'd been an uninvited guest at the party – both figuratively and literally – would do no harm, Millie thought grimly. Now that the preliminary skirmishes were out of the way, and the real fighting had begun, Millie felt a welcome coldness and alert calm settle over her. It wasn't a new sensation to her – she'd felt it before, during other significant and stressful moments in her life. And it was always welcome. Though she liked to think that she lived her life paying homage to her heart, she would always rely on her head when it came to survival.

'Oh, he didn't invite me,' Phyllis was forced to admit, but gave a small throwaway laugh to show she felt no shame about it. 'In fact, he was most put out to see me there,' she confided silkily, her voice almost purring now that she was gleefully anticipating the bombshell that she was about to explode. 'And by the way,' she added, watching Millicent like a cat at a mouse hole, 'who said he was my *ex*-husband?'

For a moment, Millie didn't seem to understand what Phyllis had just said. And then her eyes widened in stupefied understanding – the enormity of it hit her like a hurricane.

'Yes,' Phyllis said, almost gently, watching the devastation she'd caused. 'All that time that he was romancing you, sweet talking you, promising you the world, telling you that you were the love of his life and all the rest of it – he was a married man. And a father to our lovely Vicky.' Phyllis reached out and stabbed her cigarette out viciously in a large green agate ashtray.

'He walked out on us when Vicky was barely three,' she informed Millie in flat, harsh tones that did nothing to hide her bitterness. 'Just vanished – *poof* – left us in the lurch one fine day, with no financial support, nothing.' Phyllis shook her head. 'I had no idea where he was, or how long he'd be gone, or if he'd ever come back. He didn't by the way,' she added with a grating laugh. 'The bastard had no intention of saddling himself with a wife and child for the rest of his life. If it hadn't been for my parents, Vicky and I, we'd probably have … well … That's neither here nor there, as far as you're concerned, is it?' she added flatly, mimicking Millicent Vander's frozen pose by leaning back in her chair and crossing one leg elegantly over the other.

It was a nasty replication, designed to hurt and undermine the older woman in her own home, but it went largely unnoticed. Mainly because Millie was, at that moment, incapable of speech – let alone capable of appreciating the insult.

Sensing the extent of her opponent's sudden vulnerability, Phyllis wasted no time in going for the coup de grâce. 'He really was a stinker,' she informed Millie, her voice almost sad. 'He had no morals at all. You know,' she added mildly, 'I really wouldn't have put it past him to have actually gone ahead and married you, knowing it would be bigamous. I really wouldn't.'

Again she sighed elaborately. 'He was just a con man really. Came from dirt too – I hope you didn't let that middle-class accent of his fool you. But he did scrub up well, didn't he? You had to give him that,' she mused.

'Yet, I do so wonder what all your friends will think when they find out,' she added softly. 'Don't you?'

Chapter 26

The moment Trudy walked into the office bright and early the next morning, she knew she was in trouble. The oldest PC at the station, Walter Swinburne, shot her a sympathetic look and gave a quick shake of his head in warning. In a matter of seconds, the door to DI Jennings's office was jerked open, and the man himself stood in the doorway, glowering at her.

She heard Rodney Broadbent snicker from somewhere near his desk, and her heart fell to her boots.

'Loveday, in here!' the inspector barked.

Trudy swallowed hard and, on legs that felt a little leaden, followed her superior officer into his lair, and shut the door firmly behind her. Whenever the inspector failed to use a person's rank when bellowing at them, referring to them only by their surname, they knew they were well and truly in the doghouse.

As expected, he went straight to his desk, sat down in his chair and reached for a piece of paper that, it wasn't hard to guess, contained the results of the toxicology reports.

'What's the meaning of this?' he bellowed. 'And why am I only finding out about it now?'

'Sir,' Trudy said stiffly, standing at attention in front of his desk. 'Dr Ryder informed me only yesterday,' she explained earnestly, 'that he'd asked a friend of his in pathology to expedite a report on Mr Parker's blood toxicology. When he handed that to me, I came to your office the moment I had it, but you were out. I left it on your desk. I tried again late last night to inform you of it, but again your office was empty.'

Jennings fumed in silence for a moment. He and she both knew that he'd barely been in the office. The ongoing staff shortages meant that he'd had – unusually – to take on much more of the hands-on stuff himself than normal, leaving him little time for doing admin at the station. But just because he had no real comeback to her reasonable explanation, didn't mean she was anywhere near off the hook.

'Can't you keep the old vulture under control?' he snapped. Even as he said it, though, he realised the unfairness of the question.

WPC Loveday was just a slip of a girl. Why should she be able to keep the old sod in line when chief constables, mayors, and for all he knew, the president of the local branch of the WI couldn't do so either? (And that woman, so it was rumoured, was such a dragon that she was known to literally breathe fire.)

'Never mind, forget that,' he corrected himself testily, waving an impatient hand in the air. 'Just tell me exactly what you've been up to whilst my back's been turned,' he gritted, 'and don't leave anything out, no matter how insignificant.'

Trudy took a deep breath and filled him in. As ordered, she went into close detail on all the interviews, as well as the conclusions that she and Dr Ryder had drawn from the facts they'd unearthed so far. She couldn't tell if he was pleased by their thoroughness or not, but as she talked, his face certainly grew darker and grimmer. When she'd finally finished, he sat in silence for a moment or two and then drew in a slow breath and let it out again.

She'd made it clear that both she and Dr Ryder believed that something untoward had happened at Millie Vander's New Year's Eve party, and that everyone's original assumption that Terrence

Parker's death was the result of an unfortunate accident due to bad weather conditions was now in serious doubt. But whether or not her superior officer agreed with her, she was about to find out.

Inspector Jennings watched her sardonically. He saw a young police officer tensed for a well-deserved rollicking, and for a moment he was seriously tempted to just let rip. But he was tired, stressed out with the weather, overworked, and, most of all, mindful that Dr Clement Ryder had a lot of friends in high places. Even this lowly WPC had her admirers now among some of the senior echelons.

There was no denying she and the old vulture had pulled a few rabbits out of the hat over the past two years or so, and who was to say this wasn't another bunny to add to the collection? And if they had uncovered something sinister, he'd look a right fool if he didn't handle it properly.

So he simply sighed, swallowed his anger and weariness, and sorted out what needed doing. 'As I understand it, the autopsy on Parker is being performed even as we speak,' he began heavily, glancing at his watch.

When he'd found the report (after having patiently worked his way through the pile of paperwork that had somehow accumulated on top of it!), the first thing he'd done was phone Dr Douglas Carey to confirm his findings and ask when the post-mortem on Mr Parker was due.

His phone call, it turned out, had been very well timed, since the doctor himself had just been on his way out the door to start that very procedure. Jennings had also extracted a promise from him that once that was done, he'd call the police station and give a preliminary verbal report, so he wouldn't have to wait for the paperwork to come through. Because who knew how long that would take?

'Once we've got the results of the post-mortem, we'll be in a better position to know what's what,' he informed Trudy. 'And if we *are* looking at a suspicious death – and the way things are shaping up, I think that's a high possibility,' he grudgingly admitted, 'then we'll have to open a more robust and official investigation. I'll assign Sergeant O'Grady to head it. He's still feeling a bit ropey from his bout of illness but he rang to say he'd be back in the office today. Since the blasted weathermen are saying there's going to be no let-up in sight from all this snow, and we're still having trouble getting staff into the city, he's just going to have to bite the bullet and take it on.'

He sighed heavily.

Trudy, at this litany of woe, felt the first blossoming of hope flutter in her chest.

Jennings, sensing it, scowled at her, but without any real venom. She had ambition, this one, which wasn't a bad thing in an officer, he supposed. 'Since you've got the best grasp of this case, you can work under the sergeant from now on, keeping him firmly in the frame, understand?'

'Yes, sir!' Trudy said smartly.

'Be his right-hand man whilst he's not at his best,' the inspector ploughed on grimly. 'You'll have to work hard, since I don't know how many other officers I can spare for this investigation.'

'Yes, sir!' Trudy said happily.

Looking at her glowing, happy face, Harry Jennings tried to remember the last time he'd felt so keen and eager to do his job. And couldn't. It made him feel vaguely depressed.

'I take it you and the old … Dr Ryder have plans for today?' he swept on.

'Yes, sir. And I'm sure Dr Ryder will be happy to continue to help us out,' she said daringly, 'especially since he knows how stretched we are.'

Jennings sighed heavily as he contemplated the old vulture's glee on hearing that he was going to be allowed to continue to poke his nose in police business. 'No doubt he's feeling very dutiful and patriotic,' he grunted bitterly. 'All right. I'll fill in Sergeant O'Grady when he comes in, and give him time to sort things out. In the meantime, until he's ready to start assigning you duties, you can carry on with what you're doing. By the end of the day we should have something organised so that you can report to the sergeant from now on. And you report instantly any *significant* findings you might come across today, understand?' He jabbed a pointed finger adamantly in her direction. 'So far, this had all been so much speculation and theory and *flim-flam.*' He indicated her reports with a derogatory wave of his hand. 'From now on, we do it by the book. Understood?'

'Yes, sir!' Trudy agreed. She didn't care that soon Sergeant O'Grady would be taking over, because she'd finally been assigned a significant and *official* role in a police murder investigation! And wouldn't it be great if she could just get a break and lay something significant and worthwhile before the sergeant that would really make him sit up and take notice?

But, she thought with a small dip in her spirits, realistically, that seemed unlikely. They'd been working for days now and they couldn't really claim to have even a prime suspect. And what, really, could she expect would happen in just the next nine hours or so?

*

Clement was philosophical about having their case subsumed when Trudy called at his house half an hour later. After all, they still had a toe in the water, didn't they? He instantly invited her to share breakfast with himself and Vincent, who obligingly popped some extra bread into the toaster and put on another egg to boil.

As he set about making another pot of tea, Vincent watched Trudy covertly. He'd approached his father about Duncan Gillingham last night, and hadn't much liked what he'd heard. Especially when his father had explained how the reporter had helped rescue Trudy and himself from a potentially very nasty situation during their last case. Naturally, the reporter had got a very good story out of it, even earning himself an award! Vincent had, however, been very heartened to hear that in spite of the good-looking reporter's slightly spurious heroics, Trudy Loveday was sensible enough to want to have nothing to do with him.

Now he watched her and his father happily and eagerly discussing their plans for that day with a growing sense of anticipation of his own. Even though he'd only been on the fringe of the case for barely a day, he could already see why his father was so energised. This sleuthing business really was addictive.

His ears pricked up when he heard his own name mentioned, but he felt a little deflated when he realised that he was still stuck with library duties.

He'd been hoping he could spend the day with Trudy.

*

Patsy Arles was feeling more and more desperate. Ever since the accident, and the subsequent visit of Jasper and Juliet Vander to her house, her nerves had begun to stretch tighter and tighter.

What had once seemed such a great and fantastically sophisticated adventure had now taken on the aspect of a nightmare.

Although Juliet had *said* that the trick they intended to play on Terrence Parker was something that he'd thoroughly deserved, how could she be so sure now that that was even true? She'd felt the tension in the air that night they'd come to her and told her to keep quiet about things, which meant they were nervous and unsure, and that, as much as anything, had really spooked her.

Juliet and Jasper had always been a law unto themselves. Superbly self-confident and untouchable, they'd struck her as beings who lived on a different plane to other, lesser mortals such as herself, and to see them acting almost, well, scared had jarred her.

And the fact that even they were rattled was frightening her most of all, because everyone knew how scary Jasper could be when he was crossed or felt under attack. Hadn't he got poor Lionel Willis expelled from school that time Lionel had dared beat him at that silly old cricket match? Everyone knew Jasper got up to all sorts of things, but the teachers couldn't touch him. He was far too clever for them, and everyone was too scared of him to snitch on him. All her friends at school had fancied him rotten, whilst at the same time being terrified by his bad-boy reputation.

And Juliet, Patsy knew, was no less intimidating. Whilst being utterly fabulous and beautiful and chic and witty, she could be as dangerous as a viper.

And why had they given her all that money? If the trick they'd planned to play on Terry James was so harmless, why all this concern that she didn't talk to the police investigating the accident?

Patsy was not so gullible that she hadn't learned, in this life, that when things went wrong, it wasn't the well-heeled and well-connected people like the Vanders who ended up paying the price, but those much further down the food chain. In this case, one Patsy Arles!

Once again, Jasper and Juliet had cleverly arranged things so that if anything went wrong, they could deny any wrongdoing – a typical trademark of theirs.

For when all was said and done, it was *she* who'd driven off into the night with Terry Parker – not Juliet. It was *she* who'd been in the car when he'd slumped over the wheel and drove them into a snow ditch – not Jasper. It was *she* who'd run off into the night, failing to report it – not Mrs Millicent Vander.

And she'd read the piece in the papers, saying that the police were still investigating the crash, and asking for people with knowledge about it to come forward. Was she breaking the law in not saying anything? She'd been to the pictures once, when one of the leading ladies had been arrested for being an accessory after the fact, or some such thing.

What if they came for her? What if she was arrested? Her

mother would be … But here, Patsy's imagination failed her for once. She was simply unable to imagine the shame and scandal.

Which was why, over the last thirty-six hours or so, her nerves had gradually stretched and expanded to breaking point. She'd now reached the point where she simply couldn't stand it any longer.

What if, even now, the twins were already telling the police lies about her? Covering their tracks and dropping her right in it, as was their wont? She'd have no chance to defend herself! Who would the police believe, after all? The oh-so-respectable Vanders, or a nobody like herself?

Surely it was far better that she looked out for herself and got her version of events in first. So it was that she slipped out of the house early that morning, taking a copy of the *Oxford Tribune* with her, and walked to the nearest phone box.

There she called the number given out by Duncan Gillingham and asked to speak to WPC Trudy Loveday. The very act of finally doing something to relieve the pressure she'd been living under made her lean against the icy glass of the phone booth in weak-kneed relief.

She almost cried in frustration when she was informed that WPC Loveday was unavailable. She'd worked herself up to the point of confession, and now there was no relief in sight after all.

Nevertheless, she managed to hold it together long enough to leave a message.

'My name is Patsy Arles.' She recited her address quickly, and in a rush, before her courage could desert her, said quickly, 'Can you asked WPC Loveday to call on me as soon as she can? I have information about that man who died in a car crash on New Year's Eve.'

She hung up before the police operative on the other end could ask for more details.

*

If Juliet and Jasper Vander had been aware of what she was doing, then Patsy Arles would indeed have every reason to be even more afraid than she already was. But right then, they had other fish to fry. And the name of this particular piscine individual was Phyllis Raynor – although they only knew her as 'Irene'.

They'd had enough presence of mind last night to scramble into their outdoor clothes and follow her back to a B&B a half-mile or so away, so they knew where she was based. And then they'd spent most of the night discussing their options.

It was truly sickening, they'd both agreed indignantly, to have one threat to their pampered lifestyle eliminated, only to have another raise its ugly head just days later.

'It's typical of that gold-digging, low-class pig to *still* be causing us trouble even after he's dead,' Juliet had raged, pacing up and down her room, fulminating with rage. 'Now his dirty little lowlife *wife* – of all things – is trying to get her grubby hands on our inheritance. I won't tolerate it, Jasper, I simply won't,' she'd all but shouted at her twin.

Not that Jasper was arguing with her. If anything, he was even more beside himself with rage than his sister.

Eventually they'd calmed down and agreed that they needed to tackle the situation head on. They couldn't rely on their mother not to lose her head entirely, and actually start paying the woman. They were both aware of how much Millie liked being queen bee in her own social set, which had, hitherto, always been a cause of merriment between them. But now it was no laughing matter. The idea that she might be exposed as having nearly committed bigamy with a low-class con man would be unthinkable for her – and she'd almost certainly end up doing anything to avoid it.

And once she started paying, the blackmailing bitch would never let up, Jasper and Juliet had both agreed. Which meant they had no choice but to nip the matter in the bud, before their mother made the first payment.

It was fortunate that their unwanted visitor had given Millie until tomorrow to think things through. No doubt she'd wanted to give her victim time to stew and get more and more anxious about the cringe-making consequences of being made a public laughing stock. It made good psychological sense, the twins had grudgingly admitted, but luckily for them, it also gave them enough time to do something about it.

And the only action they could take right now, they'd concluded after hours of debate, was to be fast and brutal. Given time, they might have come up with a more refined and subtle plan – as they had for dealing with Terry Parker – but time was a luxury they didn't have on this occasion.

As Jasper had said, the only thing they could do was make it clear to the gate-crasher that Millie Vander wouldn't be the easy mark she thought. And that blackmailers could themselves become very vulnerable to retaliation.

So now, as they approached the Raven's Rest, they were both roiling with a dangerous mixture of fear and rage.

'Remember, we've got to put the fear of the devil into her,' Juliet hissed to Jasper as they approached the front door of the respectable former Victorian villa.

'Don't you worry,' Jasper snarled. 'I'll be happy to actually throttle the cow!'

Chapter 27

As the twins enquired about their mother's 'friend' and described her to the landlady (apparently having foolishly forgotten her surname,) Geoffrey Thorpe was also on a mission.

He arrived at the police impound yard with an expression of outward calm, but feeling truly sick inside.

The yard, where the police regularly housed stolen and recovered cars and motorbikes, or where lorries and other vehicles had, for various reasons, been taken out of the hands of their owners and searched, was practically deserted.

This didn't surprise Geoffrey. In fact, he was counting on it. What with most roads still being all but impassable, the impound yard was hardly doing a roaring business. No lorries carrying contraband cigarettes or alcohol were likely to be out and about on their nefarious business these days, when the chances were very high they might get stuck in a snowdrift.

He approached the main wooden double gate, which was firmly closed but thankfully not padlocked, and with a little difficulty managed to get it open far enough to be able to slip through. Even this simple act was hard, given the weight of the snow lying across the entrance, impeding the movement of the doors.

Inside, he could see the impound yard was protected on all

sides by ten-feet-high chain-link fencing, and that a small portable cabin, which had probably once been used by the military in the last war, had been bought in and put to use as an 'office'.

Set in one back corner, the flat felt-top roof was looking a little precarious under its layer of thick snow, and the wooden steps leading up to the front door looked as if they might have begun to sag long before the bad weather had hit.

He glanced at it quickly, but could see no movement behind the two square windows that sat either side of the central door.

A quick look around revealed that the yard was only half-full. A Foden lorry stood closest to him, its massive tyres sunk in accumulated snow, and he walked quickly towards it before slipping behind it out of sight. His heart racing, he glanced around, seeking out the Riley that he knew Terry had been driving the night he was killed.

He couldn't see it at first, but then all of the cars and vans were blanketed in a thick layer of snow, disguising their colour and shape somewhat.

Crouching down, he dodged from car to car, seeking the colour and number plate he was looking for. He found it eventually, on the far left-hand side of the lot, and his heart lifted. It couldn't have been better placed, he realised with a quick lift of his heart, being furthest from the office, and at a kitty-corner to the cabin. This meant that anyone who happened to be in the office would be unlikely to crane their neck so far around that they'd see him, if they just happened to be walking past the window.

He reached into his pocket for the set of master keys he had taken from the office – and which could be used on almost any make of car they sold – and began searching for the right one that would fit the Riley.

He found it after only a few tries, and carefully inched the door open. It screeched, for the front of the Riley was bent and folded a little out of shape from the impact with the tree and snow, and the sound made him flinch then freeze.

205

He shot a quick look around the icy, dismal yard, and heard and saw nothing. Reassured, he reached forward and shuffled awkwardly until he was crouched down in the passenger seat.

He reached in and opened the glove box.

And that was when a heavy hand descended on his shoulder and made him yelp in fear.

'Hello, sir,' a heavy, rather ironic voice boomed from outside the car. 'Care to tell me what you're doing? Because if you're trying to steal a car, I think you could have found a better car and you most certainly could have found a safer place to pinch it from.'

*

As Geoffrey Thorpe was being arrested by a very alert – and rather amused – police constable, in the warmth and much more pleasant surroundings of the library, Vincent had just finished his task of looking through the Oxford newspaper archives that Trudy hadn't yet had time to finish. He'd duly noted anything that seemed to relate to the victim or any of their main suspects in any way, but his pickings were meagre indeed.

They included the report of a girl who had died two years ago after crashing a sports car, but the article, naturally, had made no mention of where the unfortunate young woman had bought the MG in the first place. And since Oxford's Cowley area was known as a motor city, the chances of it having been bought at Terry Parker's showroom had to be remote. But Trudy had said that she wanted him to make a note of anything that might even remotely be of interest or related to their case. And although there had been other motor car deaths since the murder victim had come to live in Oxford, this one was the only one he could find that involved a sports car of the kind that Terry Parker specialised in selling.

Mrs Millicent Vander had been honoured by some local arts council for her support of the arts, and had been photographed holding some sort of cut-glass vase.

And Mr Philip Prescott had won a generous prize on the Premium Bonds that he was going to invest sensibly. The accountant had been more than happy to give the reporter covering the story – and thus the newspaper's readers – a long list of very sound advice indeed. Especially on how you should deal with unexpected windfalls in order to ease the financial burden of your old-age pension years.

Gloomy at having wasted his time, and with nothing worthwhile to show for it, he returned to his father's house, delighted to find that Clement and Trudy were back in residence and in the study.

He knew they had gone back to Millicent Vander's house, hoping to get something more from their main witness – and suspect? – but one look at their faces told him they hadn't met with much success. They quickly admitted that Millie had been pleasant, but uninformative.

'The lady was definitely nervous about something though, I thought,' Trudy insisted.

'Yes,' Clement confirmed laconically. 'She *did* seem to have something weighing on her mind, apart from us. Which, when you think of it, is rather odd in itself. You'd think being questioned repeatedly over the death of one your party guests – and almost fiancé – would be a top priority with most people. But, like you, I had the feeling she was only half-listening to us.'

'She looked pale and tired, too, I thought, under all her make-up,' Trudy mused. 'I don't think she could be sleeping all that ...' But before she could continue, the telephone rang.

Clement answered it, then, with an amused smile, handed the receiver over to Trudy. 'It's for you, Constable,' he said wryly. It wasn't often he answered his own telephone and was asked to play secretary. 'The police station.'

Trudy went a little pale. 'Oh no! Don't say Sergeant O'Grady wants me back in already!'

But she needn't have worried. The moment she put the phone to her ear, she recognised PC Swinburne's voice.

'Trudy, that you?'

'Yes, Walter. What's wrong?'

'You're a very popular person, and no mistake,' Walter Swinburne said, somewhat grumpily. 'I've got two messages for you. First, do you know someone called Patsy Arles?'

Trudy frowned. The name sounded vaguely familiar. She covered the phone receiver with her hand and said to Clement, 'Do we know a Patsy Arles?'

'She's on the guest list for the party.' It was Vincent who spoke. Since getting detective fever, just like his old man, he'd been studying all the case files and notes in some detail. And he had a sharp memory.

Clement, who hadn't remembered the name, felt his spirits drop. Once, and not long ago, he too would have remembered that detail.

Trudy nodded her thanks, removed her hand and spoke once more into the telephone. 'Yes, Walter. What about her?'

'She wants to speak to you. Urgent, like. She keeps phoning and leaving messages. She says it's important. Something to do with your dead motorist.'

Trudy's heart leapt. 'Really? Did she give an address?' As she asked this, Vincent leaned over and drew a notepad and a pen closer to her so that she could use it.

Clement watched this solicitousness with a definite twinkle in his eye.

'Got it,' Trudy said triumphantly. Only a short while ago she'd been hoping something might break, but hadn't believed that it would. And now it sounded as if something promising had come up after all. 'Thanks, Walter, that's great!'

'Hey, hold on, there's something else, just come in from the impound yard,' Walter said hastily, thinking she was about to hang up on him. 'The constable on duty there found someone breaking into the car.'

'The car?' Trudy repeated blankly for a moment. Then, more sharply, 'Do you mean the car that Terry Parker died in?'

'Yes, that car,' Walter said testily. 'That's why I'm passing the message on to you. The inspector told us you and Sergeant O'Grady were handling the case, right?'

'Yes, sorry, Walter,' Trudy said meekly. 'Do they know who it was?'

'Of course they do,' Walter said, still inclined to be somewhat tetchy. 'The cove had papers on him. Do you know a Geoffrey Thorpe? He's claiming that the car is his property and that he had a right to look it over.'

Trudy smiled widely. 'Did he now? Is he still at the impound yard?'

'Yes, but we'll be bringing him down here.'

'Great – it'll be easier to speak to him if he's brought to the station,' Trudy said, and after saying that she'd be right over, she hung up.

Eagerly, she told Clement and Vincent what had happened. 'Do you think he could have tampered with the car somehow before Terry left for the party? And he was trying to cover it up?' she theorised.

'Have the mechanics gone over it yet?' Again, it was Vincent who spoke.

'Afraid not,' Trudy said with a grimace. 'Like everyone else, the motor division is short-staffed.'

'Which do you want to take first?' Clement asked practically. Although he shared her enthusiasm that things seemed to be moving at last, he was too aware of how disappointing life could be to be as excited as she was.

'Well, they're bringing Geoffrey Thorpe to the station, so I'd better go there,' Trudy said after a moment's thought. 'I don't want to risk Inspector Jennings's wrath any more than I can help, and if he *sees* you actually helping me doing police business he'll only kick up a fuss. But this girl Patsy Arles sounds desperate. Do you think you and Vincent ...?' She looked at Clement appealingly.

'We'd love to!' Vincent said happily. 'Wouldn't we, Dad?'

Clement smiled and reached out for the address she'd written down. 'Yes, *we* would,' he agreed wryly. Vincent, aware that he'd unashamedly managed to horn in, had the grace to look slightly sheepish.

Chapter 28

Geoffrey Thorpe was not a happy man. In fact, he'd never felt more uncomfortable in his life. He was feeling thoroughly cowed, miserable and apprehensive, and seeing his worried face cheered Sergeant Michael O'Grady up no end.

When he'd slogged his way back to the station that morning, feeling better than he had for many days, the sergeant had been greeted by a sour-faced Inspector Jennings, informing him that he was to take over a case currently being investigated by WPC Loveday and her pet coroner. (Not that Jennings would ever refer to the old vulture, Dr Clement Ryder, as anyone's 'pet' should the good doctor be within hearing distance.)

But O'Grady did understand the reasons behind the inspector's unhappy state. Ever since their sole WPC had been taken under the interfering coroner's wing, the pair had come up with solutions to some surprising and high-profile murder cases. Which, whilst not exactly leaving egg on the inspector's face, did tend to make him feel rather grumpy. And the fact that it was beginning to look as if they might be about to do the same thing again was definitely annoying him.

As the sergeant had listened to the inspector's very brief briefing on events so far, it quickly transpired that what they'd all thought had been nothing more than a fatal driving accident was starting to throw up some nasty possibilities. And apparently, it was now up to him to take over the investigation and sort it out.

Which was fine by O'Grady, even as Jennings had thundered away at him that he was going to do it strictly by the book. So far, far too many liberties had been taken – which included the old vulture acting as their 'medical' expert.

True, the outstanding weather conditions, coupled with so many people being off sick, had made it necessary to cut some corners. But that had only been when the case had seemed so cut and dried – and thus breaches in protocol were unlikely to raise too many eyebrows. Now, O'Grady could tell that the inspector was much more worried that, if the case did turn out to be more sinister, he would be hauled over the coals by the powers-that-be for being so lackadaisical. Which was harsh, since nobody came equipped with hindsight, not even detective inspectors – but that was life, O'Grady supposed.

Not that any of this made his own life any easier. He'd been ordered to take over the reins, which meant sending Dr Clement Ryder packing back to his office, where *he* belonged, and WPC Loveday back to her beat or filing paperwork, where *she* belonged.

Which was all very well, Mike O'Grady thought now, but he'd barely had time to start reading the files on the Terrence Parker case before he'd been called to the front desk where a suspect in that very same case had been caught attempting to tamper with evidence.

Using the time it took to book the suspect in, he'd tried to speed-read as much of WPC Loveday's reports as possible, but even so he knew he was woefully unprepared and ill-equipped to interview the man. He hadn't had the chance to absorb even the bare bones of the case yet.

So finding, on entering the interview room, that Mr Geoffrey Thorpe was already clearly downcast was a definite bonus. At least he didn't look as if he had the spirit or gumption to try and run rings around a police officer. Nevertheless, the sergeant was aware of a feeling of relief when, almost as soon as they'd established Geoffrey Thorpe's identity, address and place of work there was a tap at the door, and WPC Loveday showed her face.

She seemed, O'Grady thought with a hidden smile, slightly apprehensive as she looked at him. 'Hello, Sergeant. I, er, heard that Mr Thorpe was here, and wondered …'

'Come in and sit down,' the sergeant said gruffly. Unlike the inspector, Mike had a more generous attitude towards the WPC. He found her intelligent, diligent and willing to work, which were all bonuses as far as he was concerned. And whilst he agreed with his superior officer that she was far too junior to be working an important case on her own, he wasn't about to look a gift horse in the mouth either. Right now, she knew more about what was happening than he did.

'Mr Thorpe, you know WPC Loveday?' he said curtly.

Geoffrey Thorpe looked at Trudy miserably, and nodded.

Trudy nodded back with a small smile as she took the seat beside her sergeant and opened her notebook.

'Perhaps, Constable Loveday, you might like to conduct this interview?' Mike said, totally flooring her.

He saw the flash of sheer surprise cross her face, followed by a look happiness that just as quickly flickered into one of anxiety. He understood the reasons for all of them, of course, but no expression showed on his own face. She was surprised to be given the opportunity to question a lead suspect when a sergeant was also in the room. She was happy she was being given the opportunity, but worried she might fall short on the task ahead of her. And perhaps she was wondering just why it was that she was taking the lead? She'd been in the job long enough now, he supposed a shade wearily, to become suspicious of even her work colleagues' motives.

He could have reassured her that, because he had no idea what questions really needed asking, he had no choice but to allow her to take the lead, and that there were no hidden motives on his part. Also, that it would simply be easier for him to watch the suspect and listen, if he wasn't the one having to do all the talking.

But, of course, he could convey none of that in front of either the suspect or the constable.

And she was such a tyro he knew that he was taking a chance, but it would be interesting to see what the inspector's nemesis was made of!

Trudy, for her part, took a deep breath and tried to organise her thoughts. When she'd arrived at the station only to be told that the sarge was already with the witness, she'd believed that her only hope was that she might be allowed to at least sit in and observe. And take notes, of course.

Now that she was actually conducting a formal interview, and on such an important case, she could feel her heart beating fast in her chest, and she felt just a little bit sick. She knew if she messed this up, it might take her years to regain the sergeant's trust. If she ever did!

Which would simply not do! Why should she mess it up? She'd interviewed no end of witnesses since she'd been working with Dr Ryder, she reminded herself stoutly.

She gave the car salesman a thoughtful inspection, whilst giving him another small but encouraging smile. She knew there were only two ways to go about a formal interview – hard and threatening, or coaxing, and this man, she felt instinctively, would be far more forthcoming if handled gently.

'As I understand it,' she began mildly, 'you were apprehended a short while ago, breaking into the car in which Mr Parker died. Is that true, sir?'

She had no idea if that was the right question – or even the *first* question – that the sarge would have asked, and didn't dare look at him in case she saw disapproval in his face.

'I didn't break in,' Geoffrey denied at once. 'I had a key. It's

214

one of a set of master keys that we keep at the car showroom. It allows us access to all vehicles. Obviously, we have to have one.'

'I think that's rather splitting hairs, Mr Thorpe, don't you?' Trudy chided him gently. She might not be conducting the interview in the same way as the sarge would, but she had the distinct advantage of having met this man before. She'd talked to him in his own home, and had seen him in a family setting. She'd heard his grandchildren playing in the next room, and believed he was basically a good man at heart, who'd probably just been caught up in a bad situation. And she believed he wanted to confess to whatever it was he needed to confess to, if she just helped him along a bit.

'You must have known you were entering an unauthorised police facility, Mr Thorpe,' she insisted softly, and saw him flush guiltily.

She leaned slightly forward and laid her hand on the table not far from his own. She didn't touch him, but it was enough of a gesture to suggest support and encouragement. 'Don't you think it would just be easier if you told us what you were doing? Why did you want to see the crashed car, sir? Did you want to make sure that whatever sabotages you'd committed on it had been destroyed in the accident, perhaps?'

Geoffrey Thorpe who'd begun to feel slightly more comfortable with Trudy's presence and her softer voice, suddenly went white and sat bolt upright.

'What? What sabotage? What do you mean?' he squeaked. He looked appalled – first at Trudy and then at the large sergeant, as if to silently ask the other man if he too had heard the same thing. But the sergeant, with his quiff of sandy-coloured hair and pale blue eyes merely returned his look with a blank, apparently uninterested gaze.

'Did you tamper with your business partner's car, sir?' Trudy persisted gently but firmly. 'We know that he had already stolen a significant sum from your partnership, so it's understandable that you were angry with him.'

Beside her, O'Grady listened with acute interest. His time with the case files hadn't been long enough for him to get to that bit yet, and he began to feel hopeful that they might just tie up this case in record time. His old training sergeant had always said that there were only ever two real motives for murder – sex and money. And here was a financial motive, right enough, staring them in the face.

'What? No, he was paying me back. I told you that,' Geoffrey said. 'Don't you remember?'

'Yes, I remember what you *told* me, sir, but that might not have been the case. Perhaps he refused to pay you? Or, if he had indeed begun to do so, did you trust him to pay it *all* back?' Trudy put to him. 'After all, if he'd betrayed you once, he could do it again. Maybe you found out that he was planning to steal more money – or perhaps get an accomplice to steal the cars themselves. He could put you out of business and disappear overnight with the proceeds, couldn't he?'

'No, no, it wasn't like that.' Geoffrey, his voice rising higher in pitch as he panicked, looked from one to the other of them helplessly. 'We'd sorted it all out. I *told* you!'

'We can quite see if you decided enough was enough, sir,' Trudy carried on, as if he hadn't spoken. 'By your own admission, you knew Mr Parker was going to that New Year's Eve party. The weather was atrocious, and you knew his habit of taking one of the heavier, older cars when the weather was that bad. It wouldn't have been hard for you to suggest that he take the Riley. Perhaps you tampered with the brakes, only wanting to frighten him, not thinking—'

'No! I tell you, I didn't touch the car!' Geoffrey almost leapt to his feet in his anxiety to be believed, but a sudden threatening movement by the big-boned sergeant made him slump back helplessly into his chair once again. 'I'm not a mechanic,' the older man said, trying a different tack. 'I only *sell* cars, I don't know anything about the actual workings of the things! We have a mechanic at the shop to do all that! I wouldn't have a clue what you'd have to do to a car to make it crash!'

'Then what was so important about the car that you needed to break into a police impound yard and search it, sir?' Trudy asked reasonably. 'If it wasn't to cover your tracks, what was it?'

'I only wanted to find the letter!' Geoffrey Thorpe yelped in frustration and panic, and then went abruptly white. Slowly, he leaned forward and dropped his despairing head into his cupped hands and let out a long, low moan. 'Oh Lord,' he muttered, shaking his head, 'I wish I'd never *written* the damned thing!'

Trudy, caught by surprise at this, couldn't help but cast the sergeant a quick, searching look. O'Grady, in response, simply nodded his chin towards the broken man in the chair opposite, indicating her to get on with it.

'What letter is this, Mr Thorpe?' Trudy asked gently.

Geoffrey sighed heavily and rubbed a tired and visibly shaking hand across his face. 'It was when I first learned what he'd been up to. I was so angry that I wrote him a formal letter, threatening to take him to court, threatening to see his reputation ruined and the scandal splashed across the papers ...'

Geoffrey sighed again and raised his head, his face lined with worry. 'Of course, once I'd calmed down, I changed my mind. As you know, I told you all about it when you came to my house. Exposing him would mean ruining the business, which wouldn't do me any good, would it? Instead, we worked out the repayment scheme that I told you about. But when Terry died, and you came asking questions, and wouldn't let it go, I realised something might be ... well, funny, about the accident. And I felt afraid.'

He drew in a wavering breath and shook his head. 'I just became obsessed by that damned letter,' he admitted heavily. 'I thought, if you found it, and something, well, *funny*, had happened to Terry, that you, the police, would find the letter and think it was me who was responsible. *But it wasn't!* I didn't do anything to Terry or his car.'

217

He looked at Trudy with wide, utterly tired eyes, and then glanced at O'Grady. 'But I was the obvious suspect, wasn't I? Like you said, he was stealing from me. Who else would you suspect? I couldn't find the letter at the office, and it wasn't in his house. So the only other place it could be was in the car.'

Trudy looked at him thoughtfully. 'Are you admitting to having broken into the deceased's house as well, Mr Thorpe?'

'What? No, he kept a spare key in the shed ... Oh what's the use?' the older man said, lying his head tiredly down on his hands which were now resting flat against the tabletop. He reminded Trudy of a little boy who wanted nothing more than to go to sleep and pretend that the bad things weren't really happening to him.

Trudy regarded the back of the man's head for a moment, and then said gently, almost reprovingly, 'Mr Thorpe, why are you so sure that Mr Parker kept the letter at all? Surely, the most logical thing for him to do, once you'd come around and stopped threatening to sue him, was to simply destroy it?'

*

'Of course, he was obsessed about it,' Mike O'Grady said from behind his desk, some twenty minutes later. Mr Thorpe was being officially charged with tampering with a police investigation, and Trudy would now have to type up the notes. 'I've seen it before. Once someone gets an idea in their head ...' He shrugged at Trudy. 'In his own mind, the letter was out there, and he had to stop us getting it. He'd probably got himself worked up into a right state, thinking he was about to be arrested any minute.'

Trudy nodded. 'But the silly man had an alibi for New Year's Eve!' she pointed out in exasperation. 'And now that we've got a mechanic working on the car at last, he'll soon be able to confirm one way or the other if the vehicle was or wasn't tampered with.'

'Do you think it was?' O'Grady asked, genuinely curious to see what she thought. She'd come through the interview with flying colours as far as he was concerned, and he was still happy to mine her for any insights she might have.

Trudy mulled it over for a second or two and then reluctantly shook her head. 'No, I don't think so. I think the killer was relying on the overdose of sleeping stuff to do the trick.'

O'Grady nodded and reached for her stack of files. 'Well, I'd better get on reading this lot ...'

But before he'd finished speaking, PC Swinburne came over and interrupted them. 'Sorry, Sarge,' he muttered, then turned to Trudy. 'You really *are* popular today,' he said with a grimace. 'You're needed up at Summertown. Does the Raven's Rest Bed and Breakfast ring a bell with you? Because the landlady there knows you! She's just been on the telephone demanding that you get over there right away. Apparently, that guest you were inquiring about is causing an almighty ruckus about something, and the landlady isn't happy.'

Trudy blinked. 'What? Phyllis Raynor?'

'Yeah, that's the name.'

'But that doesn't make sense ...' Trudy said, turning to look at the sergeant. 'Do you want me to go and see what it's all about?'

'Who's this woman and what is she to the case?' O'Grady asked her sharply.

'She's the gate-crasher at the party,' Trudy said, confusing the sergeant, who hadn't got that far in the notes either. 'But she denied it. Being at the party that night, I mean. I can't think why she should be drawing attention to herself now though. I'd have thought, if anything, she'd have been anxious to keep her head down and lie low. Do you want me to go and see what it's all about, Sarge?' she asked again eagerly.

O'Grady sighed heavily. Damn it, he needed to get up to speed on this case! How could he take control when he didn't know what he needed to take control of!

'Yes, I suppose you'd better. But take Broadstairs with you,' he added flatly.

Trudy felt her heart sink. Not Rodney! The last thing she needed was his sneering, superior attitude, and sniggering handsome face getting in everybody's way. 'But, Sarge,' she began.

'Take Broadstairs,' O'Grady growled. 'If there is a ruckus going on, you may need a second pair of hands.'

Whilst the sergeant might not always agree with Inspector Jennings's opinion of women in the police force, he did agree that they should never be knowingly put in harm's way. And young WPC Loveday, although she might be an intelligent and diligent officer, simply couldn't be expected to have the necessary brawn when it came to any rough-housing.

And the inspector would have convulsions if she got hurt in the line of duty!

Rodney Broadstairs might have a high opinion of himself, but he was a big and beefy lad who could be relied upon to use his fists if need be.

'Yes, Sarge,' Trudy said, seeing the set and resolute look on his face.

Chapter 29

As Rodney drove the Land Rover gleefully towards Summertown with Trudy Loveday sitting mute and resentful beside him, Patsy Arles was sitting in the back seat of the coroner's big and impressive car. It was parked outside her house, and she was telling her story to the astonished father and son pair, Vincent and Clement Ryder.

'It all started, you see, when the twins asked me to vamp that dead man,' she began helpfully.

Vincent, who was turned to kneel fully on the front seat so that he could look at her sitting in the back, wondered if he had heard her right.

They had arrived at her house only a few minutes ago. She'd obviously been waiting and watching out for them, for she had come outside before they'd even had the chance to knock on the door. Clearly, she didn't want whoever was inside the house to be made aware of their presence.

Since it was perishing outside, after introducing themselves, Clement had suggested they sit in the car, with the engine and heater running. Patsy had taken one look at the younger man's good looks and manly form, smiled at him widely, and quickly agreed.

Even as they walked to the car, she was assuring them that she needed their protection, and had clung on to Vincent's arm throughout the short walk. She was adamant that she had important information about the dead man, and that he had probably been murdered. And that she should know. She'd been with him that night!

That alone had been enough to make father and son exchange surprised and slightly wary glances.

Both of them were thinking that this headstrong and rather voluble young lady was, perhaps, too good to be true. *An eyewitness at last – and at this late date?*

And with this latest breath-taking statement, father and son again shared a worried look between them. They'd both heard about witnesses coming forward to confess to crimes they hadn't committed, or trying to insert themselves into criminal cases out of some sort of compulsion or quest for attention or to get into the limelight.

Was that what they were dealing with now?

Clement, unlike his son, still sat facing forward, so he positioned the driving mirror so that he could see the back-seat passenger's face clearly.

'I'm sorry, Miss, er …'

'Arles, Patsy Arles,' the young girl said cheerfully. 'How do you do – again.' She giggled.

At this, Clement suddenly remembered that they'd introduced themselves to her at her doorstep, and that she'd confirmed that she was indeed Patsy Arles, the same girl who'd telephoned and asked to speak to someone about the Terry Parker case. And he'd forgotten her name.

He felt a nasty jolt rip through him at this further sign that his mental capacities were being slowly but surely nibbled away by Parkinson's, and pushed the thought aside violently. It might not, after all, be necessarily true. He was of an age, anyway, when short-term memory started to lessen.

'Yes, Miss Arles, of course,' he forced himself to say calmly, and to keep his mind firmly on the matter at hand. 'Did you say that someone had asked you to er ... *vamp* the dead man?' Clement asked cautiously. 'That is, Mr Terrence Parker?'

'Not just someone. The twins! I told you,' Patsy corrected him kindly.

'Er, yes, so you did,' Clement acknowledged. 'The twins being Jasper and Juliet Vander?' he clarified briskly.

'That's right. I nearly died when they asked me!' Patsy sighed as she remembered that wonderful night. 'That Juliet remembered me from school, and actually sought me out and spoke to me! She's so glamorous and popular. I was so flattered, I can't tell you!'

Vincent stared at the young girl, utterly fascinated. Her mop of fair ginger curls, the freckled open face flushed with excitement and big wide eyes all made her appear to be more of a child than a grown woman. Her hands, flapping around in the air as she spoke, had nails painted a bright crimson to match her lipstick. (Which did very little, Vincent thought, for her colouring.) She seemed totally oblivious to the sensation she was creating. Surely, this was all so much pie-in-the-sky though?

Clement, for his part, was wondering if the young woman was perhaps drunk, or worse. But after observing her closely, he decided that she was probably no more than overexcited, and of a highly strung disposition – and maybe not the most intelligent of youngsters.

'Perhaps you could just tell us, from the beginning, what it is that you know, Miss Arles,' Clement said, trying by his flat tone and calm demeanour to try and rein her in a bit. 'You say you were with Mr Parker on the night he died? You were at the party at Mrs Vander's house?' This, at least, had been confirmed by her appearance on the guest list.

'Oh yes – it was heavenly. Mrs Vander is such a fashion icon, isn't she? You can see where Juliet gets it. That house! Yummy – like

223

something from a magazine. And there was so much champagne there – I mean, *real champagne* – and the food was—'

'Yes, yes,' Clement cut in hastily. 'I take it the twins invited you?'

'Oh yes.'

'So you knew them socially?'

'Oh no. Well, not until they needed my help because of that awful man trying to rob them of their inheritance and all that,' Patsy said eagerly.

'Er ... by that man, you mean Mr Parker?' Clement said, resigning himself to the fact that this wasn't going to be easy. Just keeping his witness to the point was going to take most of his – admittedly limited – patience.

'That's right. He was dead set on marrying Mrs Vander and spending all her money,' she responded earnestly. 'Juliet told me so. He was so infra dig it was sickening.'

Clement could hear Juliet Vander's voice in that last sentence, and wasn't surprised. By now it was becoming abundantly clear that Juliet had taken advantage of this girl's hero-worship to inveigle her into some sort of scheme or other. The question was – what had that scheme been? And did it include collusion in murder?

'I see. Seems he was a gold-digger,' Clement said. 'And Juliet and Jasper took you into their confidence?'

'That's right. I was so flattered that they did. I mean, *me*!' Patsy gushed. 'I felt so sorry for them. It must have been absolutely galling to have some lounge lizard become engaged to your mother, mustn't it? I mean, my own mother is so annoying and plebeian, you wouldn't believe it' – Patsy rolled her eyes theatrically – 'but at least the dear old so-and-so wouldn't fall for the charms of some gigolo *years* younger than herself. Poor Juliet was devastated! I mean, can you blame her?'

'Er, quite,' Clement said. Beside him, he could see Vincent was trying to hold back a huge grin, and he shot him a quelling look.

'So, what did the twins plan to do about it, exactly?' Clement asked, careful to keep his voice casual. The last thing he wanted to do now was frighten this rather scatter-brained young lady into uncharacteristic silence.

'Oh, like I said. They asked me to do them a massive favour and vamp him for them,' Patsy said airily. (She was, in fact, rather pleased with the way she sounded so casual and offhand about it. Like she'd been a femme fatale for years and years! She could tell by the way that the handsome younger man opened his eyes wide that he was impressed.)

For a moment Clement was thoroughly nonplussed. He considered himself a man of the world, but this strange young woman, who seemed to be such an odd mixture of child and sophisticate, had him stumped.

Manfully, he took another deep breath. 'When you say "vamp", by that do you mean that they wanted you to, er …' But here, even Clement Ryder found himself floundering. And this time his son, damn the youth, was openly grinning at him.

But, luckily for the coroner, he didn't have to grope for the right words after all, because Patsy saved him the trouble.

'Oh yes. They wanted me to seduce him, you see,' she admitted matter-of-factly. 'Or let him seduce me. I'm not quite sure.' Patsy frowned. 'It was all so clear and easy when Juliet explained it to me.'

'Yes,' Clement grasped the proffered straw with both hands. 'Just what *did* Juliet explain to you? And just *what* was it that she wanted you to do that night? If you could be specific, Miss Arles, it would be very helpful.'

'Well,' Patsy took a deep breath and leaned forward in her seat. 'I was to sweet-talk that horrible Parker man and get him to take me home. Then I was to, you know, string him along a bit and get him interested in me,' Patsy's voice speeded up a little over this admission, as if she didn't really want to dwell on exactly what that entailed. 'But make sure, you know, that I got him so interested in me, we started dating. And when I had got that far, we were going to set him up in a sting!' she concluded happily. 'Wasn't that just thrilling? Juliet and Jasper were going to rent a room in a nice hotel, and I was going to invite him in, and then, when he was kissing me and stuff, they'd sneak in and take photographs. Just like in one of those old black-and-white movies with Humphrey Bogart and Lauren Bacall in it!'

Clement and Vincent exchanged bemused, somewhat helpless glances.

In the back seat, Patsy sighed happily. 'It would have been so wonderful. The twins would have shown the photographs to Mrs Vander, who'd finally see what an oily oik he really was, and a philanderer and all that, and she'd chuck him and the twins would be so grateful to me we'd be friends for ever!' She paused to take a much-needed gulp of air. 'Only ... well ...' Her expression fell and she began to look pensive.

'Yes?' Clement encouraged her. 'Well, what?'

'Well, things went wrong, didn't they? I mean, it started off all right,' Patsy said, her little chin coming up gamely. 'I played my part just right, and I made sure I followed him out when he was leaving the party and asked him if he could give me a lift back home. I was staying that night with my aunt in Wolvercote, you see, because Jasper said that the Parker man lived only a stone's throw from there. And I was all set to be scintillating and fascinating and get him to agree to take me out on a date and stuff but ...'

'But?'

'Well, he sort of got all sleepy on me. His voice started to slur and once or twice I had to grab the steering wheel to stop him from hitting some parked cars. And then, finally, when we got close to Wolvercote he turned down this road and went straight into a tree!'

She sounded very aggrieved by this.

'And what did you do?' Vincent finally spoke, too caught up in this wild and weird tale to be able to keep silent anymore.

'What do you mean?' Patsy asked, looking and sounding puzzled.

'I mean, what did you do when the car crashed? Were you hurt yourself?' Vincent persisted.

'Oh no. We weren't going *that* fast because the roads were so bad, and I had time to see what was happening, and I braced my hands on the dashboard. My shoulder felt a bit stiff for a while, but it didn't last long.'

'OK. So you got out of the car,' Clement said, realising that those vague footprints really had been caused by a passenger after all. 'What did you do then?'

'What do you mean?' Patsy repeated, again looking and sounding puzzled. 'I walked to my aunt's house, of course, and went to bed.'

Clement felt his mouth drop open, and snapped it closed. It was left to Vincent to ask the obvious question.

'But, didn't you call the police? Or an ambulance?' he asked.

'Oh no,' Patsy said airily. 'I couldn't do that, could I? I didn't want to get into trouble.'

And she looked from the young handsome man to the older handsome man, and smiled, waiting confidently for their approval.

Chapter 30

'But you can't have done *nothing*!' Vincent said, staring at the girl as if she'd just grown an extra head.

Patsy, suddenly aware that the atmosphere in the car had changed – though she couldn't tell why – looked at him helplessly. 'Well … what do you think I should have done?' she asked, sounding a bit petulant.

'You left a man unconscious in a crashed car!' Vincent said exasperated. 'Er, he was unconscious, wasn't he?'

'Well, he wasn't moving,' Patsy said cautiously, thinking back. 'I sort of shook his shoulder a bit, but his head was lolling against the steering wheel and he didn't make any sound.'

Clement sighed heavily. 'But you must have realised he needed help?'

Patsy frowned, and her lower lip began to tremble slightly. 'But I was sure somebody would find him! There were houses all around! I thought people must have heard it, and would soon start coming out to find out what was what, and find me there with him, and my mum would kill me if she found out!' she wailed. 'She didn't even know I was going to the party – she thought I was spending the night with Auntie!'

Again, she paused for a much-needed breath.

'But it was late, and bitterly cold. People would have been asleep, with their windows tightly shut. And you said yourself the car wasn't going fast, and the snow would have a blanketing effect. How loud could the crash have been?' Clement spoke slowly and clearly, trying to bring it home to the girl the seriousness of her actions that night.

At this, the girl began to cry. 'You're being ut-utterly b-beastly to me,' she accused, sniffling heavily.

At once, both men felt acutely uncomfortable.

'Come on now ...' It was Vincent who tried his best to stem the tide. He offered his handkerchief, reached across to pat her shoulder, murmured apologies for being so beastly and offered vague reassurances.

It took him a few minutes, but eventually he succeeded in calming her down. Before she could set off on another round of tears, Clement thought it best to get the rest of the story from her as quickly as possible.

'So what did you do later?' he asked gently. 'When you realised ... er ...'

'That he was dead?' Patsy asked helpfully. 'Oh, I was so *sorry*. I mean, I know he was a horrible man, and a gigolo and all that, but I didn't want him *dead*, did I? Well ...' She wiped her eyes with Vincent's hankie and a stubborn look crossed her expressive face. '*I* certainly didn't want him dead,' she repeated with heavy emphasis.

Clement caught on before his son. 'But you think that maybe the twins did?' he asked softly.

At this, Patsy began to squirm. 'Well, no! I mean ... not really. I mean ... well, Jasper can be very mean sometimes. I'm sure Juliet wouldn't have done anything ...' But her voice trailed off uncertainly, because, of course, she remembered that it certainly didn't pay to get on the wrong side of her either.

'So why did you phone the police station now?' Clement tried to keep her to the point.

'Well, I'm scared, aren't I?' Patsy said, and for the first time, she sounded more like a normal young girl, and not someone playing a part. Her voice was unsure and all her ebullience was gone. 'And when they paid me to keep quiet, and sort of … well, they didn't threaten me. But …'

Patsy heaved a sigh.

Clement and Vincent exchanged another appalled look.

'*They paid you?*' Vincent repeated, stunned. This was just getting worse and worse. Was this scatty but surely harmless-looking girl really an accessory to murder?

'Yes. Afterwards. They said the police had come sniffing around their house, and I was to just keep my mouth shut about stuff. And I mean, we didn't actually go ahead with the plan, did we?' she said self-righteously. 'About the naughty photographs and everything, I mean. So I thought that was sensible. But the more I thought about it, the more scared I became. I know Jasper and Juliet are so much cleverer than me, you see,' she said with devastating honesty. 'And I did begin to worry … and wonder …'

'If they were setting you up for something?' Clement asked gently. 'Yes, I could see how you might think that. That was very astute of you.'

Patsy visibly brightened. 'So you think I was right to call the police?'

'Absolutely,' Clement said firmly. 'In fact, I think we should take you to WPC Loveday at the police station right now so that you can make a proper statement.' He didn't have the heart to tell the girl that she might well be facing charges herself. He only hoped that her full cooperation would go a long way in her favour, because he was fairly confident that there was no real harm in her.

At least he felt pleased to be contributing something worthwhile towards moving the case forward, finally. Lately, he felt that both he and Trudy were beginning to wonder if they'd ever get a break. Right now, he suspected that Trudy was feeling bored to death back at the station, and just longing for something to actually happen.

*

At that moment, however, WPC Trudy Loveday wasn't at the station, and she certainly wasn't feeling bored. Instead, she was in the bedroom of a B&B in Summertown getting her hair pulled out by the roots!

When Trudy and Rodney arrived at the Raven's Rest, they found a scandalised and highly indignant landlady waiting for them in the hall. Even from there they could clearly hear the raised and angry voices emanating from somewhere above.

Naturally, they sprinted up the stairs and towards the room, following the violent sounds, and pushed open a half-closed door to discover a young man and woman volubly harassing an older woman, whom they'd succeeded in backing into a corner of the room. All three were shouting violently and heatedly at each other.

At the sudden interruption by the police officers, they fell momentarily silent, staring at Trudy and Rodney in astonishment.

The older woman, relieved at seeing much-needed reinforcements, recovered first. 'It's about time some help arrived,' she said shakily, and then asked them to arrest the two younger people, who had been about to assault her.

At this point, Juliet recognised Trudy, and rallied quickly. 'You can't do that! She,' she said, pointing dramatically at the older woman, 'is the gate-crasher from Mother's party! And if anyone did something to Terry Parker, it has to be her! It's *she* who should be arrested.'

Counter-accusation on hysterical counter-accusation quickly followed, and ended with Jasper being foolish enough to try and drag Phyllis away from the wall in order to aid in her arrest.

Phyllis promptly slapped him and tried to fight back. At this, Jasper, shockingly and resoundingly slapped her back. As the sound of it echoed around the room, the older woman stared at him in stunned surprise, her hand going up to her reddening cheek.

Trudy, reacting faster than Rodney, immediately rushed forward to separate them. For all that she'd never liked Jasper, she'd never thought he would physically attack a woman. Oh, she knew drunken husbands beat their wives, but the sight of a well-brought-up, wealthy young man acting like a thug made her absolutely furious.

But Trudy had not reckoned with the bond of twins, and as she moved to tackle Jasper, so did Juliet rush to go to his defence, and with fingernails poised for action, she jumped on Trudy, trying to rake her face. In fending her off, Trudy felt her police cap dislodge and fall away, and for some reason this small act really annoyed her.

Putting her back into it, Trudy jabbed her elbow back, and felt it connect with Juliet's ribs. Very satisfyingly, Juliet howled in surprised outrage and pain and staggered back.

Seeing his sister fighting with the constable – and getting the worst of it – he forgot all about his original target and snarled at Trudy, 'Get off her, you cow!'

A moment later, Trudy felt her right arm being yanked back and upwards in a vicious twist that made her shriek in pain. For a moment, white lights flashed behind her eyelids and she felt as if she might be sick.

Rodney chose that moment to stride in, like the hero in a wild west film, and peeled Jasper contemptuously away from his colleague, only for Jasper to then turn around and kick his shins viciously and headbutt him in the nose.

Rodney responded to this unexpectedly expert fighting prowess by throwing a massive punch to Jasper's handsome face, which shocked the spoilt Jasper rigid and sent him into a howling rage.

Trudy, recovering a little from the pain inflicted on her, turned instinctively to watch, just in case her colleague needed help, but promptly paid the price for turning her back on Juliet, as the young girl reached out, and, grabbing a handful of her hair, yanked hard.

'Owww!' Trudy yelped and, grabbing Juliet's hands, sought for and found one of her assailant's thumbs. She yanked it back nastily and without a qualm of guilt.

This time it was the other girl who let out a yell of pain and abruptly let go of her.

Over in one corner of the room, she could hear Rodney and Jasper exchanging blows and grunts. Her heart was hammering in her chest and she felt a little absurd, but mostly angry. They were all scrapping like cats, and with as little dignity!

Trudy spun around and faced the girl, who was panting hard. 'Juliet Vander, I'm arresting you for assaulting a police officer,' she began with grim satisfaction. 'You …'

Before she could finish the official warning, however, the other girl went scarlet with rage, screamed more abuse at her and launched herself at Trudy like an avenging fury, fingernails once more outstretched and intent on scratching her eyes.

But Trudy had had more than enough of this little madam's tricks! It was time, she thought grimly, to get the upper hand once and for all. So, just as she'd been trained, she let Juliet get close enough, then ducked under her outstretched hands, grabbed a wrist and twisted up and backwards sharply, just as Juliet's twin had done to Trudy not more than a minute or so ago. This made the young girl stagger and half-turn, in order to avoid having her arm wrenched out at the shoulder.

Now that Juliet was in a vulnerable, half-crouched position, Trudy stepped smartly behind her assailant, and literally kicked her legs out from under her. She then followed the writhing, cursing, furious and petite girl down onto the carpet in a more controlled landing.

Juliet, not looking remotely svelte or smug now, reminded

Trudy even more of an outraged cat, she was screeching and hissing epithets so hard.

With one bent knee either side of her twisting body, Trudy hastily used her one free hand to open her satchel (which had long since dropped to the floor beside her,) and reach inside for the handcuffs that made up part of her accoutrements. She snapped them on the girl's wrists with a satisfied sigh and a reassuring 'click'.

The noise of the handcuffs finally brought home to Juliet the full ignominy of her situation, and she closed her eyes for a few moments, forcing herself to calm down.

Trudy, meanwhile, saw that her police cap was within reach, and so retrieved it and put it back on her head. For some reason, this small act made her feel much better! As she was tucking her now messy hair firmly back under the cap, she caught Phyllis Raynor's grim face watching her from a safe distance, and glared at her.

'Don't look at me like that,' Phyllis said, aggrieved. 'None of this is *my* doing!' The older woman had had the good sense to get out of the way, and was now half-hiding behind the bed. 'I want these two charged!' she added loudly.

At this, Juliet howled in protest. 'No, arrest her! She's the blackmailing bitch!'

Rodney finally managed to get Jasper into the same position as his unfortunate sister, and grunted in satisfaction. The man might be small, and he might talk like a public schoolboy but as PC Broadstairs had been finding out to his cost, the little sod fought like a back-street villain from Naples!

Now, finally, some sort of calm began to settle. Trudy was kneeling over the handcuffed Juliet, and Rodney was doing the same to her twin, and making a formal arrest – the charge being the same as that being delivered to his sister, that of assaulting a police officer and resisting arrest.

'I tell you, she's the one who should be handcuffed,' Juliet hissed viciously, nodding her chin (the only part of her body she could easily move) in the older woman's direction. 'She's been blackmailing my mother. We can prove it – we overheard her.'

At this, Phyllis Raynor began to look a little less relieved at her rescue.

'Is this true?' Trudy asked her curiously, looking at the woman who was still maintaining a discreet distance from all four of the other people in the room.

'Of course it isn't,' she denied at once. 'They came here, threatening me with all sorts, including bodily harm,' Phyllis added for good measure. 'I think they're either drunk or off their heads on something. Take them away. I'm entitled to police protection, aren't I?' she challenged.

Trudy, who was now rapidly recalling how unhelpful and uncommunicative this woman had been before, began to smile. This little episode, annoying and painful though it had been, was at least giving her a wonderful opportunity to turn the tables on the gate-crasher. 'I rather think, madam, that we'll have to sort all this out at the police station,' she said sweetly. 'I'm sure my inspector has a lot of questions he'd like you to answer.'

Phyllis's lips firmed into a thin, displeased line. Juliet smirked at her in triumph.

Chapter 31

'What now?' Inspector Jennings yelled angrily, some quarter of an hour later. He'd been drawn to the door of his office by the loud and still-complaining twins, who were hurling threats, insults and pleas about in almost equal measure, as Trudy and Rodney brought them in. He stood surveying the scene with a scowl that didn't bode well.

'Sir,' Trudy said by way of brief apology, then turned and spotted Sergeant O'Grady at his desk. 'Sarge, this is Juliet and Jasper Vander,' she called, finally managing to silence the twins, who watched cautiously as the sergeant got to his feet and lumbered over.

Jennings's eyes sharpened. 'What's going on, Constable?' he demanded briskly.

'Sir,' Trudy made her report smartly. 'We were called to a disturbance at the Raven's Rest Bed and Breakfast. We arrived to find Miss and Mr Vander in a guest's bedroom – this witness,' she added, nodding at Phyllis.

She'd kept a close eye on Phyllis, both when she'd escorted everyone to the Land Rover, and when they'd disembarked at the station. She wouldn't have put it past the older woman to try and give them the slip. Luckily, though, it was very hard to run away when everywhere was as slippery as an ice rink.

'They were all involved in a violent altercation. When we tried to break it up, the twins then assaulted PC Broadstairs and myself,' she added, in no mood to soft-soap things. 'Mr and Miss Vander have also positively identified this lady as the woman who gate-crashed their mother's party on New Year's Eve, Sarge,' she added warningly.

O'Grady, who by now had read all the files, looked at Phyllis Raynor with much more interest. Now that he'd taken over the case, he'd seen at once that interviewing everyone who'd seen or spoken to the dead man in his final hours was a top priority. And this woman, in particular, was high on the list of witnesses he wanted to hear a detailed and thorough account of that fateful night from.

'Did they now?' O'Grady said, smiling like a wolf at the more and more discomfited Phyllis.

'Sarge, Mr and Miss Vander have also alleged that she is currently engaged in trying to blackmail their mother, Mrs Millicent Vander,' Trudy swept on, rather enjoying the sensation this occasioned in both of her superior officers.

'That's an out-and-out lie,' Phyllis responded defiantly. 'Let them try and prove it,' she added viciously. She was fairly confident that, under normal circumstances, Millicent would deny any such accusation as well. After all, only someone with some nasty secret to hide could be a victim of blackmail, and Millicent would be desperate to deny any such thing was possible. But these were not normal circumstances, Phyllis knew. Soon Millicent would be informed that her precious children had been arrested. Would the stupid, wretched woman land herself in the soup in order to confirm their allegations and try to get them out of trouble? Or would she brazen it out and hope for the best?

She wouldn't like to call it. Phyllis thought that she'd recognised in Millicent a woman who was soft and selfish but shrewd. And, as she knew herself, there was no denying that maternal instincts could be the very devil!

237

But, she tried to comfort herself, even if Millicent *did* back up her children's claims, she was still sure that none of the Vanders could provide actual *proof*. Not real evidence. No money had yet exchanged hands, after all, so it was her word against theirs. All she had to do was keep a clear and cool head.

Except, of course, she would have to come clean about who she was. And when they realised she was Terrence Parker's legal wife …

Phyllis could quite see that she was going to be in for an uncomfortable time. And worst of all – any chance she had of getting any cash out of Terry's philandering ways was well and truly up the spout now.

'These two people assaulted me in my room and threatened me with physical harm,' she said flatly, nodding at the twins, who sneered back at her. 'I want them charged.' That, she hoped, would at least give the police something else to chew over, besides her!

Jennings sighed heavily. Blackmail, assault, threats? What the hell else was this damned case going to throw at them? 'Sergeant,' he said wearily. 'If you would like to interview Mr and Miss Vander, I'll deal with Mrs …?'

'Ms Raynor,' Phyllis said reluctantly, wondering if she could possibly get away with it if she didn't give out her married name. Oh, she knew eventually that they'd track her down through marriage records, but by the time they did, who knew what else might have happened?

The inspector eyed her knowingly. He hadn't been a police officer for nearly twenty years without knowing a chancer when he saw one. This one was going to be slippery, he could just tell.

'Yes, sir,' Sergeant O'Grady said. 'Right then, you two, let's get comfortable downstairs, shall we?' Ideally, he would have separated the two, but there was no one else available to help him out with the interviews. WPC Loveday was too young, and Broadstairs too junior for something like this.

'Sir,' Trudy said to Jennings, as the inspector ushered an unhappy Phyllis into his office.

He turned to give her a jaundiced look. 'Constable?' he said heavily.

Trudy blinked, feeling nonplussed. 'What do you want me to do, sir?'

'You?' Jennings had so many things that he would have liked to have said to this thorn in his flesh, that it was impossible to arrange them in order. Yet he was already feeling too tired to care – and he wasn't even halfway through his shift yet! 'Oh, just go and do something *useful*, Constable Loveday!' he finally growled, slamming the door to his office in her face.

Rodney sighed, and slouched over to his desk. 'What's eating him?' he muttered. He limped as he went, because his shins were still sore from the kicking he'd taken, and that at least did a little bit to cheer Trudy up.

She was just sitting – a shade forlornly – down at her own desk when she looked up and saw Clement, Vincent and a pretty girl with masses of curly ginger hair approaching her desk.

'Hello Trudy,' Clement said mildly. 'This is Miss Arles. You remember, she had something she wanted to tell us? Well, apparently, it was the fact that she was a passenger in the car when Mr Parker crashed.'

And having thoroughly taken Trudy's breath away and having made her jaw literally drop, he calmly pulled out a chair for Patsy and indicated that she should sit.

'You might want to take notes,' Clement added helpfully – and in massive understatement.

*

By the time she'd taken and neatly typed up the girl's statement, and got her to sign it, Trudy's head was reeling. Was it only that morning that she'd wondered just how much she could realistically expect to happen in just a day?

239

Realising the outrageousness of Patsy Arles's testimony would test Inspector Jennings's patience to the limit, she prudently asked them all to wait, and sent a note to be given to the sergeant that something urgent had come up that needed his immediate attention.

He duly abandoned the Vander twins and the moment he sat down at her desk, shot a questioning glance at Trudy.

Both Clement and Vincent enormously enjoyed watching the usually phlegmatic sergeant's face as he read Patsy's statement.

*

Half an hour later, Trudy, Clement and Vincent were sitting in Clement's kitchen, drinking hot chocolate. After the sergeant had gone into the inspector's office with Miss Arles, and they'd heard the subsequent roar from Jennings as he'd been given the latest developments, all three of them had deemed it prudent to leave.

'After all, the inspector has ordered me to do something useful,' she'd pointed out reasonably as they'd scarpered through the door. 'And reviewing the case so far is fairly useful, yes?'

Now that they'd discussed the day's events at length, they set about trying to make sense of the various strands.

'The twins and Patsy were trying to set up Terrence Parker in some sort of love-sting,' Vincent recapped. 'This Phyllis woman – presumably a past or jilted lover or something of the sort – was probably trying to put the bite on him, given her love of acquiring money. His current fiancée or lady-love, who was actually hosting the party, was likely suspicious and curious about her mystery guest, whilst the victim himself must have been desperate to keep them apart. Oh yes, and by the way, one of them, somehow, sometime, managed to slip a heavy dose of sleeping powder into his champagne? Now that's what I call a party!' he finished with a wry grin.

Clement and Trudy had to laugh, although neither of them felt much like celebrating.

It was Trudy who put their malaise into words. 'Well, it's not our problem any longer. It's Sergeant O'Grady's.'

'So that's it? We're off the case?' Vincent asked, scandalised, looking and sounding as disappointed as the others.

'Afraid so. Now it's all got so complicated and convoluted, and it's clear that we're dealing with murder …' Trudy sighed heavily and shrugged. 'A mere WPC won't get a look-in anymore.'

'Or a semi-official outsider like me,' Clement added heavily.

'That's so not fair,' Vincent said, sounding like a sulky schoolboy. 'You've done most of the work for them. You even got into a fight,' he said admiringly to Trudy. 'And to think, most of the time this was all going on, I was just sitting quietly in the library doing background research. Not very glamorous at all, is it?' he added wryly.

Trudy, who had in truth forgotten that she'd handed over the completion of that thankless task to Vincent, felt an onrush of guilt. 'It might not have been interesting, but basic legwork and painstaking attention to detail is the backbone of policing.' She trotted out the saying that had been drummed into her throughout her training.

'In that case, you're welcome to it.' Vincent grinned at her whilst handing over the notebook she'd given him, which contained the meagre fruit of his morning's work.

Idly, Trudy began leafing through it.

Clement gazed fondly at his son. 'I thought you didn't approve of your old man playing sleuth?' he teased. 'You thought it was beneath my lofty talents to go poking around in criminal cases. Now you're all indignant because we've been stopped in our tracks. Come on, admit it, you're as hooked as I am.'

Vincent flashed him a sheepish smile. 'All right, let's say I can see the appeal now … Trudy? What is it?' he suddenly asked sharply, causing his father to turn and look at her too.

Clement saw that Trudy had sat bolt upright, staring at a page of the notebook, a look of horror, uncertainty and a flash of excitement in her face.

'Fairweather,' Trudy said.

'Huh?' Vincent said.

But Clement felt only an answering flare of excitement race through his veins, because he'd seen that look on his young friend's face before, and knew that it spelt something interesting, at the very least.

'What if *none* of them did it?' Trudy said, looking excitedly from father to son. 'I mean, none of the ones who are at the station now? What if there was even something more going on at that party that night? Someone *else* who wanted Terry Parker dead?'

Chapter 32

Katherine Morton didn't look particularly surprised to see them – not even Vincent, who had insisted on coming along despite having absolutely no worthwhile excuse to be there.

After they'd made their way to her flat once she'd buzzed them into the building, she simply stood in the door, gave the trio a brief, almost humorous glance, and then theatrically stepped to one side, making a sweeping gesture with her hand.

'Come on in,' she invited with a smile. 'I have mulled wine or iced vodka aplenty, depending on your preferences.'

That the lady had already been generously imbibing one or the other (or maybe both) beverages was rather apparent by the way she walked very carefully to her chair and sat down. Sure enough, on the little table beside her chair, was a half-full bottle of vodka and a half-full glass.

The glass she lifted at once and took a sip. 'Well, don't hover over me,' she admonished them with a smile. 'Sit down. And who is the handsome young Adonis?' she asked, looking at Vincent, who promptly looked uncomfortable.

The artist was wearing a long warm woollen gown of various knitted shades that alternately clung and floated around her in a way that he found odd. Her make-up had been applied a little lackadaisically, and her hair was rather mussed, but there was no denying she had a definite sexual allure.

He reminded himself that she was old enough to be his mother, and glanced at his father, who was watching the artist thoughtfully.

'This is my son, Vincent. I hope you don't mind me bringing him along, but he was dying to meet you,' he lied urbanely. 'He's an admirer of your work.'

Vincent, who wouldn't know a Mondrian from an El Greco, blinked and nodded enthusiastically.

Katherine regarded both men with a mocking, cynical smile. 'And that's why you've come to see me?' she asked, her voice just a little slurred, and a lot more sceptical. She glanced across at Trudy in her uniform and sighed gently.

'Not quite, Miss Morton.' Trudy, knowing that she couldn't ask for a better cue, stepped in cautiously. 'Or should I say Mrs Fairweather?' she added calmly.

'No, you should not,' the artist responded tartly. 'I was born Morton, and go by Morton. Besides, I'm divorced.'

'Yes. But your daughter would have used your husband's surname.' Trudy stated matter-of-factly.

'Amy Jean?' Instinctively, Katherine's head swivelled to regard the photograph resting on the sideboard that Trudy had noticed during their first visit to the flat. It depicted a pretty teenage girl, laughing straight at the camera. 'Yes, Amy Jean was very fond of her father,' the artist said. She sounded, to Trudy's sensitive ears, a little bitter about this fact. 'For some reason, we always seemed to rub each other up the wrong way. Even when she was little.'

'I was so sorry to read about her death,' Trudy said gently. She could feel both men become tense and uneasily alert as she started to get down to the nitty-gritty. 'She died in a car accident, didn't she?'

Trudy, of course, already knew that she had. Vincent had read about it in the library that morning.

'Yes,' Katherine confirmed with a long, wavering sigh, and took a hearty gulp of her neat vodka. 'She was only eighteen.'

'I can't imagine it,' Clement said softly, glancing at Vincent. 'I have a daughter too,' he added.

For a moment, the artist and the coroner looked at one another in complete understanding. Then Katherine Morton shook her head and looked away. 'I try not to think about it,' she said.

'This happened nearly two years ago, didn't it?' Trudy continued, carefully feeling her way now.

'Yes, it happened one night. One night that should have been just like any other night. Only it wasn't. And it still feels as if it happened only yesterday,' Katherine added, nodding.

'What happened?' Trudy asked, although, again, she already had the details. The eighteen-year-old girl, who'd only passed her driving test the previous month, had lost control of her MG sports car and crashed into a lorry on a busy main road not far from the market town of Banbury. She had been killed instantly. The shaken lorry driver had suffered only very minor injuries. But what, Trudy wondered with a pang, did such a thing do to someone? She doubted that he was still driving lorries today, even though her colleagues in Banbury had quickly established from the many witnesses that he had in no way been to blame.

'Her father gave her the money to buy herself a car – and of course she chose a silly little low-slung sporty thing in bright red,' Katherine said, her voice taking on a hard, nasty edge now. 'I told him she was too young and wild for it, but he always indulged her. And she, the little minx, knew how to twist him right round her little finger.'

She drained her glass and topped it up from the bottle, her hand shaking visibly.

'So what happened?' Trudy led her as gently as she could.

'Oh, she'd been to a party and had been drinking too much.' At this irony, the artist regarded her newly full glass and gave a sudden harsh, despairing bark of laugher. '*Mea culpa*, obviously.

245

Her father, the swine, wasn't easy to live with and … Well, from an early age she'd seen us both drink liberally. So you see …' She tossed a defiant, heartbreaking and wretched smile at them. 'It was all my own fault that I lost my little girl.'

She took another gulp and leaned her head tiredly back against the headrest of her chair.

'But it wasn't *entirely* your fault, was it?' Trudy remarked calmly.

Katherine rolled her eyes Trudy's way, and a small, odd, almost whimsical smile played across her lips. 'Wasn't it?'

'No. There was your husband who gave Amy Jean the money to buy it in the first place and, of course, the man who sold her the car.'

The words hung in the air invitingly. All four inhabitants of the room listened to them echo, each chasing their own thoughts.

Trudy was thinking that it was now or never. If her hunch about why Terry Parker had been killed was correct, then right now, right here, was the time that she was going to learn if she was right or wrong.

Clement was wondering if the artist had reached just the right stage of drunken indiscretion to be of use to them, or if, perversely she'd turn belligerent and silent.

Vincent was marvelling at the delicate skill with which Trudy was handling her witness.

And Katherine … Katherine hovered on the brink of some kind of precipice that she'd long since wanted to throw herself over, whilst at the same time, was terrified of confronting. It made her both angry, and somehow coolly amused.

Ever since Amy Jean had died, she'd felt as if she was half-dead too. Oh, her subsequent paintings were fantastic (didn't they say that all the greatest art came out of great suffering?) but she could enjoy them no longer. The booze deadened nothing. Life dragged and seemed pointless. And all the while, the black cloud of guilt that loomed over her pressed down, a little harder, a little darker, every day, slowly smothering her that little bit more.

A mother was supposed to succour and protect her child,

wasn't she? Not set a bad example that gave her carte blanche to go and do something so utterly stupid and wasteful as get herself killed before her nineteenth birthday. What she wouldn't do to have those last few days of her daughter's life back again. The things she'd do differently …

She felt something tickle her cheek and raised a hand to it, surprised to find her fingers came away wet. Tears had begun to roll down her face without her noticing.

Angrily, she wiped them away with her palm, and drew in a deep breath.

She'd known ever since she'd woken on New Year's Day that somehow, someday, this moment would come, but had not made any plans for what she would do when it did. Spontaneity was her chosen path in life, be it in her art, her love life, or her occasional forays into gambling.

She had always crossed her bridges only when she came to them, trusting in her instinct and feelings to guide her. And now she'd come to this, perhaps the last bridge of all.

She looked at Trudy, feeling almost puzzled. Funny, but a pretty young girl in a smart police uniform was not what she had been expecting of fate. And yet here the pretty young girl was, looking at her so … *knowingly*.

Ah well, Katherine thought. *So be it*.

It was not as if she had much to lose, was it? Every day was a struggle to get through. What did it matter where the struggle took place? Here or in a prison cell?

'Mr Terrence Parker was the man who sold your daughter that car, wasn't he?' Trudy said gently. Yet again, she already knew the answer. Before leaving Clement's house, and after explaining her suspicions about this woman to both men, she'd rung Geoffrey Thorpe. Luckily he'd been in his office, and still feeling thoroughly cowed, had been more than anxious to help. A quick rifle through the appropriate files had soon provided the positive answer that she'd been expecting.

'Yes, the bastard sold her the car,' Katherine heard herself say. It sounded as if her voice was coming from a long way off. 'He must have seen how young she was. He must have known from taking down her details that she couldn't long have taken her driving test. And he knew cars, damn him. He knew that sporty little bit of fluff of nonsense would be too much for any inexperienced teenager to handle. And it was so flimsy – all light and airy and built for speed. It crumpled like tissue paper when it hit that lorry,' she added horrifically. 'Amy Jean had no chance,' she concluded flatly.

She regarded her glass and took another hearty swig. She wished she could get blind drunk and just forget, just for a few hours … But it was odd. Nowadays, no matter how much she drank, she never seemed quite able to lose touch with reality anymore.

'Did you know he'd be at the party?' Trudy asked quietly, hardly daring to move in case she distracted the older woman or gave her pause to rethink what she was doing.

'What? Oh, that stupid little New Year's Eve bash? No, I had no idea,' Katherine said, and Trudy believed her. 'I'd met Millie Vander vaguely out and about, as you do. This is a small city, after all, and she was something on an arts council or some such thing. But she wasn't exactly my "type". A repressed society matron, with plenty of money but probably bored out of her skull, poor cow,' Katherine said, with what sounded to Trudy and Clement like genuine sympathy in her voice.

She sighed heavily and took another, more thoughtful sip of vodka. 'No, it's like I said. I had a whole stack of invitations to various parties, but because the weather was so bloody awful and hers was the only party within easy walking distance, I ended up going there.'

She gave a sudden brief bark of laughter. 'It wasn't too bad though, now I come to think of it. The food was good – trust Millie to get the caterer just right. And the champagne was even better – bloody good vintage. I was beginning to pick up a bit of salacious gossip from some of her so-called "friends" at the do that she was making a bit of a fool of herself over a younger man,' she added with a smile. 'And I remember thinking to myself that I should congratulate her on living it up a little. But then, when *he* arrived …' There was no mistaking who she meant, for her voice became like ice, and all three of her visitors felt a similar coldness crawl over their skin. The venom and hatred in her voice was so powerful and raw it was almost like another presence in the room with them.

Katherine shook her head and again gave that harsh, bitter bark of laughter that made Trudy feel like crying. It sounded so hopeless and lifeless.

'I recognised him at once, of course. Not that *he* knew *me*,' she informed them. 'I attended Amy Jean's inquest wearing this big floppy hat and enormous sunglasses so that the press vultures wouldn't get a good likeness of me. And I wore the same thing about a month after my daughter died. I went to the place where she'd bought the car, you see – I just couldn't help myself. I remembered how she'd laughed when she told me that a handsome young man had sold it to her, and I just wanted to see him for myself. Oh, I knew that it wasn't healthy, but I just couldn't stop myself.'

The artist sighed and shook her head. 'It was a mistake, of course. I watched him on the forecourt, going about his business without a care in the world, and felt so impotent and so full of rage. What did it matter to him that a lovely young girl had died so young, just so long as he'd made his pieces of silver on the sale of that damned car?' She looked out of the window, clearly battling tears. At last, she turned once more to face them. 'I never went back there again,' she said quietly. 'I think, even then, I realised that it would be dangerous – both for him, and for me. Something deep inside told me that I was close to a deep and dark precipice, and that I must never allow myself to look over it. So I forced myself to put him and his bloody cars out of my mind. It wasn't easy, but I managed it.'

Suddenly, she gave another harsh bark of laughter. 'And then, just when I thought all that was behind me, I went to a party and there he was. Just right there, right in front of me. When I first saw him, I froze. Just as well I was sitting down with a drink in my hand, I can tell you,' she added bitterly.

'It must have been awful for you,' Trudy murmured, meaning it. 'Suddenly finding yourself in the same room as the man who'd played a part in your daughter's death.'

Katherine's eyes flickered. 'I know what you're thinking,' she said, her voice more slurred now, but still perfectly understandable. 'You're thinking that his part in Amy Jean's destruction was so small. That I was the more guilty one …'

Trudy, in fact, hadn't been thinking anything of the sort, but she didn't correct the other woman. She could plainly see that Katherine Morton was so steeped in guilt and self-loathing that it would be pointless to try and comfort her. Besides, what could she possibly say?

'And you're right, of course,' the artist swept on wearily. 'I *was* to blame. But at least I am suffering for it,' she added defiantly, almost proudly. 'And so is her father, in his own way, I suppose,' she conceded grudgingly. 'But as I watched *that man*, laughing and drinking, I could see that he hadn't suffered for even a moment. And when he began to dance with that rich widow he was soon to marry, I realised that his life was only going to get better and better.'

Slowly, she leaned forward in her chair and placed her drink, with just a little difficulty, squarely back in the middle of the table. She fixed her gaze intensely on Trudy, who stiffened slightly under the onslaught. The artist's face was now ravaged by some emotion so strong it made Trudy want to cringe back in her own chair to avoid being contaminated by it.

Of course, she didn't move a muscle.

'I could see it all, you see, Constable,' she said softly. '*He* was going to enjoy all the many years that *he* still had left, helping to spend Millie Vander's money, dining at the Ritz, going on holidays in the south of France, enjoying everything that this world had to offer. Whilst Amy Jean, my Amy Jean, was lying in the ground, in the dark, with all those years she should have spent doing the same sort of things now lost to her, forever. And do you know ...'

At this, Katherine's voice lowered and she leaned forward even further in her chair. Around her, the two men in the room instinctively leaned forward too, ears straining, both utterly fascinated and repelled but desperate to hear what she was going to say next.

'As we began to wait for the clocks to strike midnight, I knew, *just knew with an absolute certainty*, that I couldn't allow him to live one minute longer than necessary,' Katherine said simply. 'It wasn't something I'd ever thought of before – taking revenge, I mean. Like I told you, I've tried and tried not to think about Amy Jean and that car crash at all – that fatal night when everything changed. And that included trying to forget everything to do with it, including her father and *that man*. But at that moment, with the old year counting down, and seeing him laughing and cosying up to Millie Vander ... it was as if something just came over me. I can't really describe it. It was like a blanket, only it wasn't warm and comforting, but rather the opposite. Cold and lifeless. A compulsion, a certainty, a ... oh, it's no use, I can't explain it in words. Without planning it, without even almost knowing it, I just knew I had to stop that man from living one day longer in a world where Amy Jean no longer existed. I felt so calm it was almost inhuman. It was as if a ... a ... fatal chill had crept into my blood. It was all-consuming and overpowering, and I didn't even try and fight it.'

Remembering that moment must have been more than she could take, because Katherine reached desperately for her glass and drained it again. Then she slumped back into her chair.

251

'So what did you do?' Trudy asked, her voice little more than a whisper now.

'Hmmm? Do?' Katherine looked at her vaguely, then smiled wryly. 'Oh, I didn't do anything, really, except think. *How could I kill him?* I had no weapon, and even if I got a knife from the kitchen or something and launched myself at him, all the others would stop me. His car was outside, and I'd have loved to see him die the same way my Amy Jean died, all alone at night in his car, but I'd no idea how to go about sabotaging it. The only things I had on me were in my handbag.'

As she spoke, her eyes went to that very item, lying on the floor beside her chair, large and voluminous and bulging with items. Trudy remembered how full of stuff it had been on their first visit.

'I keep practically everything you can think of in there,' Katherine said, and smiled slowly. 'Including the pills my doctor gave me to help me sleep. Bloody things stopped working after a time and I had to take more and more of them in order to get any sleep at all. But the funny thing is, that gave me a good idea of how they worked, you know, about doses and things. And suddenly it was obvious. All I had to do was wait until everyone had raised their glasses after midnight, then kept a close eye on that man, and his glass. The moment he set it down – in order to take the last dance with his lady-love, as it happened – I slipped two and a half doses into it, being careful not to be seen, of course, and simply waited.'

Everyone in the room let out a small sigh.

'Of course, it would have all gone wrong if he'd drunk it and then stayed for more than ten minutes or so,' she said, almost casually. 'But I was counting on the weather, and our Millie wanting her other guests to see him leave in good time. Just to prevent any more gossip than usual, obviously,' the artist said drolly. 'They couldn't have anyone thinking he was going to stay the night! Oh no. Too, too shocking!' She laughed mockingly. 'And sure enough, just as I thought, he obligingly drank the rest of his glass down, and made a show of saying goodnight and leaving. And I ... I just watched him leave the house, then said my own goodbyes and went home myself.'

Katherine said this last sentence as if it surprised her somehow. 'It felt ... odd. Walking home. Wondering if it would work. If he'd crash the car before he got home. If it would be enough to kill him – and if not, trying to think of some other way of killing him.'

At this blunt, matter-of-fact, indeed almost offhand statement, Vincent gave a slight shiver.

'And you would have tried again?' Trudy asked quietly.

'Oh yes,' Katherine Morton said, looking at Trudy with a slight smile. 'I'd made my mind up, you see,' she said simply.

Chapter 33

Trudy, afraid the other woman might become too drunk if she didn't act fast, quickly wrote out a statement of that night's events, as the artist had described them, into her notebook in longhand and got Katherine to sign it. Clement then witnessed it.

They then guided the malleable, now almost content Katherine to the police station in Clement's car. Trudy sat in the back with her, but asked no further questions. She knew the sergeant would want to conduct his own, formal interview as soon as they arrived.

She wasn't surprised that Katherine seemed to feel almost satisfied now. Content even. The relief of confession must have been enormous.

In the front seat, Vincent looked at his father's tight but composed face, and couldn't help but admire his old man. He himself felt distinctly shaken. Never in his life had he ever thought that he would sit in a room with a killer and hear her confession – let alone feel genuinely sorry for her. Even though, at times, he'd felt chilled to the bone by what she'd said.

At the station, once they'd all trooped in, Trudy saw at once that Sergeant O'Grady was back at his desk. The door to Inspector Jennings's office also stood open. Relieved that both men had dealt with the Vanders and Phyllis – who were probably booked and in cells by now – she led Katherine gently but firmly to the sergeant's desk and sat her down.

O'Grady regarded his visitor with sharp, assessing eyes, then looked up questioningly at Trudy.

'Sergeant, this is Miss Morton. She's just confessed to the murder of Mr Terrence Parker,' she said calmly. 'I've taken down her preliminary statement and she's signed it.' She handed over her notebook, knowing that she'd have to type it up later.

The sergeant's eyes, which had been widening more and more throughout her short report, flickered to the suspect, who gave him a brief smile and an even more brief nod of her head.

'I see,' O'Grady said calmly, beginning to read Trudy's neat longhand. 'You'd better report to Inspector Jennings,' he ordered her, without looking up.

With not a little trepidation, Trudy got up. Whilst she couldn't help but feel proud of herself and happy to have solved the case, she wasn't expecting any rosy congratulations or heartfelt thanks from her boss.

Clement and Vincent, she noted with an inner smile, were wisely nowhere in sight as she headed through the open door!

*

Later that night, Clement stood at the sink washing up the supper dishes. He wished he'd been able to see Harry Jennings's face when Trudy had told him they'd just brought in the killer, a confession already in hand, but he was pretty sure his imagination was up to the job!

He was still grinning widely at his mental image of Harry Jennings spluttering, as he wiped up one of the glasses. Then his hand began to tremble uncontrollably, and before he could prevent it, the glass slipped through the folds of the tea towel and onto the kitchen floor, where it broke noisily.

'Damn!' Clement growled. Behind him, he heard his son

255

approach and turned around quickly. 'Pass me the dustpan and brush, will you?' he asked casually.

'Later,' Vincent said firmly, taking the towel from him. Quickly Clement turned away, hiding his hand between his side and the kitchen sink.

But Vincent calmly reached around him, took his father's still-trembling hand in his and pulled it out into the light. Clement stiffened.

For a few seconds, both men watched his trembling fingers, and Vincent felt dread kick off inside his stomach.

'All right, Dad,' he managed to say through a throat tight with alarm. 'Don't you think it's about time you told me just what's the matter with you?'

Keep reading for an excerpt from *A Fatal Affair* …

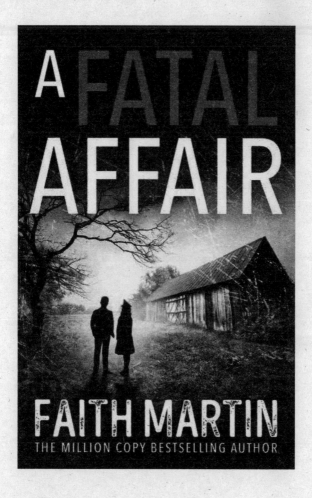

Prologue

Tuesday 1st May, 1962

No one in the city of dreaming spires on that chilly May Day morning would have been thinking about death. Why would they, when the birds were singing, and everyone was congregating around Magdalen Tower, counting down the moments until it was 6 a.m.; that magical moment when the city began its celebrations in earnest?

Certainly, the excited young choristers clustered at the very top of the college building had no reason to ponder on tragedy. Rather, their minds were firmly fixed on their soon-to-be-given rendition of that lovely piece, '*Te Deum Patrem colimus*', the singing of which had been customary from Magdalen Tower on May Day since 1509.

Even the influx of foreign visitors to the city on that special morning were far more interested in watching, with bemusement and disbelief, the quaint and colourful antics of the morris dancers that thronged the city streets, with their jingling bells and clacking sticks, than in contemplating murder.

After all, who in that beautiful and ancient city could believe on such a wonderfully auspicious and bright spring day that anything dark and fatal could be happening anywhere? Weren't the daffodils and tulips, the forsythia bushes and polyanthus, blooming in multi-coloured glory in all the gardens, proclaiming that life itself was good? Little children, perhaps bored with Latin hymns, were laughing and playing and singing their own, far more down-to-earth, songs, every bit as traditional to May Day, and carried on the breeze – 'Now is the Month of Maying' competing with 'Oh the Little Busy Bee' for dominance.

Tourists took photographs. The choristers, flushed with triumph, eventually left the tower. The people in the streets, flushed with having witnessed proper 'English culture' sought out any cafés that might be open so early in the morning in search of that other British stalwart, a hot cup of tea.

And less than seven miles away, in a small country village that had for centuries celebrated May Day almost as assiduously as its nearest city, a plump, middle-aged woman made her bustling way through the quiet lanes and barely stirring cottages, towards the village green.

Margaret Bellham had lived in Middle Fenton for all her life, first attending the village school there, and then marrying a lad who'd grown up four doors from her down the lane, and moving into a tied cottage on one of the farm estates.

In her younger days, she had missed out on being chosen May Queen for the day by the narrowest of margins, and had long since mourned the fact. Still, such disappointments hadn't stopped her from cheerfully ruling the roost on the May Day Committee for the last twenty years.

It was her job to see that the May Day Procession, including all the infants and juniors from the school went like clockwork, with the flower-festooned 'crown' and four lances being allocated to only the most responsible (and strongest) children to carry. It was she who organised the village ladies who would be producing the food for the afternoon picnic, traditionally held around the village duck pond. And, naturally, it was her responsibility to ensure that the village maypole, a permanent structure erected in pride of place on the village green nearly two centuries ago, was ready for the maypole dancing by all the village maidens under the age of eighteen, which would start promptly at noon.

Margaret puffed a bit as she crossed the lane in front of the school, and looked across to check the time on the church clock opposite – barely 7 a.m., so she was well on schedule. Nevertheless, she was mentally making a list of all the things she still needed to do as she turned the corner that would take her past the duck pond and on to the village green proper.

She only hoped, she thought with a scowl, that Sid Fowler had remembered to secure the ribbon-bedecked wooden crown on top of the maypole before it got dark last night. For whilst the stone maypole itself was left in situ to withstand the weather all year round, the wooden piece at the top, with multiple slats carved into it through which the long, colourful 'ribbons' were secured, was always kept stored in the school shed.

Sid wasn't the most reliable of men, though, and she had the spare key to the school shed in her pocket, just in case. She had delegated Rose Simmonds, the barmaid of the village pub, to make sure that all the many ribbons, traditionally the seven colours of the rainbow, had been cleaned and would be bright and sparkling for when the children began their dances.

As a child who had once danced around the maypole herself, weaving and ducking around her fellow schoolmates in order to create the intricate patterns so iconic of the maypole, she knew how much better it all looked when the ribbons were bright and fresh. Spider's Web and Gypsies' Tent were her favourite dances, but the Twister …

At that moment in her reverie, Margaret looked towards the maypole to check all was as it should be, and stopped dead in her tracks. For a second or two, she merely stood and blinked, not really sure that she was seeing what she thought she was seeing.

Falteringly, her brain buzzing like a hive of disturbed bees, she stumbled forward, but as her feet stepped onto the soft green grass of the green, she felt the strength leaching out of her, and she sank awkwardly onto her knees.

She felt her mouth open, but was incapable of making a sound.

Instead, she just stared at that year's May Queen.

Nobody had been surprised when Iris Carmody had been chosen. Traditionally, all the village men (in a closed ballot) elected a village girl between the age of sixteen to twenty to be Queen of the May. And Iris, with her long pale fair hair, big blue eyes, heart-shaped face and hourglass figure had been breaking the hearts of local boys since she'd hit puberty. And probably even before then! Now, at the age of seventeen, she had swept all other challengers before her.

As May Queen, she was to rule the village for the day, for tradition had it that the May Queen's every wish had to be met. Of course, in the past, this had led to some jolly japes, with one May Queen famously ordering that all the pigs must be 'painted' green, and all lads must have daisy-chains for belts!

Margaret, for one, had had severe misgivings about giving Iris Carmody, the little minx, so much scope to make mischief, and she didn't believe that she was alone in that. There had been more than one wise matron who had taken her aside and muttered darkly about the village's choice this year.

But looking at Iris now, dressed in a long white gown embroidered with a swathe of tiny colourful flowers and her long, waist-length hair topped by a crown of violets, bluebells, primroses and narcissus, even Margaret had to admit that she epitomised youthful beauty and the spring.

Even the colourful ribbons, hanging from the crown of the maypole, and which were now wrapped tightly around and around her body, holding her fast to the stone edifice, looked pretty.

But underneath the swathe of beautiful fair hair that was

framing her profile, Margaret Bellham could see a string of darkly smudged bruises around Iris's neck, and even more horrifically, the congested, contorted face and lolling blue tongue that made the dead girl look like a grotesque parody of what a May Queen should be.

Finally, the monstrousness of what she was seeing freed Margaret Bellham from her paralysis, and she began to scream, before wailing pitifully.

Chapter 1

It was a week and four days after the murder of Iris Carmody, and DI Harry Jennings was beginning to feel the strain. His officers had been working on the case non-stop, with the press breathing down their necks every inch of the way. He wasn't particularly surprised by this, as a beautiful girl dressed as a May Queen and found strangled and bound to a village maypole was many a newspaper editor's dream.

But it was just one more headache that he didn't really need.

And he knew that another one was about to walk through his office door at any moment. He sighed heavily and leaned back against his chair, feeling the lack of sleep catching up on him. The trouble was, for such a spectacular crime, the investigation of it was turning out to be frustratingly pedestrian.

For a start, nobody had seen the dead girl on the day of her death. The girl's parents had no idea why she'd dressed so early and left the family home when she had such a busy day ahead of her. And nobody in the village had heard anything untoward occurring at the village green, either the night before she was found, or early in the morning – not even those sleeping in the cottages surrounding the crime scene.

And whilst there had been gossip and speculation aplenty

within the village about the dead girl – and her love life – there was very little confirmatory *proof* to actually go on. Oh, it quickly became very clear after the PCs had finished interviewing everyone in the small village that everyone and their granny had a lot to say about the dead girl – and not much of it flattering. Or *too* flattering, depending on who was doing the talking. According to most of the women, she was a flighty girl at best, a man-eater at worst, but nobody could actually point the finger with any conviction at the supposedly long list of her potential victims or lovers. And whilst a fair proportion of the men had liked to hint that they knew Iris rather well, on being pushed for times, dates and proof, nobody would actually go so far as to admitting to being the girl's paramour.

Everyone agreed that her 'official' boyfriend of the moment had probably been taken for a fool, but unsubstantiated gossip didn't provide rock-solid motives for murder.

And now, piling tragedy upon tragedy, there had been a second death that was almost certainly connected to the murder of the May Queen. Although this one looked, thankfully, far more straightforward to deal with, and the inspector had high hopes that it could soon be closed. Especially once his next visitor had been tactfully dealt with.

Well, perhaps …

Here DI Jennings heaved a massive sigh. As he did so, there was a sharp, peremptory rap on his office door, and before he could bid anyone enter, the door was thrust open and a tall, brown-haired man walked in. Dressed in a slightly rumpled, charcoal-grey suit, he was not fat but not particularly lean, and although he was a handsome enough individual, he looked noticeably pale and hollow-eyed. He also looked much older than the fifty-two years that Harry Jennings knew him to be.

As well he might, poor sod, the inspector thought grimly. Jennings hastily shot to his feet. 'Superintendent Finch, sir,' he barked out awkwardly. 'Er … won't you sit down?'

The superintendent nodded and sat very carefully and precisely in the chair in front of the inspector's desk, a clear indication of how rigidly he was controlling himself. The superintendent had already given his formal statement to Jennings yesterday morning, which had been painfully awkward for both men concerned, but Harry hadn't been surprised to have received the call from Keith Finch late yesterday afternoon asking for another 'informal chat' today.

'Sir, again, I'd like to say how very sorry I am about your son. I assure you, his case is being treated with the utmost care and respect,' Harry said flatly, retaking his own seat.

His superior officer grimaced. 'Yes, I'm sure it is,' he agreed. Then his shoulders slumped slightly. 'Look, let's not beat about the bush, Harry,' he said wearily, suddenly dropping the formality and looking and sounding more like the bereaved father that he was, rather than a still-serving police officer of some rank. 'David's death has left us, my wife and me, I mean … well … all at sea, as you can probably imagine.'

Harry cleared his throat helplessly. He was beginning to feel a shade angry and resentful at being put in this position, but he knew it was hardly the Super's fault. Even so, he wished the man would just take some leave and keep well out of things. It would make things so much easier for everyone all around. But he knew, just from looking at the other man's face, that that was not going to happen any time soon.

'Let's put our cards on the table, shall we?' Superintendent Finch said grimly. 'There's no denying that my boy, David, was head over heels about this Carmody girl. He'd not yet brought her home to meet us, even though they'd been stepping out together for some weeks, but we were all well aware that he was well and truly smitten. And I don't mind telling you, his mother was worried about it. Even before her murder, we'd been hearing rumours about her. You know what it's like – women gossip and delight in bringing bad news to your door, and a number of people went out of their way to warn Betty that, well, this girl he was seeing might have been two-timing him.'

'Very distressing for you and your family, sir, I'm sure,' Harry said soothingly.

'Yes, well, his mother was concerned, as I said, but for myself I thought … well, David was a good-looking lad, young, doing well at university … and frankly, Harry, I thought it would all blow over. When I was his age …' He trailed off and shrugged.

Again Harry nodded, wishing that this was all somebody else's headache. But it wasn't. The mess had been dropped well and truly in his lap, and now he had to try and steer a course that kept a superintendent happy, whilst showing no bias or favour in his pursuit of closing the Carmody case.

And the best of British luck with that, he thought sourly. On the one hand, he had his immediate bosses braying at him to close the case, and on the other, he had Superintendent Keith Finch, who was not going to be happy if he solved the case at the expense of his family and his dead son's reputation.

'You thought that he would soon get tired of Iris and find someone more suitable sooner or later.' The inspector followed his line of thought easily. 'Yes, sir, I understand, and who's to say you wouldn't have been proved right?' Harry was careful to keep his voice neutral.

The superintendent eyed him with another weary smile. 'I realise this isn't exactly an ideal situation for you either, Harry. Especially now. David's death has hit us all hard, but there's no denying …' He paused, took a deep breath and sat up straighter in his chair. 'You know, of course, that they're saying that David killed her? And then killed himself out of guilt?'

Jennings nodded miserably. Three days ago, this man's son had been found hanging in a barn belonging to a close friend of the family. So far, although it was early days, there were no signs to suggest that it had been anything other than suicide. Naturally, the village was aflame with speculation, and the newspapers were only too happy to stoke the fires.

'I find that impossible to believe,' Keith Finch said. Then he held up a placatory hand as the inspector opened his mouth to respond, adding quickly, 'And yes, I know, how many times have we heard family members of suicide victims or murder suspects say exactly the same thing?' He ran a hand helplessly over his face.

The inspector, aware that he could put it off no longer, said, 'Sir, I assure you that we're going to conduct a proper investigation into everything, but, obviously, I can't keep you apprised of anything …'

Luckily, he didn't have to continue. Usually, telling a superintendent things that he didn't want to hear wasn't a smart move for a man with ambitions, and Harry Jennings hadn't been looking forward to doing it. So it was with something of a relief that he stopped speaking as his superior officer again raised a hand.

'Don't worry, Harry, I'm not here to ask you to keep me updated. The chief constable has already made it clear that I can't be involved in this thing in any way. Especially with David being a murder suspect in the Carmody case.'

Harry let out a relieved breath. 'Yes, sir.' But he was very much aware that he was in a uniquely awkward and unenviable position. He wanted to be able to tell his superiors – and the press – that he'd found the killer of the May Queen; and when a murdered girl's boyfriend hangs himself a few days later, that's usually taken to be as good as a confession. Which meant that, normally, he could be confident of closing the case once they'd been able to collect some evidence cementing the hypothesis that her lover had killed her in a jealous rage.

But when the dead suspect was the son of a superintendent of police, and an old acquaintance, it could hardly be business as usual. Especially when dealing with a man who, before now, could claim to have high-ranking friends in both the police force and society in general.

But Harry was well aware that the superintendent would not be able to weather this particular storm unscathed. Unfair or not, the chances were that Keith Finch now faced not only a personal loss, but a professional loss too. For surely the powers-that-be were already making plans to pension him off – the usual fate of anyone who caused them such public embarrassment?

Harry had been careful to make sure that there were no newspapers on his desk that morning, but it was impossible that the Finch family wouldn't have read the speculation in the local press. He knew David had had a sister, and he could only guess the hell she was going through right now. He suppressed a shudder and sighed gently.

'The thing is, of course, that I *don't* believe for one moment my son killed her, Harry. Of course, I know you have to consider the possibility that he did, but I have every confidence that you'll find no evidence supporting this. And that you will eventually find out who did,' the superintendent added hastily, although there was nothing on his face to indicate whether he believed this to be true or not.

Harry swallowed hard, unable to meet his gaze.

'So, to get down to brass tacks. I'm here about the inquest on David. It's set for this Monday, yes?' Superintendent Finch said briskly. Whatever his personal tragedy, he was determined to keep a stiff upper lip, and for that Jennings was grateful. He wasn't sure, given the circumstances, what comfort he could give to a grieving father in imminent peril of breaking down.

'Yes, sir. Starting at 10 a.m.'

'And it's the old vulture presiding?'

Inspector Jennings nodded. 'Yes, sir. He's the best, as you know.'

'I agree. I've always rated Dr Ryder very highly – even when he's being the proverbial pain in our necks,' Keith Finch said heavily but with a wry twist of his lips.

Jennings merely grunted. In the past, he'd had to have more to do with Dr Clement Ryder than he'd ever wanted. Why the man couldn't act more like a regular coroner, and just do his job and leave the police to do theirs, he didn't know. But no, he had to stick his nose in – and, even more annoyingly, often come up trumps.

'And that brings me to the purpose of this visit. I've had a word with the chief constable, and he's agreed with my proposal.'

At this, Harry Jennings felt his heart rate began to ratchet up a notch or two, and a slow, sick feeling sidled into his stomach, making him swallow hard. 'Sir?' he asked warily.

'We might turn a blind eye to things, Harry, but that doesn't mean to say that the powers-that-be haven't noticed that that girl of yours and our coroner have developed a habit of, well, shall we say, "supplementing" our more normal lines of inquiry?'

At this point, Harry Jennings got a *really* bad feeling. 'Sir,' he began to object, but wasn't allowed to finish.

'Now, I know we can't expect WPC Loveday and Dr Ryder to help you on the actual Iris Carmody case—'

'No, sir, we definitely can't! WPC Loveday has barely completed her probationary period and—'

'But Dr Ryder, as city coroner, has before now done some, shall we say, follow-up inquiries on a number of his inquest cases, isn't that so?'

'Yes, sir,' Harry admitted miserably.

'And with some considerable success?'

'Yes, sir,' he was again forced to agree.

'Very well then. As I said, the chief constable is with me on this, Inspector. After the inquest on my son is over – *no matter what the verdict may be* – you will approach Dr Ryder and ask him to make further discreet inquiries about my son and the circumstances of his death.'

'Superintendent, sir, I don't think that's really wise …'

Keith Finch gave a harsh bark of laughter, and for the first time looked seriously angry. 'It may not be *wise*, Inspector,' he snapped, leaning forward in his chair, 'but everyone's going around saying

that my boy – *my boy!* – murdered that girl and then killed himself.'
Suddenly he slammed the flat of his palm down on Jennings's
desk so hard and fast, that Jennings nearly went into orbit. The
sharp ricochet of sound had the heads of the police officers in
the outer room swivelling in their direction.

'*And I'm not having it, Jennings*. Is that clear?' Superintendent
Finch said through gritted teeth.

Harry nodded wretchedly. 'Yes, sir,' he agreed. Clearly the Super
still had some clout with the higher-ups, and he was in no mood
to be thwarted.

'Very good. So, continue your investigation into the Carmody
case,' the superintendent said mildly now, standing up and looking
as if nothing dramatic had happened. 'Let nothing interfere with
that. Continue regarding my son as a suspect if you must. But
let that clever girl of yours and the old vulture sniff around my
son's case without any impediment. Understood?'

'Yes, sir,' Harry said, standing up politely.

It was clear, all right, but that didn't mean to say he had to
like it. And, whilst he might have to tread carefully – for now,
anyway – that didn't mean he would always have to toe the line.
Especially if they finally got some proper evidence as to who had
murdered Iris Carmody, and why.

He watched his superior officer leave the room and then
slumped back down behind his desk with a groan. Great! As if
he didn't have enough troubles already. This was infuriating –
another case with his station's annoyingly efficient and pesky lone
WPC and the old vulture snooping around in police business.

Just what he needed!

Dear Reader,

We hope you enjoyed reading this book. If you did, we'd be so appreciative if you left a review. It really helps us and the author to bring more books like this to you.

Here at HQ Digital we are dedicated to publishing fiction that will keep you turning the pages into the early hours. Don't want to miss a thing? To find out more about our books, promotions, discover exclusive content and enter competitions you can keep in touch in the following ways:

JOIN OUR COMMUNITY:

Sign up to our new email newsletter:
http://smarturl.it/SignUpHQ

Read our new blog www.hqstories.co.uk

🐦 https://twitter.com/HQStories

f www.facebook.com/HQStories

BUDDING WRITER?

We're also looking for authors to join the HQ Digital family!
Find out more here:

https://www.hqstories.co.uk/want-to-write-for-us/

Thanks for reading, from the HQ Digital team

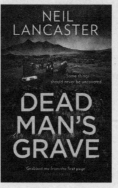